Will flashed those dimples again.

Kenzie's breath did a little fluttery thing in her throat.

She took a swallow of hot coffee that seared away all remnants of that fluttery feeling. But it didn't incinerate the sudden memory of the conversation she'd had in class only a few nights ago.

Lust at first sight?

Oh, please...it didn't exist. Well, okay. *Maybe.* Which came at her sideways.

She watched Will return the floor plans to the folder, shuffle through the papers with those long fingers as if checking to make certain everything was there.

Then he slid the folder toward her. "This is yours. Everything you need to know about Family Foundations, the lease and the proposed floor plans. And a lot of contact information in case you think of more questions. My cell number is in here, so you can call me anytime."

And she so wanted to call him...but not for business.

Dear Reader,

I had the honor of visiting St. Gerard House, "A Sanctuary for Families Facing Autism." To say I was touched by the engaging charm of the students doesn't come close. To say I was humbled by the dedication of the folks who work and volunteer there would be another understatement. The atmosphere of love and hope filling every corner of this special place is what I most wanted to share in my fictional world. While St. Gerard House provided the inspiration, any lack of understanding in my presentation of autism is solely my responsibility.

Unfortunately, a lack of understanding plays a big role in the lives of those who deal with this disorder. Enter Will Russell, a dad pulling out all the stops for his son. He meets Kenzie James, a woman with a unique twist on family life. Their attraction draws them together, and what they learn from each other helps them redefine happily-ever-after.

Ordinary people. Extraordinary romance.

Harlequin Superromance is the place to explore the sort of life issues only love can conquer. I hope you enjoy Kenzie and Will's love story. Visit me at www.jeanielegendre.com.

Peace and blessings,

Jeanie London

Right from the Start

JEANIE LONDON

HARLEQUIN®SUPER ROMANCE®

Recycling programs
for this product may
not exist in your area.

ISBN-13: 978-0-373-60767-9

RIGHT FROM THE START

Copyright © 2013 by Jeanie LeGendre

Printed in U.S.A.

www.Harlequin.com

ABOUT THE AUTHOR

Jeanie London writes romance because she believes in happily-ever-afters. Not the "love conquers all" kind, but the "we love each other so we can conquer anything" kind. Jeanie is the winner of many prestigious writing awards, including multiple *RT Book Reviews* Reviewers' Choice and National Readers' Choice Awards. She lives in sunny Florida with her own romance-hero husband, their beautiful daughters and a menagerie of strays.

Books by Jeanie London

HARLEQUIN SUPERROMANCE

HARLEQUIN BLAZE

*Falling Inn Bed...

HARLEQUIN SIGNATURE SELECT SPOTLIGHT

Other titles by this author available in ebook format.

To the folks at St. Gerard House in Hendersonville, North Carolina—kids, families, administrators, faculty, professionals, staff, volunteers, benefactors, community partners and all who contribute to this ministry in any way.

You inspire with your courage, your breathtaking faith and your generosity of spirit.
May God bless you all.

CHAPTER ONE

"I'M GUESSING YOU don't believe in love at first sight?" the student asked.

Not much of a guess from where Kenzie James stood, which was at the front of the classroom. The room was filled to maximum capacity with students of both genders. They ranged in ages from barely-legal-to-drink to middle-aged. They represented demographics from the young woman with facial piercings who had asked the question to an army officer wearing a knife-creased uniform.

Kenzie's classrooms were always full—a bittersweet commentary on the state of marital affairs. As a rule she didn't share her opinions during divorcing parent classes, but occasionally a group would actually be interested in participating rather than simply marking time in the court-ordered class.

Participators could motivate others, so Kenzie seized the teaching moment.

"No, I'm not a believer in love at first sight," she admitted. "In my opinion a love that will weather life's storms involves a lot of things—respect, caring, commitment, self-sacrifice to mention a few—none of which are spontaneous."

"Fair enough," the pierced young woman said genially. "What about lust at first sight?"

There was a titter of movement from the back of the classroom, where several obviously bored men showed life signs. An impatient woman wearing a business suit narrowed her gaze disapprovingly at the shocker question, or the appearance of the girl who'd asked. Maybe both.

The army officer's expression didn't flinch. Clearly the man was well trained in controlling his responses. Not a bad thing in Kenzie's opinion.

And questions meant to shock were all part of her job, so she leaned a hip against the table where her handouts were stacked and said, "Lust at first sight is another beast entirely. Chemistry is a natural, physical response. The only problem with lust is how often people confuse it with love. Because they both begin with the letter *L*, do you think?"

That got a laugh from around the room. Even the officer grinned. Not the impatient businesswoman.

But Kenzie had the class's attention. "Lust can certainly be a part of successful love, but the feelings are in no way interchangeable. Human emotion operates on impulse and instinct, at the maturity level of a seven-year-old. I call it the inner child. We all have one."

Stepping to the whiteboard, she grabbed a dry-erase marker and drew circles. "Think about your children. Those of you who have teens will know what I'm talking about. Those of you with babies who haven't yet hit the toddler phase get ready."

She turned to the class. "Think about when your children want something. They want to watch TV now, not later. They want to go out and play now, not later. And what happens when you tell them no?"

A woman with a ponytail raised her hand. "My son is three. I can get anything from tears to a full-blown tantrum."

"My daughter is thirteen," the impatient business-woman added. "I get a nasty look and an attitude."

"Exactly." Kenzie spread her hands in entreaty. "The responses vary with the age group, but basically all children want immediate gratification. When they're denied, they can respond with tears or tantrums or any emotion in between. As they get older and more socially aware, they can manipulate. It's common for children in divorce situations to play one parent against the other."

Kenzie used the marker to point at the largest circle on the board then wrote two words inside it. "*Inner child.* The feelings and reactions you see in your children never go away. All of our inner children want immediate gratification. They want to pitch a fit when they're told no. They're willing to move heaven and earth to get their way."

She pointed to the next smallest circle. "There's absolutely nothing wrong with our inner children. We should acknowledge how we feel and embrace our feelings. They're what make us human. But the difference between children and adults is that adults learn how to channel those feelings constructively."

Kenzie wrote *adult* in that circle. "Self-control is the key here. Adults learn to step back and make sense of a feeling before taking action."

A simple concept that managed to be so complicated.

Kenzie didn't share that opinion with the class, but after eight years as a divorce mediator with the state of North Carolina and now owner of her own agency, Positive Partings, she knew how underutilized emotional coping skills could be.

"Adults understand consequences. There are plenty of mornings I wake up and don't feel like coming to work," she said. "I make a choice. Do I want to risk losing my job so I can stay in bed, *or not?* Do I want to sacrifice my reliable reputation so I can roll over and go back to sleep, *or not?*"

Kenzie wrote the word *parent* in the smallest, farthest circle on the board. "Parents take their choices one step further. Not only must they think about the consequences to themselves, but they have to think about what's in the best interest of their children. That's why you're here tonight and why the court appoints these classes."

Setting down the marker, Kenzie faced the room. Every eye was on her now.

"Bottom line, people, you're divorcing your spouses, not your children. Just because you won't be married to your husband or wife anymore doesn't mean you'll stop parenting together. You're still a family. You'll *always* be a family. Life goes on. There'll be decisions to make about schooling and a thousand other things. There'll be birthdays and graduations and holidays and weddings and births and on and on as long as you live."

If people realized this fact from the start, they might see how much simpler life would be if they resolved problems together rather than divorcing and dragging the same problems into another relationship.

"The goal of these classes is learning to navigate divorce in a healthy way so you and your family don't suffer. That starts by understanding our inner children and assuming control in ways that help us to be productive adults and effective parents. Most kids don't want their parents to divorce. They're scared and don't know how to articulate their fears. They need the adults in their lives to act like responsible parents who will work together to reassure them they're loved, they're still part of a family and they're not responsible for the divorce.

"Adults who are effective parents learn to step back from divorce drama and manage whatever feelings they have for their former spouses in private. That's hard to do if you're hurt or angry or worried. But that's what you signed up for when you became parents."

There was a collective pause, the classroom so silent Kenzie could have heard a pin drop. She smiled.

"And that's why I don't believe in love at first sight,

to get back to the original question. Lust at first sight is the domain of our inner children, who want passion and excitement and immediate gratification. They want to feel good *now*. Love is the domain of adults who recognize those shiny new feelings will eventually fade. Life's going to have ups and downs and joys and sorrows.

"Successful love will require people to place the needs of their spouses and families ahead of their own desires, and unless a couple has healthy emotional coping skills, they'll likely have trouble succeeding at marriage."

Precisely why Kenzie's classes were always full.

Reaching for her handouts, she went down the center aisle setting small stacks on each table to be passed around.

"I want you to take a look at how quickly most of you will jump into your next marriage and the percentage of those marriages that will fail. I just updated with the latest statistics, so this information is current. The fact is when families become blended, there will be more complications, not fewer, so now's the time to get healthy coping skills in place."

Unless they wanted to spend another four hours sitting in this court-appointed class.

Love at first sight?

Not a good idea in Kenzie's book.

WILL RUSSELL BRACED himself for the meeting ahead while opening the front door of the unassuming two-story house. He barely noticed the plaque by the door anymore.

Angel House.

A Sanctuary for Families Facing Autism.

Tucked behind a church, this house had become another home to him and his son, Sam. In many ways Angel House was more of a home than even their own with just Will and Sam and an ex-wife who could only be a drop-by mom.

He and Sam certainly spent enough time here between classes and evaluations, Will's nighttime support groups and ongoing fund-raising meetings. The fund-raising was as important as everything else because without money, no work would get done, no kids or families helped to make sense of the unexpected and complicated journey that came with this disorder.

Will took another deep breath and plunked himself in a chair in the reception room. He'd arrived nearly fifteen minutes early. All afternoon he'd been in City Hall at a council meeting. Rather than tackling five o'clock traffic, he'd walked the six blocks. Hadn't taken long. He'd practically jogged here because he was still wound up from the meeting. *Not* because he was eager to hear news he expected to be all bad.

Leaning forward, Will steeled himself to deal with even more pressure. Was it even possible he could feel more? He suspected the answer would be an unfortunate yes. Angel House had reached the literal end of the line. Only a miracle could save them now, and miracles were damned slow in the making.

He'd been working on this particular miracle for two years already—a meticulous process that involved a lot of factors coming together in the right way at the right time. His luck had held, and now the end was finally in sight. He needed a little more time...and didn't hold out much hope he'd get it. Time depended on money around here, and both were in short supply.

"You're here already," a harried voice said.

He glanced up as Deanne emerged through the open doorway.

"You should have rung the bell, Will. I wasn't busy."

He doubted that. In their entire acquaintance, he'd never known her *not* to be busy. "Just got here. Barely sat down."

She glanced at his suit. "Looks like you came from City Hall."

"I needed some exercise."

She smiled, and something about her smile seemed forced. Will knew right then the luck had run out. He knew it as surely as he'd come to know Deanne Sandler, the executive director of Angel House, a determined and accomplished woman with a cloud of dark hair that wisped around her face, lending to the rushed, high-energy impression of someone who never sat still. To Will's knowledge she didn't. At least not often.

"Come to my office." She led the way toward the back of the house on quick steps.

As a hardworking mom slash administrator slash advocate for needy kids and their families, she was dressed casually. Her neat khaki slacks and button shirt with rolled-up sleeves were the perfect uniform for carrying out the myriad functions that made up her days. Long hours spent in her office with faculty and therapists. Impromptu chases after kids who could bolt like sprinters. Presenting issues to various media sources and politicians. Reassuring stunned parents after a diagnosis of Autism Spectrum Disorder.

Will knew firsthand how reassuring Deanne could be because she'd been a lifeline for him, a caring guide during the three years he and Sam had been affiliated with Angel House. She was a mentor who had become a much-valued friend.

At the moment, the classrooms were silent and empty in such a striking contrast to the normal daytime activity.

"Have a seat, Will," Deanne said as they entered her office.

There was no missing the cracked plaster molding that hinted at foundation instability or the discolored patches on the ceiling, water damage from roof leaks.

As a contractor, Will noticed it all.

Sinking into a chair, he loosened the tie that suddenly choked him. "You have the final numbers from the golf classic?"

Deanne clasped her hands on the desk, mouth pursed, gaze leveled, an expression Will had come to recognize as her we'll-forge-ahead-and-figure-out-how-to-make-it-happen look. "You want the good news or the bad news first?"

"Good news always." At least there actually was some.

"I have a lead on an agency that sounds as if it was custom made to fit the criteria for Family Foundations."

"Unexpected, but very good news."

She nodded. "And I got the numbers. Not so good."

"How long?" Not how much. The amount they raised only translated into how long they could remain operating.

"Enough to cover expenses until December."

"With or without the projection from the festival?"

"With."

"Damn." They faced each other without speaking because there was nothing to say. They'd hoped the revenue would cover operating expenses until at least next April, giving Will time to put the last pieces in place on their miracle. They could get one more school year out of this location.

No such luck. He hated how this always happened. Every quarter they projected costs for the upcoming quarter and decided whether or not they could keep the doors open. Then he got to go home to his son, knowing he had no way to provide everything Sam needed. Not without Angel House.

Living hand to mouth, his mother had always called it, and she would know since she'd reared three boys with no help from a deadbeat dad. Robbing Peter to pay Paul. That was another way to phrase what boiled down to plain not having enough money.

"Any possibility of squeezing another event into the calendar?" he asked. "Something big enough to tie us over until the McKay money gets here? That'll carry us through to the apple festival in September. Everything will be in place by then."

"I don't see what else our parents can do," she admitted. "The schedule is crammed already, and you know how labor intensive the festival is. There aren't enough hours in the day. Not without sacrificing all our time at home with the kids, and they're the whole point of everything we're doing. I don't know how we accomplish what we do already. It's not as if we get nights and weekends off."

That much was true. Sam's learning wasn't confined to a classroom during a normal school day. He didn't get to come home, do homework then spend the rest of his night being a kid. No, the learning was an ongoing process that took up every waking second of every minute of every day, and Will was Sam's teacher when he wasn't in school.

Even the simplest things, such as getting Sam to brush his teeth, required an action plan and consistent reinforcement. It had taken months for him to brush after breakfast without a meltdown that made it impossible to get out the door. Now Sam brushed before bed, too. The ultimate goal was to brush after each meal. Then they could move on to learning the next skill.

Slow progress, perhaps, but progress nonetheless.

Will was grateful for every move in a positive direction. And grateful that he only had Sam to worry about, and work. He wasn't the norm. Most parents juggled marriages and siblings in addition to their jobs and kid's special needs. As a parent with less on his plate than most, he'd felt obligated to help Angel House get on solid financial footing.

"What did the accountant say? Can't he pinpoint where the problem is?" That's exactly what Will's financial officer did for his contracting company, and those projections were hugely instrumental in sidestepping trouble.

"It's the economy, plain and simple," Deanne said somberly. "We're devoting more time to fund-raising for a lot less money. That's never a winning combination."

Will sighed. No arguing that. Even his company felt the pinch. New construction was down, and with so many people struggling to pay mortgages, renovations were a luxury many couldn't afford.

Or maybe Will had been so involved trying to solve Angel House's problems that he hadn't been focusing enough on his business. That was also a possibility.

"Whatever happens, Will, you should be at peace. You've gone above and beyond to help us qualify for this grant. Even if we can't apply with the Ramsey Foundation, you'll find some way to raise awareness about autism. I know you will, and we have no way of determining what good might come from that."

"Not after all this work." He'd won a seat on the city council to make this miracle happen—one more job he didn't have time for. "I'm not going to let a few months take away our chances. That's really all it amounts to. The deadline for the annual walk-through isn't until August thirty-one—"

"August *thirtieth*, remember? The thirty-first falls on a Saturday."

Great. Not even the calendar was on board with the plan. "One day isn't going to matter. If we can't keep operating here until next summer, then we have no choice but to move up the timetable and make this year's deadline."

Deanne sank back in her chair and stared at him. "Is that even possible?"

Not without a *real* miracle because the manufactured kind didn't seem to be cutting it.

But what was Will supposed to do—let Angel House close its doors? Sam needed more help than the government offered with all their special services, and the insurance company fought him every step of the way on additional therapies. But without the extra help, Sam wouldn't be accepted into a regular school. He'd be labeled "intensive needs" and sent to an exceptional center that still didn't have the services he needed.

Angel House filled that gap. It provided the extra training necessary to help Sam become higher functioning so he could get by with the level of special services the school system provided and continue to progress in the least restrictive classroom environment.

That's what Will wanted for Sam. He wasn't going to accept anything less. Period.

"We've got everything else in place, Deanne. All we need is a permanent location that fits specs for the grant. We've found that, too. We just need to move in."

She frowned. "You're talking about extensive renovations on a building that covers nearly an entire city block."

"Did I mention I own a construction company?"

Of course, he couldn't start the renovations until he had a partner to share the space and offset the private status of Angel House, thereby fulfilling the last requirement for tenancy.

"Tell me about this agency. Give me something to work with here." Stretching his legs in front of him, Will rubbed his temples. A tension headache on the way. What was new?

Deanne must have recognized the symptoms or was getting a headache of her own because she shoved away from the desk and stood. "You want coffee? I need a cup."

"Please." Maybe caffeine would constrict the blood vessels and cut off the throbbing before it worsened.

She headed off to the nearby staff room then returned with two foam cups.

"Here you go." She handed him one. "Judge Parrish sits on the board for the Young Leaders Camp Initiative. I presented to the board this week about developing more opportunities for our lower-functioning kids." She took a tentative sip as she sat. "After the meeting we talked about our potential involvement in Family Foundations, and Judge Parrish mentioned a divorce mediator who has an independent agency based here in Hendersonville."

"What's the name?"

"Positive Partings."

"Why does that sound familiar?"

Deanne shrugged. "Maybe you read about it? Apparently the owner has been active lobbying for divorce reform."

"Maybe." Not that he read much anymore. Not unless an issue involved the City of Hendersonville. For those issues he stayed tuned to the local radio station whenever he was in his truck and pored through council briefings in any spare moment. There weren't many of those.

"The agency fits the criteria for both Family Foundations and the Ramsey Foundation?" he asked. That was critical, and so far they hadn't had much luck.

"Looks like Positive Partings might be the answer to our prayers. Judge Parrish spoke highly of the owner and said they'd worked together with the family court. I did some research. The agency opened two years ago and serves a huge network of professionals from all over the state."

"Does it need more space?"

"Possibly. The owner teaches divorcing parent classes for the court. Apparently that's a part of all the lobbying she does—she's trying to standardize the system of court-ordered education."

"Those classes need reform. I attended one with some guy who managed to make four hours feel like two lifetimes of completely wasted time."

Deanne chuckled. "Yeah, well, it was probably good for you to sit down and relax for a change."

"Right back at you. But the coffee wasn't too bad if memory serves. Not as good as this, of course." He took another swig of brew that could have rusted a galvanized nail.

"It was good a few hours ago." She thoughtfully swirled the dregs in the bottom of her own cup. "Besides, I never argue with free. Smile and be grateful."

The coffee was a donation from the café on Main Street and demonstrated exactly the sort of community spirit and generosity that made Hendersonville special. A city small enough so people didn't get lost in the crowd, yet infused with new blood because of tourism and some-timers who kept vacation homes in the mountains. This sort of community was largely responsible for bringing Angel House into existence and keeping it going.

Until December, anyway.

"So Positive Partings might need more class-rooms," he said. "And you think the owner might be interested in a historic building the city's willing to cut her a break on rent for?"

Once *he* renovated it, of course.

"That's what Judge Parrish said. She thinks a location close to the courthouse would be attractive. And no question Main Street would be visible for folks who come to those classes. We've got a lot to offer. The low-rent lease. The location. Positive Partings would be crazy not to at least consider a move."

"Is the owner from around here?" Why else would anyone set up shop in Hendersonville? He could think of a lot of places in North Carolina with better access to the state capital.

"Hendersonville born and bred, according to the website." Deanne reached for her laptop. "Take a look for yourself. You won't believe the list of profession-als the agency serves. Would be great exposure for Angel House."

Will tossed his cup in the trash before heading to Deanne's side of the desk. He half sat on the edge and waited while she called up the site. "Can't get much more public service than family court."

"I know, right."

Given the demographic it served, Angel House would have been a shoo-in to benefit from the Fam-ily Foundations Project, which targeted five areas of focus for revitalization of Hendersonville. There was only one problem with Angel House: its affiliation with a Roman Catholic Church.

Will hadn't been involved with Angel House back then, but he knew the story well. Deanne had been looking for help after her daughter's autism diagnosis. Ten years ago there hadn't been an Angel House to help a parent maneuver the minefield of information and misinformation.

But she'd refused to settle for the meager services the government offered, which simply weren't enough to affect any progress in her daughter's treatment. She also refused to accept that she couldn't help her child.

So she traveled around the country to investigate every program that dealt with autism then approached her pastor to put her knowledge to use for her daughter and other families experiencing similar difficulties.

Angel House had started as a ministry in some unused classrooms of the parish school. And through the generosity of caring parishioners and the dedicated involvement of parents and professionals, Angel House flourished.

The church gifted the center with the house and land it occupied now. Deanne had reached out into the community to fund the renovations. The center had outgrown the old house, and there was no expanding. They needed to level the old structure and start from scratch and, given the costs involved, that simply wasn't possible as a ministry of one church.

No, for Angel House to grow and serve more kids,

it needed to grow into a real not-for-profit organization. That's when Will had conceived of letting the City of Hendersonville provide a new location through Family Foundations.

The church affiliation was the problem.

While Angel House served kids based on need, it was still perceived as a religious organization. If there was any better way to trigger a firestorm of controversy about how the city allocated funds, Will couldn't think of one.

No one wanted to hear that Will's company would fund the building renovations, or that Angel House supported itself through donations, fund-raising and private grants that came from all over the community, and the nation, too—*if* they could secure the all-important Ramsey Foundation grant. But applying for that grant meant they needed a permanent location in an area that served its community.

The chicken and egg.

In order to make this work, Will had to couple Angel House with another organization with a strong public service affiliation in the new location to bridge the distance between the city's private and public sectors.

Positive Partings?

"Here you go." Deanne tilted the laptop his way then stopped. She placed her hand over his. "Seriously, Will. Before we go one step further, do you really think it's possible to get all that work done?

I know what renovating this place was like and we didn't knock down walls."

She met his gaze with the quiet desperation and determination of a mother who took every breath to clear obstacles out of her daughter's way and give her a chance to learn. There was no time for fear in the journey, no room for doubts, only the grinding day-to-day, minute-by-minute, steps along the path.

And lots of hard-won triumphs to light the way.

Deanne had helped Will see those, too, to accept that, while his journey as a parent differed from what he'd expected, the differences brought unique joys, and so much love.

She devoted her life to helping her daughter and to paving a smoother way for others until the medical community and insurance companies and the local, state and federal governments caught up with their services.

"I won't lie, Deanne. Even if this agency proves to be the right one, and we can convince the owner to sign on fast, we'll be making a leap. The building has to be updated before I can bring it up to specs for Angel House. And I won't even know what I have to do until I get inside and start taking things apart. But how can we not at least try when we're this close?"

All the uncertainty melted from Deanne's expression. She understood shooting for the stars. She knew what it meant to hope against hope.

And she went for it every time and taught others

to take those insane leaps of faith, to believe in miracles because there was always hope.

How could Will do any less for the woman who'd given him so much, for all the families who relied on Angel House?

How could he do any less for Sam?

CHAPTER TWO

KENZIE SAT ON the bench across from the two-story building that occupied nearly the entire block between South Main and West Orchard Streets.

She loved this building with its brick front and chipped white-paned windows and faded blue canopies. A few coats of paint would restore the windows to their former glory as easily as new fabric would replace faded with bright.

Well worth the effort, Kenzie knew. No question. She'd loved this building ever since first setting eyes on it as a child when her parents had brought her to an open house to decide if she had any interest in dance lessons.

She'd taken lessons from Madame Estelle and the other professionally trained instructors in ballet, jazz, lyrical, tap and musical theater. She'd competed and performed year after year and had even taught classes during summer technique camps.

But that had all been before college graduation when she'd struck out to establish her career, and gotten so busy that even squeezing in dance classes as exercise proved a challenge. Before Madame Estelle had passed away and her estate had sold the building to the city.

Once this former dance studio had symbolized dreams in Kenzie's young mind. Now she had fond memories and an appreciation for its killer location in Hendersonville's historic downtown.

Kenzie thought of all those long-ago afternoons getting lost in Mast General Store with her friends, gathering at the soda shop after school functions and enjoying the various music, art and food festivals that took place in practically every season.

As far as Kenzie was concerned, Hendersonville was the model for healthy family living, abounding with opportunities to engage in community and outdoor activities and culture. Not too rural. Not too urban. *Perfect*. Which was why she'd chosen her hometown as the base for her agency.

Because she liked living here.

The very thought of working in this beautiful building made her breath catch, which is why she'd arrived a few minutes early to her appointment. She needed to wrap her brain around this unexpected opportunity so she could think clearly and weigh the offer with reason, not emotion.

The Family Foundations Project.

The certified letter had arrived just before the close of yesterday's business day with an invitation to participate in the project by relocating her agency into this building. If she understood the letter correctly, the city would cover the cost of renovations to meet her agency's specific requirements, and she'd contract for an extended period at a very reasonable rent.

An opportunity of a lifetime?

She'd heard of the Family Foundations Project but was sketchy on details. She didn't care for walking into any meeting unprepared, but there had simply been no time for research. By the time she'd gotten home from last night's class and finished prepping for today's meetings, she'd barely been able to keep her eyes open. So she'd jotted down a list of questions to ask the mayoral representative. Lots and lots of questions.

Her cell phone beeped, and Kenzie glanced at the display. Time to go. Would not do to keep the mayoral representative waiting. She'd barely crossed the street and knocked when those glass-paned front doors flung wide and a man appeared.

"Good morning, Ms. James." His voice was rich-timbered and male, a voice equally comfortable at hushed conversations by candlelight or projecting over a crowd. And a bit throaty, too, as if he hadn't been awake long. "Thanks for coming today."

Kenzie barely had time to shake off that ridiculously personal thought before he extended his hand. "Will Russell."

The first thing Kenzie noticed was how big his hands were, long-fingered and strong with the rough skin of a hardworking man but a grip unexpectedly gentle.

The second thing she noticed was that his name

sounded familiar. For a suspended instant, she racked her brain to remember why—an effort because his fast smile blinded her.

Figuratively, of course, but she mentally shook herself. By the time she'd slipped her hand from his and realized she hadn't yet replied because she was too busy staring, she belatedly said, "Kenzie James."

He motioned her inside, and she stepped past him into the once-familiar reception area. "You're the mayoral representative for Family Foundations?"

"I am." He shut the door and beelined to the refreshments set up in the former reception window.

Kenzie stared at the neat line of Will's business haircut. He was a big man, physical in an earthy, I-work-with-my-hands sort of way. Not so much crazy tall or overly muscular, just a bit off scale. Athletic, broad-shouldered. Larger than life in a way that made her think of old movie stars like Clark Gable, debonair and charming.

"I know it's early," he said genially. "But with the short notice I was afraid I wouldn't make it on to your schedule, so I brought coffee."

He seemed so eager to make up for the perceived inconvenience that Kenzie didn't have the heart to decline. Particularly since he looked as if he could use a cup himself.

"Black, thank you."

While she waited, marveling over her remarkable awareness of this man, Kenzie remembered why Will Russell was familiar.

A man for the people.

She could practically see his face on the campaign propaganda that had arrived in her mailbox during the last municipal election. His expressions had ranged from smiling to thoughtful to somber, depending on the issue.

He'd campaigned on his blue-collar roots because he hadn't had political experience. A local business owner, if memory served. He'd won his seat. Coming face-to-face with that blinding smile and those dimples suggested a reason why.

Even so, Kenzie hadn't voted for him.

Well, weren't they off to an interesting start? Will probably had no clue that this process would have been so much simpler had the mayor pro tempore or any of the other council members shown up.

Someone who hadn't already crossed Kenzie's path.

Did Will even know his ex-wife—his *last* ex-wife—had consulted with Positive Partings during their divorce?

The man certainly didn't act as if he knew. He seemed perfectly cordial as he offered her the first cup before pouring one for himself and taking a sip.

"Why don't we look around, Kenzie?" he suggested. "I'll tell you about the council's offer then address your questions. Sound good?"

She nodded and placed a firm lid on her reaction. She didn't know Will personally, so judging him based on one side of a story wouldn't be kind or fair. If the mayor sent him to represent her, then Kenzie needed to give him a chance. She had a high regard for the mayor—Hendersonville's first female mayor—who was as laid-back and delightful to be around as she was politically effective.

So Kenzie followed Will through a doorway and stepped inside an open room that looked exactly as she remembered. Floor-to-ceiling mirrors made up the rear wall with a ballet barre running the length.

"Great light and lots of space," Will said. "Building was outfitted with central heat and air-conditioning a good twenty-five years ago, judging from the system. It'll get new units and ductwork once we confirm how to parcel up the square footage. Place needs updates, but the building is structurally sound."

Kenzie took in the windows at intervals along the one wall, allowing light in. The early-morning sun illuminated dust motes of a building too long unused, wistful from the memories of the bright lights and all the activity of her memories.

"Have you heard anything about the Family Foundations Project?" he asked.

Kenzie sipped the coffee then admitted, "Not much, I'm afraid. Family Foundations was an issue during the last election. The project addresses some areas targeted for renewal by the mayor."

"That's actually more than most people know. Unfortunately, turnout for local elections is dismal. Easy to get the impression no one cares. Glad that's not the case."

"It's a challenge to keep up with the issues," she said. "I don't come close, but I do make a point of attempting to catch up before I head into my precinct to vote."

"Did you vote for me?" He flashed that smile, blinding her with the glare.

What was up with her and this man's smile? "I did not."

"I'm crushed." Humor showed deep in his striking eyes, gray and so clear they seemed to sparkle. "May I ask why? Just generally. Was it district or about a specific issue? The council is nonpartisan, so accountability? Availability? I'm guessing it wasn't about political experience because the guy I ran against had less than I did, which is saying something."

Did he grill every voter? She supposed it was a natural politician question, but he surprised her with his candor. She sidestepped answering by asking a question of her own. "I was unaware of your experience."

"A three-year term on the Historic Preservation Commission. That's why I know so much about the Main Street Advisory Board. They've been working on revitalization of the downtown district since long before I came on board. It's largely because of the new historic status of the area that we've been able to get funding. We're improving the infrastructure trying to grow tourism and new business. All good stuff. You're invited to be a part."

"First question."

"Shoot."

"Why me?" Her agency hadn't yet celebrated its second anniversary, and one typically had to be involved in government bureaucracy to even know Positive Partings existed.

Or be familiar with the divorce process.

Which Will Russell was, with not one but two divorces behind him. And he couldn't be much older than she was. Thirty-ish? He'd never attended her classes. Of that she was certain. There was simply no overlooking this man.

Idly sliding a hand along the barre, he gave an occasional tug as if testing the stability. Then he met her gaze in the mirror, addressing her question with his undivided attention.

"Family Foundations targets public services, downtown revitalization, economic growth, infrastructure and family support. You're a locally based agency doing public service work for our community that's directly related to families.

"This building sits on the outer boundary of the Main Street Historic District, so it qualifies for renovation funds. But we can't allocate those funds until we have tenants to provide steady revenue and, because we're using the city's money, there are guidelines for tenancy."

Kenzie was suddenly glad for the coffee, which provided a chance to glance at her cup and avoid the intensity of his gaze. "The letter mentioned sharing the space."

"The other tenant will be Angel House. It's a local resource center for families and a preschool for exceptional students."

Sipping her coffee, she kept her gaze fixed on her cup and asked, "What sort of exceptionalities?"

"Primarily autism but other pervasive developmental disorders along the spectrum like Asperger's."

Kenzie considered that. "Two local businesses that serve the community through family support. Divorce and special needs. One provides services through the public court. The other through private education. One business deals exclusively with adults, while the other deals with children. Family Foundations is covering all the bases, isn't it?"

He raised his cup in a mock toast. "Very good. People may not always agree on the issues, but everyone wants their tax dollars at work where they can see it. We're trying to hit as many demographics as possible."

Kenzie could practically feel approval radiating off him. This man wore his heart on his sleeve. She had no idea why, but his inner child was instigating her inner child in a big way. She could feel his intensity straight to her toes.

Chemistry. *Honestly.*

Running a hand along a windowpane, she glanced out at South Main Street, at the traffic rolling past, at the people on the street even this early in the day. Such an incredible location. "So who decides how space will be allocated? Preschoolers need room to run around."

"This is a big building. A former dance studio." He pulled on the barre to emphasize his point. "There's a recital hall in the back. When you count the parking lot, this place encompasses an entire city block. We'll create two separate facilities. The exact square footage will depend on your needs."

"Who gets the parking lot?" The lot was to the side of the building, cleverly accessible from West Orchard Street rather than Main, which could have created difficult traffic situations or limited accessibility during rush hour.

And there was usually plenty of activity on the street, so Kenzie wouldn't feel so isolated getting to her car after night classes. A definite minus for her current location.

Most folks were pleasant enough, usually inconvenienced to attend court-ordered classes and wanting to get in and out as fast as possible more than anything else. But her career hadn't been free of stressful incidents. Such was the nature of dealing with the adversarial divorce process.

"The lot will be accessible to both tenants," he reassured her. "There's plenty of room even for the school staff, and, if for some reason you need overflow, there are the metered lots nearby." He covered the distance between them with a few long strides. Then he was so close she had to tip her head to meet his gaze.

She resisted the urge to step away.

He gazed out the window toward the parking lot in question, which was barely visible from this vantage. The morning sun backlit his profile, cast his expression in shadow.

"We've got some preliminary plans drawn up," he said. "Nothing firm, of course, but every possibility sections the building from front to back, not side by side as you might expect with this much square footage. Your agency will benefit from the visibility of Main Street since you deal primarily with the general public. Angel House will have considerably more square footage, but they'll take the back portion of the building with the recital hall entrance on South Wall Street. It's more appropriate for a school setting. How does that sound to you?"

"Definitely can't beat the address."

That pleased him. She could tell by the way his expression eased, turning down the intensity a notch. "Come on."

Motioning toward the door, he led her into the other smaller studios and administrative offices that made up the remainder of the first floor. "I want you to see the whole place so you can imagine your agency here. I understand you need more space for classrooms. Is that right?"

"Eventually," she said noncommittally. Not only did she intend to expand service by hiring more instructors, but also to start training educators from all over the state. Divorcing parent education needed consistency to be effective.

She'd already laid the groundwork with the state. In fact, that was one of the main reasons she'd ventured into opening her own agency. Through the years, she'd garnered a lot of support to fill the need for quality education.

She hadn't dared to hope for a location so close to the city center, an address that lent her credibility in such a big way.

Without Family Foundations, she could never afford such a high-visibility location.

"Who knew dancers needed so much space, right?" Will commented. "There are a lot of mirrors."

"And ballet barres."

A dimple flashed. "These rooms are perfect classroom size, don't you think? The square footage ratio for your students is something like ninety or a hundred to one, I believe."

At least one of them had done his research. Kenzie wasn't sure how she felt about that. Or by the way the deep-throated sound of his voice made it difficult to concentrate.

She didn't mention that she and this building were old friends, allowed him to tour her through the familiar rooms and do most of the talking, explaining the merits of relocating, talking about the work that needed to be done.

"If you require a really big classroom, we could leave this room as is. It's already designed for the public with the separate restroom facilities. All we need to do is get some fixtures in this second bathroom. Plumbing is already there."

"Oh, sounds easy enough." Once upon a time that bathroom could hold at least ten girls, all laughing and dodging practices. The other room had been a dressing area where the students could change out of their street clothes.

"Can you use a classroom this size?" he asked.

The man was getting more direct, probably wanted to gauge her interest and had realized he was doing most of the talking.

"I could."

"Good." He met her gaze with a curious one of his own, and she wondered if he thought she was being purposely evasive.

She wasn't. She simply was taken aback. By this unexpected offer. By Will Russell. By the way she kept getting distracted by the sparkly color of his eyes and the throaty sound of his voice and his big hands that seemed to swallow the cup he held.

"Come on. Let's get a refill," he finally said. "Don't know about you but I could use more caffeine. We'll go by way of the second floor so you can see upstairs. Then I can show you where we propose to divide the building."

Had she not already known something about this man's character, she might have felt reassured and not as if he was trying to sell her. But Kenzie did know something. From what she'd heard, he was a ruthless charmer used to getting his way.

And he wanted something from her. He had something at stake here. She could feel it as surely as she could feel her own unexpected awareness of him.

"How did you hear about my agency, Will?" she asked as he allowed her to precede him up the staircase that opened to an area that had once held racks upon racks of costumes.

"Divine intervention." He chuckled, a rich sound that echoed in the confines of the empty room. "A judge with the family court apparently thinks highly of your work. She sits on a board with another affiliate of Family Foundations. Your agency came up as a possibility."

Judge Geraldine Parrish had likely been the one to toss Kenzie's name into the hat. Geri wasn't only a longtime supporter, but also an equally longtime family friend.

"So are you a possibility, Kenzie? How do you like what you see so far?"

No more subtle probing. She glanced around the room with two lovely canopied windows that opened over the alley. Since the shop next door was only one floor, the room got plenty of light over the pitched roof. Perfect for a mediation room, she decided, spacious and private enough to fit couples, attorneys, advocates if they had them.

She answered Will's question with a question of her own. "Were those firm numbers on the lease?"

Inclining his head, he reached out to take her cup. "Within the range. Can't say whether it'll be high end or low, but it won't be any more, or less. That I can promise. Once we parcel up the building and determine the exact square footage, I can give you solid numbers. The Main Street Advisory Board and the Historic Preservation Commission set the scale."

"I see." And she did. Crystal clear. Even accepting the smaller portion of the building at the high end of the rent range, she'd be nearly doubling the square footage of her current offices in a strip plaza near the railroad depot for not substantially more than she currently paid.

Kenzie followed Will from the studio downstairs into what had once been Madame Estelle's office. There would be an office for Kenzie, one for her assistant Lou, and a comfortable reception area. An improvement already from her current location.

"Here's the end of the line. The proposed end, anyway," Will said. "We'll insulate the walls, make sure everything is solid and soundproof. No worries there."

"How do the percentages break down?"

"Roughly seventy-thirty." He rolled his eyes. "Okay, more like seventy-two, twenty-eight. If you don't have enough space, we can always take a second look. Angel House could negotiate."

She only nodded. Twenty-eight percent translated into something like fifteen thousand square feet. The building certainly appeared designed to be split, with the entrance in front and the recital hall entrance in the rear. Kenzie remembered Madame Estelle's conversations about refinishing the recital hall floor, and knew that hall alone was over seven thousand square feet.

As they continued to the rear of the building and the space that would eventually belong to Angel House, Will explained the changes that would take place. He sounded like the host of any of the home improvement programs she watched on television.

"When you're not conducting city council business, what's your line of work?" she asked.

"I own a construction company. WLR General Contracting and Development."

"WLR?"

"William Lord Russell."

"Lord Russell? A middle name?" The question was out of her mouth before she thought better of asking.

He pulled a face. "My mother's maiden name. She thought it was hysterical. Still does."

That made Kenzie laugh despite herself. "Oh, I understand. Trust me. I live with my parents' attempt to be modern. And all I do is explain that Kenzie isn't short for anything."

The dimple flashed, and Kenzie had to ask herself why she was sharing personal information with this man when she'd already decided to stick to the facts.

But Will Russell was charming. There was no getting around that. She'd have had to be dead not to notice. And this meeting was proving she definitely wasn't dead.

A distraction was in order.

Inside the recital hall, she took in the full effect of all this space, with the tiered seating and well-worn curtains, the overhead lighting big and bulky, reminiscent of another era.

He couldn't know that she had years and years of memories inside this hall. The short dances and cute costumes of the preschool dancers, many of whom began their dancing careers too shy to perform so older students buddied up to coax them on stage.

The performances had grown more challenging as students aged and skill levels progressed. Those shows had served as practices for competition routines and award ceremonies to celebrate hard work and discipline. By the time Kenzie had been in college, she'd danced in recitals, choreographed her own sections, taught beginner classes and emceed many of the dances as Madame Estelle had grown old and needed help.

This hall had been the one place students could shine and show off and revel in the applause of an always appreciative audience. No matter what happened during competitions, the unexpected problems, the heart-breaking disappointments, the stomach-churning anxiety and the companionable and fun celebrations, this space had been a safe place for all Madame Estelle's dancers.

Here each and every one of them had been a star.

"What's going to happen to this hall?" Kenzie asked.

"Reallocated into classrooms. Lots of them."

His admission drove home the reality that Madame Estelle's would vanish into history, her legacy and everything this studio had been to so many people would end forever. In some ways more final than even her death five years ago.

But Madame Estelle would have never wanted this recital hall to sit empty, and as Will flipped off the house lights for what felt like the last time, Kenzie thought of special needs preschoolers who would utilize this space. Madame Estelle, with her French accent and larger-than-life laughter, would likely be pleased to know new generations of children would make a home in the building she'd loved so dearly. Her true legacy lay in the hearts of all those who had danced here, all who felt welcomed and encouraged and cared for by an instructor who challenged them to dream big.

The thought made Kenzie smile.

Following Will to the reception area in the front of the building, she considered the possibility of making this her new home.

"More coffee?" he asked, and when she declined, he poured himself some. "What do you think so far? Got any questions for me?"

Family Foundations was a dream come true in just about every way. Positive Partings had begun with a solid network of professionals and her contract with the state, but a business was a business.

Overhead. Licensure. Staff. Insurance. Supplies. The list went on.

Kenzie had known her strip plaza wouldn't suit her long-term goals when she'd originally signed the lease. And she'd quickly outgrown the place thanks to her network of professionals who, like herself, believed the adversarial divorce process needed reform. Judges, attorneys, mediators and psychologists from counties all around Hendersonville kept her calendar full.

But mediation wasn't ever going to make her rich. Despite her crazy-busy schedule, the agency was still new, which hadn't left free capital to make a move to any place more substantial. Certainly not to a prime location such as South Main Street.

"At first glance, this deal couldn't have been packaged any more perfectly if someone had tailored it to my needs." Although now Kenzie suspected she had a very good idea who that *someone* was. "So perfect, in fact, had the invitation come from any organization other than the City of Hendersonville, I would have thought it was a scam. But everything in the proposal is legitimate city business."

Will arched an eyebrow as if surprised by her frankness. "Completely legitimate. Cross my heart."

Kenzie wanted to believe him.

"Tell me your concerns," he coaxed. "I can address them."

"What's the catch?"

"Too good to be true?"

She nodded.

He set the cup on the counter. "Well, maybe at first glance. But the building's really old. Renovations will update a lot, but things will still go wrong. You can count on it. That's the nature of the beast with any building that's been around awhile. The city will cover some of the maintenance, and that will be detailed in the lease, but it won't cover everything. You'll want to consider carrying more insurance than you probably do now or you'll be asking for trouble."

Fair enough. She could find out what decent insurance cost and crunch the numbers. "That's it?"

A beat of silence. "You won't get much time to debate this decision. Seventy-two hours, otherwise the project committee will move to the next candidate on the list."

It took Kenzie a moment to process *that*. "Wow. Seventy-two hours. That's not a lot of time."

"We've got to get the renovations underway. Angel House needs to be relocated before the next school year begins and we're already pushing our luck. Can't have the kids start school in one location then move while they're in session."

That made sense, but seventy-two hours? She would barely get enough time to research everything she needed to make a rational decision. Not when she already had a full day of work ahead of her. She wouldn't even be able to begin until tonight.

She wondered if she should push for more time. He'd already said they couldn't lease to any business, so she had to wonder how long the list of potential tenants actually was.

Then again, did she really want to risk losing an opportunity to move into this building? This completely perfect location?

To preserve some of the legacy of the woman who had taught her to reach for her dreams?

"When can I realistically expect my part of the building to be ready?" she asked.

Will reached for a laptop case and withdrew a folder. "City won't release funds to start the renovations until both tenants sign the leases. Give me an idea about what you think needs to be done so you can function in your space."

Motioning her to the counter, he spread out a sketch of some floor plans. "Take a look at these. I'd like an idea if I need to start knocking down walls."

He'd be knocking down walls?

Kenzie saw a problem. "You're in charge of renovations?"

He nodded.

Maybe that shouldn't have surprised her. Maybe she should be relying on what she'd heard about him instead of trying to be *too* fair. "You mentioned spending the city's money, yet you hired your own firm?"

"There's no conflict of interest if that's what you're asking. I promise. The mayor and the other members of the council are all fully aware of the situation. We've worked out an equitable arrangement.

Of course, you're welcome to confirm that with the mayor or the council. There's the Historic Preservation Commission and the Main Street Advisory Board, too. And Angel House. A lot of people to be accountable to and to govern the budget. Give any or all of them a call."

"In my seventy-two hours?"

He smiled at that and she took a step back instinctively. She was too close to this man whose charm oozed off him in a physical wave. *Way* too close.

"So, do I need to knock down walls?"

Would she be foolish not to take advantage of an opportunity to create a new floor plan when the city footed the bill?

She indicated the plans. "May I?"

"Please." Will stepped back from the counter, clearly willing to give her whatever time and space she needed.

Kenzie studied the floor plans.

Various options were laid out from barely changing anything except constructing the walls that would separate Positive Partings from Angel House to literally restructuring the main studios into smaller rooms, similar to how they'd reallocated the space in the recital hall.

And Kenzie knew right then that if she decided to seize this opportunity, she would fit her business around the rooms that had served Madame Estelle so well for decades.

Big classrooms. Smaller classrooms. Spacious and

comfortable mediation rooms. And an office with a view.

"No need to knock down walls. I'd rather see your efforts spent on updating what we've got."

"I was hoping you'd say that." He sounded relieved. "Really? Why?"

"Because I can get you in here more quickly. I'll do preliminary work like the air handlers and painting, but the rest can be done once you're in. That will give you a chance to see what you want done. I can work around your schedule so I don't interfere with business."

He spoke as if she'd already signed on, when Kenzie hadn't even decided if she could make such a big decision in seventy-two hours. She'd call her parents and ask their opinion. Singular. They'd only have one. They'd discuss, debate then decide on one common opinion to suit them both. They were an excellent example of a longtime couple who had worked hard to master the art of marriage.

And her dad was insurance savvy having been the owner of a title insurance company until his retirement. He'd figure out the coverage she'd need and what it would cost.

"It's my understanding the lease on your current property is up in April, Kenzie. Did I get that right?"

She nodded. The fact he'd taken the time to research her bore up her impression that he was personally invested in the outcome of her decision.

"Okay, so making a move is coming at a pretty

convenient time for you. I mean, you won't have to deal with prematurely ending a lease and may have only a few months overlap. Were you planning to stay where you are now?"

She considered how forthright she cared to be. There was really no comparison between her strip plaza offices and this building, as he surely already knew.

"I hadn't really decided. This opportunity is convenient in the sense that if I wasn't going to sign my lease again, I'd have to notify the management company by the end of this month. They require ninety days written notice to vacate."

"Did you want to spend another year there?"

She shook her head. "Not really, but I might have stayed simply because I haven't yet contacted a real estate agent to begin scouting a new location."

"Why not?"

"Too busy. And I'm not sure if I'd be better served buying my own location. Real estate being what it is right now, I can get more for my money with a mortgage than a lease."

"Except with the City of Hendersonville. Best deal around." Those dimples again.

Her breath did a little fluttery thing in her throat and she had the sudden memory of the conversation she'd had in class only a few nights ago.

Lust at first sight?

Oh, please… Well, okay. *Maybe.*

Just because lust at first sight wasn't a good idea

didn't mean it didn't happen. Even to someone who had her inner child firmly under control.

Will returned the floor plans to the folder, shuffled through the papers with those long fingers as if checking to make certain everything was there then he slid the folder toward her. "This is yours. Everything you need to know about Family Foundations. The lease is there for you to review along with the proposed floor plans. I put a lot of contact information in there in case you think of more questions. My cell number, too, so you can call me anytime."

"Thank you." She *wanted* to hang her shingle outside this building, so the real questions were whether or not the move was viable and if she could determine that in seventy-two hours.

There was also Will Russell to consider. If the man's company was renovating, he'd be around. In her building. Did she really want to involve herself with a man whose integrity she'd questioned enough to not even consider voting for him?

A man whose charming presence had unexpectedly whipped her usually well-mannered inner child into a frenzy?

"I'll get back to you with my decision in seventy-two hours." She extended her hand, and he took it.

Unfortunately, invisible sparks flew.

"I'll look forward to hearing from you."

Kenzie had no doubt he meant what he said.

CHAPTER THREE

WILL STOOD AT the front door of the suburban-style home, a well-landscaped yard and sizeable house that looked similar in size and style to the house next door. And the one across the street. And the one up the street. Why builders never used architects who designed houses with continuity of style rather than cookie-cutter designs was a mystery to him.

He didn't bother ringing the bell again, knew the effort was wasted. Guadalupe would get to the door when she got to the door. She had her hands full inside. That much he knew.

He heard her voice even before the locks started rattling.

"Coming, Will. Coming. As fast as I can, which isn't fast enough."

Guadalupe Santiago was the only person Will knew who could stretch his name into two syllables. *"We-el."*

Better yet, when she referred to him with the kids, she managed to turn his name into lyrics.

"Me-ester We-el."

The last lock jangled and the door opened to reveal the short, rounded form of Guadalupe wearing a patterned housedress, her wild salt-and-pepper hair barely contained under a kerchief.

"Come in. Come in," she said. "Sorry to keep you waiting."

"No problem, *chica*."

Will entered and toed off his shoes to add to the heap already in the foyer. A sacred house rule. Guadalupe didn't like people tracking in dirt on her clean floors. Her floors were always clean because people didn't track in dirt.

She could have covered her windows with aluminum foil for all Will cared because this home had the most important things as far as he and Sam were concerned: accessibility for a child with special needs, hearty laughter and lots of love.

"I told him he could finish his coloring." She wiped her hands on a dish towel. "You in a hurry?"

Will shook his head. "Not today."

"Good. Then come to the kitchen and tell me how it went this morning. You never texted me, so I fretted all day. Did you charm her with this cute smile?" Guadalupe reached up to grab his cheek and gently tugged.

Will didn't think he'd charmed Kenzie James. Unfortunately. Not for lack of trying, though, but he didn't want to make Guadalupe worry more than she already worried. She was as invested in Angel House as he and everyone else.

A Cuban native, Guadalupe's thick accent accompanied a heart of pure gold. She'd come to this coun-

try after her husband's death to assist her daughter
and son-in-law in caring for their son, Rafael, who
was two years older than Sam and further along his
journey to higher functioning.

Thanks to Angel House.

In fact, it was Deanne who had arranged for Guadalupe to help Will during those first dark months
when he'd been alone playing both dad and mom and
failing miserably. And trying to work. And run his
company. And deal with the house. And feed them.
And get Sam to and from doctors' visits and therapy
sessions and Angel House. They would have never
made it if not for Will's mother who, although she
also worked full-time, had cared for Sam when she
wasn't working and cooked and cleaned and helped
Will get their lives under control.

Then Deanne had suggested Guadalupe as a possible solution to the care-giving problem. She already knew the drill because she took care of her
own grandson. Guadalupe had become the living
manifestation of Deanne's favorite saying.

God provides.

A day didn't pass when Will didn't reply with a,
"Thanks."

Rafael had found his language and proved an excellent role model for Sam. And while they didn't see
each other much at Angel House, they'd become great
friends during their afternoons together.

"Go sit at the table while I check on the boys and
make sure they're not getting into mischief," she said,

leading him into the kitchen where something that smelled really good simmered on the stovetop. "I'll let Sam know you're here."

Hanging the dish towel on the refrigerator handle, she slipped from the room.

Will sat and checked his phone for messages.

She reemerged as he sent off a text to a subcontractor on a remodeling job stalled while they waited for an inspector who hadn't shown up for the second day in a row.

Will would place a call to Building Services. Of course, he'd have to wait until Monday now. Damn.

"Going to be a few minutes," she said. "There's still some white space on the page. You look hungry. Will you eat?"

He nodded, grateful. All he had at home was leftover delivery pizza from last night's supper. There hadn't been time to cook while he'd been researching Kenzie James, preparing her proposal for today's meeting and moving Sam through their nightly routine.

Guadalupe set a bowl of steaming beef and beans in front of him along with a napkin and silverware. "Now tell me how the meeting went. Deanne wouldn't say a word when I picked up the boys."

"Thanks." He snapped open the napkin and grabbed the fork. "Deanne didn't say anything because she didn't know anything. I haven't spoken to her yet."

"Now you're making my heart hurt. The lady

didn't like the building? How could she not like the building? It's beautiful, and big."

"The lady liked the building. I'm sure she did."

"Then why don't you look happy?"

He had to think about that. "I'm not unhappy."

Guadalupe gave a huge, disgusted sigh and yanked open a cabinet hard enough to make the hinges squeak.

"Relocating a business is a big decision, *chica*," he said. "I didn't expect the lady to make a decision on the spot." In his dreams maybe… "She's a businesswoman. As it was I didn't give her much time to think things through."

"How long?"

"Three days. We should know something Monday."

"If she liked the building, then why do you look worried?"

He used a mouthful of Guadalupe's shredded beef and beans as a distraction to avoid answering her question. Will wasn't sure he knew himself. But Kenzie had bugged him. He hadn't expected her to be so…unapproachable.

Guadalupe knew he was dodging her question. Setting a glass of iced tea in front of him with a sniff, she left the kitchen to check on the boys again.

Will dealt with people. Always had. He could read them. Win them over if he put his mind to it. Even the tough ones who took some time and effort. Not that he was God's gift or anything, but people had always come easily to him.

Not Kenzie James.

She had some sort of invisible wall around her. As if right from the start she'd decided to keep her distance. She'd been polite and businesslike and *remote*. Only once had he gotten even close to an unguarded response from her. He'd told her his name and they'd connected for an instant, one fleeting interaction when he saw humor twinkling in her hazel eyes, heard amusement in her sudden laughter.

She was a lovely woman, fresh-faced and a lot younger than he'd expected a divorce mediator with such a stellar reputation to be. But when Will thought about it, which he hadn't had time to all day, he realized she was likely good at what she did because she had such a gentle, unflappable calm about her.

Was that what he hadn't been able to get around?

Maybe her distance had nothing to do with him personally and everything to do with a career that dictated she be the calm in the middle of storms. By definition when a couple needed mediation, they weren't agreeing on something. After two divorces Will knew that firsthand. In order to be an effective mediator for people who were at each others' throats, Kenzie James probably had become an expert at wielding her calm the way he wielded his charm. Like a weapon.

Only he hadn't wielded enough to make a dent this morning, the one time in his life it really counted.

Guadalupe returned and dropped into the chair adjacent to him with a sigh. "You were hungry."

"The meeting this morning put me behind. I spent the day running from job site to job site playing catch-up."

"You should pack a lunch."

He supposed he could have thrown a few slices of leftover pizza and an ice pack into one of Sam's lunchboxes. Cold pizza from a superhero lunchbox. Better than starving.

"This is really good. Thanks."

She leveled her dark gaze at him. "What's bothering you?"

He shrugged. "Meeting went okay. I guess I wanted more than *okay*. Maybe some indication she was going to sign on and solve a big problem."

"Is there something wrong with this lady? Why wouldn't she want to help us?"

Guadalupe lived to care for people. A born nurturer, so obviously her thoughts were about helping and that's how she would have talked to Kenzie. But Will hadn't slanted his presentation that way. He'd been all about what she could get out of the deal. He didn't think he would have gotten any further had he appealed to her charity and asked her to help a bunch of kids and their families. Not when it meant relocating her business.

"Maybe she will. We'll know in a few days, anyway, so no more fretting."

But, like the rest of the parents, grandparents and

caregivers of Angel House's kids, Guadalupe would continue to worry until Angel House got on solid financial footing or shut its doors, whichever came first.

"Well, if the lady turns down that big building, we can find someone else who's not so silly."

"Sounds like a plan." Will wished the solution was that simple. Despite what he'd told Kenzie about moving down the list of businesses interested in Family Foundations, the truth was that list consisted of one name.

Positive Partings.

The criteria were just so damned specific. And if he didn't get to work on that building yesterday, there would be no earthly way to make the deadline.

"I'll light a candle at church." Guadalupe pushed up from the chair. "It's the weekend, so I can slip out of here for the morning mass. Now, you take some of my apple bread home. I baked it this morning. Sam ate two pieces after school today."

Fickle taste buds came with the territory. Rafael had already transitioned to a gluten-free diet, which was encouraged by Angel House's nutritionist. But Sam wasn't even close, compliments of Will's epic failure. They'd failed every time Will had tried to introduce and transition Sam to new foods. Time was the biggest deterrent. No time to cook. No time to deal with Sam's behavior when he didn't want to eat something. Texture was a big issue, so until Will could make the time to consistently travel the long road to behavior modification, Sam's taste buds would dictate the menu. At the moment, they were both lucky they didn't starve.

Will scarfed down the last few bites then grabbed his bowl and glass from the table. He set them in the sink then dropped a kiss onto the top of Guadalupe's head. "There's a halo under that kerchief, isn't there? Don't know what we'd do without you."

"Starve for sure." She waved him off, a fierce-looking gesture as she held a knife to cut the bread, but she beamed. "You know if you need extra time to work on the building or to find another business to help us, Sam can stay here. Even overnight. Gabriella and Jorge don't mind. They like when Rafael has friends over."

"Thanks, my little Cubanita." Will only hoped he would get to take Guadalupe up on her generous offer.

For all their sakes.

WITH SO MUCH at stake and so much to gain, Kenzie had enlisted the aid of almost everyone she valued in her life to help her make an informed decision. With only seventy-two hours to gather research, answer questions and assess the consequences of becoming a part of Family Foundations, she'd needed help.

So she'd put both her parents to work even though they were still wintering in Punta Gorda. And Geri, who had recommended Positive Partings for consideration. And Nathanial, her lifelong best friend and sweetheart. And Lou, her proficient administrative assistant.

On the surface the decision was a no-brainer. Opportunity knocked, too good to pass up even for the few months overlap with her current lease. That overlap would enable her to move her offices around her current work schedule, which was a plus.

Classes were scheduled in advance, so she would have plenty of attendees to contact about the move, which was a minus. But the overlap gave her the option of working between the two buildings while Will and his company renovated—another plus.

Unfortunately this move was not a surface decision. And some of her most basic questions required ridiculous effort to answer because her seventy-two-hour window fell on a weekend.

Had Will Russell intended for her to be challenged by the inability to talk to her bank or easily access public records or consult with a real estate agent? Or had the timing simply been an oversight on his part? She supposed the reason didn't matter when the end result meant more work for her.

But there was the real problem—Will Russell. Her opinion of his integrity and her unexpected reaction to him had muddied the water of her decision.

All weekend Kenzie had operated like the president being briefed on the issues by an attentive staff. The fax machine churned out documents for her perusal. The phone rang constantly with calls and texts coming in during other calls and texts.

Geri had been in charge of providing information about Family Foundations. As a close personal friend of the mayor, she was in a unique position to get the inside scoop. Through her, Kenzie had learned that not only was Will the mayor's representative for Family Foundations, but he'd actually conceived of the original proposal as part of his platform to run for city council.

"I knew it," she said to Geri late on Sunday during one of their many phone conversations. "He's personally invested. I got the sense he was more than just someone presenting the offer. So his run for city council was to push his private agenda?"

"I'm not psychic so I can't tell you what prompted his run for council," Geri said drily. "What I can tell you is that Family Foundations is an insightful and intelligent approach to meet the mayor's areas of focus for renewal that wouldn't have gotten attention if he wasn't on the council."

Which sounded suspiciously as if he'd run to push his private agenda. Kenzie sat at her desk, suddenly feeling all the long hours of processing information that had kept her from much sleep.

"I'm not sure how I feel," she said. More emotion. Great. Was it any wonder she couldn't make a rational decision?

"What's bothering you, Kenzie?" Geri had never been one to dance around an issue. Add the twenty-plus-year age difference, and Geri easily fell into the role of mentor. "It's not as if he'll be around to bother you. So what's worrying you?"

Kenzie wouldn't mention how her knees turned to jelly every time Will had smiled. Such a ridiculously chemical reaction had been unexpected but not the end of the world. "I'm not worried per se. It's just I have a bad taste in my mouth about this man. Any other representative from the council and we wouldn't be having this conversation."

"Do you know him? Everything I've heard from Sally has been positive. She says the council has accomplished more in the past year with Family Foundations than she'd hoped to accomplish in her first *term*. That's high praise coming from someone who's achievement-oriented on a good day."

As mayor, Sally Morse knew what she was talking about.

"Okay, this is between you and me, Geri. But I consulted with his second wife during their divorce."

"Oh. Any conflict of interest?"

Kenzie spun around in her chair to stare out her office's only window. The view was of the alley running behind the strip plaza to the automotive parts store on the street behind. There was a big bay with enough room for a tractor-trailer to back in and deliver supplies. "No. Nothing like that."

"Then what?"

"It's just that I met his wife. She was a very friendly, very professional woman who was looking for a collaborative divorce to make the transition as easy as possible for their son."

"Admirable. I didn't even know he had a son."

"My point. I don't know about you, but I had a ton of campaign propaganda show up in my mailbox. I got phone calls, too. And I'm not talking automated. The man personally called his potential constituents. I'm serious, Geri. I had voice mails on my house phone and my cell. He left his number to call him back if I had any questions."

"Did you?"

"No. The only question I wanted to ask was why in all that campaigning, he never once mentioned he had a family."

"A divorce could be perceived as a negative."

"Two divorces."

"Twice as negative."

Kenzie slipped off her shoes and propped her feet on the desk. Much better. "You don't think it's odd he never once mentioned his son? The son he has primary physical custody of."

There was a beat of silence on the other end. Finally, Geri said, "That's unexpected. What part of the divorce was collaborative—the ex giving custodial rights to the father?"

"She didn't. We consulted and came up with a very equitable settlement that jointly split physical and legal custody. No sooner did we get everything documented and set a date for mediation than she calls me to say her soon-to-be ex hired Les Schlesinger because he wanted sole physical custody. The poor woman was in pieces and so panicked she sacrificed my fee and ran off to get herself a bulldog attorney to go to battle so she didn't lose her son."

"But she didn't win? There must be more involved in the situation than you were aware of."

"Absolutely. I only heard one side of the story. But I do know there wasn't any kind of negligence happening. Nothing on record. One of the attorneys in my network mentioned the case, which is the only reason I know of the outcome. I'd like to say no judge would give primary physical custody to a father without due cause, but you know as well as I do it doesn't always work that way. Sometimes the parent with the most money wins, which is why we need divorce reform."

"I hear you, Kenzie. And when you consider that Les is one of the original good old boys around here, you may even have a point. But I still don't get why you're taking this so personally. That doesn't sound like you."

"I know. I don't have all the facts, and it's not my place to form opinions, anyway. But I felt so bad for that mom and horrible I couldn't help her. When I saw how Will sidestepped the entire family issue, I got a bad taste in my mouth. For a man who's asking people to trust him…well, I didn't vote for him."

"And now he's asking you to become involved with his brainchild. I get it."

Not all of it. Not even Kenzie understood why she had practically melted at the sight of the man. "Just want to make sure I don't miss anything since I do have this information."

"Smart girl. What did your father say?"

"He said I should go for it."

"I think you should, too, as long as you don't have any other hesitations except for Will's potential character flaws. He'll be out of your hair after the renovations. And who knows, maybe this is his way of contributing to society for past indiscretions. The private school that'll be sharing the building was affiliated with a Catholic Church. Maybe the man's having a conversion experience."

Kenzie remembered what he'd said about covering every demographic. He'd been up front about that at least.

"Kenzie, if you're still undecided after a good night's sleep, stall for a few hours in the morning. We'll be together all day tomorrow reviewing cases. We'll make time to talk." Geri chuckled. "We always make time to talk."

"True, true." Kenzie smiled. "You're right. A good night's sleep to process this abundance of information and I'll be able to think more clearly in the morning. Thanks for all your help."

"What else did I have to do with my weekend?" Geri asked. "Aside from catch up on everything I haven't done because I spend every waking moment in the courtroom or my chambers."

"You're the best."

"Ditto, kiddo. Whatever you decide will be the right thing to do. Remember that."

Kenzie crossed her fingers.

A DECENT NIGHT'S sleep and Kenzie did indeed feel refreshed and more confident in her ability to brush aside impressions that shouldn't factor into business decisions about her agency.

Will Russell's personal life was none of her business.

Would she have been so troubled by the specifics of his custody battle had she not reacted so unexpectedly to the man? In the dawn of a new morning, Kenzie suspected not.

So, feeling more at peace than she had since coming face-to-face with the man representing Family Foundations, she headed into town at the crack of dawn. She was scheduled to be in Geri's chambers when the courthouse opened, so this was her last chance to be alone with her choices before her time was up.

After parking at the courthouse, Kenzie walked down Main Street to the bakery, where she treated herself to a piping hot latte and croissant. Then she walked to the city park in the brisk morning air.

Hendersonville resided on a plateau in the Blue Ridge Mountains at an elevation that produced a frigid chill on this early morning. But she embraced every second of being outdoors, knowing what the day ahead held in store for her. Long hours in Geri's chambers, where they would review cases and tailor the educational programs Positive Partings provided parents party to custody and visitation action.

Between case reviews they would chat. Geri had laughed about how much time they spent talking, but they simply didn't get together often enough, which turned every meeting into those of the marathon variety. Kenzie normally packed enough food for lunch and dinner so they wouldn't have to waste time leaving the courthouse for a restaurant.

The cold air and steaming latte cleared away the traces of fog in her brain. There were plenty of people in the park although many of the businesses hadn't yet opened. Main Street with its parks, squares and flower-filled easements made for an environment where people would feel welcomed and comfortable visiting Positive Partings.

Sipping her latte, she watched a young mother in sweats jog while adeptly pushing a double stroller holding toddlers.

There was an elderly couple, dressed to meet the morning air with scarves wrapped around their necks, an example of longtime love as they strolled along hand in hand, looking so comfortable together. Kenzie knew that look well since her own parents had been married over fifty years.

A group of women who were likely tourists with wide-brimmed hats and cameras gathered in front of the focal point of this small park—a memorial statue of a long-dead city patron—to take photos. Whether old friends or friendships in the making, they chatted animatedly and appeared to be having fun.

Then Kenzie saw *him*.

Suddenly he was all she could see, as if the world vanished from her periphery when he materialized, a manifestation of all the weekend's deliberation and effort and uncertainty.

He crossed the street at a steady clip, wearing a business suit similar to the one he'd worn while touring her through Madame Estelle's. He carried a child's ball under one arm, but it wasn't until he emerged from around a parked car that she saw the young boy whose hand he held.

His son?

A few more steps and Kenzie realized the adorable little boy couldn't have been anyone else. The same glossy black hair. The same dimples. He hurried along on sturdy legs, visibly excited, clearly sharing the same brisk energy of his dad.

The son who had been fought over by his parents. Will had won custody. Kenzie wondered why. There was a reason. That much she knew. A legitimate placement for this little boy's well-being? Or simply the result of one parent outmaneuvering the other through an adversarial, and often-flawed, divorce process?

She set down the croissant, suddenly without appetite, and reminded herself—yet again—that Will Russell's personal life wasn't any of her business.

That didn't seem to make a difference. Not when

she couldn't keep her eyes off him. He didn't appear to notice her, though, clearly not suffering the same malady of heightened awareness and curiosity. He stopped in a clearing, deposited his son and took off with long-legged strides.

The other day, she'd had the impression of big, but seeing him now, both his muscular build and easy athleticism pegged him as a very physical man. Masculine, but with a strength that was visibly contained, gentled somehow, as he rolled the ball to his son, who caught it eagerly and rolled it back.

Back and forth. Back and forth.

Their game wore on for a surprising length of time, a steady, repetitive effort that seemed to please the boy. Maybe six, Kenzie guessed, somewhere around kindergarten age.

She distracted herself by breaking off pieces of croissant to feed the squirrels who ventured near, tails twitching as they looked for a handout. The attempt at distraction was a failure, but Kenzie persisted, thoughts trailing to her initial consultation with that little boy's mother.

"We've been formally separated for over a year but haven't lived together for closer to two," the woman explained.

She was beautiful in that classic, porcelain-complexioned way that Kenzie, with her fuzzy red hair and freckles, had spent most of her life dreaming about. As if the woman had stepped off the cover of a magazine stylishly dressed with her long, slim skirt and silky blond hair. She smiled warmly, and Kenzie had no trouble seeing why this confident woman made a successful career in public relations.

"I want the divorce to happen as seamlessly as possible," she said. "There's no conflict. My husband and I both want what's in the best interest of our son."

Kenzie appreciated the sentiment and where this woman, and supposedly her husband, placed their emphasis. "Then you've come to the right place. Positive Partings specializes in the collaborative divorce process."

"I did my homework. Your agency comes highly recommended."

"I'm pleased to hear that. Today's consultation will let you know what the agency can do for you. Positive Partings has the resources and network to navigate you through a smooth divorce from start to finish."

"Smooth sounds good."

"I'll send you home with information today, so you can begin to give some thought to parenting arrangements, division of marital property and the support you expect from your husband. If you decide to retain my services, we'll meet again to review your information and prioritize. Basically we'll determine your range, Mrs. Russell, the things you're willing to negotiate and the things you're not."

"My son," she said earnestly. "Not negotiable."

Kenzie met her gaze, recognized the sudden glint in big blue eyes, the tension that made a porcelain expression seem brittle enough to crack.

"Of course," she said softly. "Your son's well-being is most important. You can familiarize me with the situation before scheduling our first conference with your husband. Sound good?"

The woman only nodded, still managing her reaction.

Kenzie stepped into the breach. "Generally we'll meet for up to two hours during that initial discussion then table anything that doesn't get worked out. We'll keep meeting until we come up with an equitable arrangement. In between these conferences, you'll meet with an attorney who practices collaborative family law to have your legal questions answered. Positive Partings provides access to the family court and divorcing parent classes and any other professionals who may be needed along the way."

"My son," Mrs. Russell said with effort. "He's really the only thing I care about. A little boy needs his mom."

The sound of laughter dragged Kenzie back to this moment, and with the memory of Mrs. Russell's heartfelt admission still ringing in her ears, Kenzie glanced instinctively toward the sound to find Will laughing as the ball soared past his son.

To her surprise, Will was the one who went after it, running past his son and heading straight toward her.

He caught the ball in an athletic lunge just as she extended her legs to block it from rolling under the bench and toward the street.

"Sorry about that." Laughter echoed in that deep,

resonant voice, but he didn't immediately realize who she was. Likely because he was looking at her legs. By the time his gaze made it to her face, recognition sparked in his clear eyes. "Kenzie."

"Good morning, Will." So much for stalling until the last possible second.

He glanced at his son, then he straightened with the ball clasped in his hands, so she had to tip her head to meet his gaze.

Her heart started to race.

"An unexpected pleasure." His charm was turned on full force in one fast smile. "Hope I'll be hearing some good news from you this morning."

He didn't put her on the spot exactly, only voiced his hopes in a simple, forthright way in that full-bodied voice that struck her in such an absurdly physical way.

But that observation came through the filter of Kenzie's adult mind. Her inner child felt as if he were extending his hand in welcome, slipping those warm, strong fingers around hers and inviting her close.

Suddenly, three days of weighing pros and cons were forgotten. Her intention had been to push the decision to the last possible second, but when Kenzie opened her mouth, she said, "I believe you will."

For one suspended moment, he stood motionless, so utterly still as if comprehending her words took effort. Then he flashed that high-beam smile again. "That is the best possible news. The absolute best. I'll give you a call later this morning, and we can set up a time to go through the paperwork. How does that sound?"

She nodded mutely, afraid to open her mouth lest something else unexpected pop out.

But her response seemed enough for him and everything about him seemed so earnest when he said, "Thank you, Kenzie."

Then he took off, leaving her staring after him as he returned the ball to his son, and resumed his place, saying, "Five more times, Sam, then we go to the truck."

Sam only rolled the ball toward his dad again, who returned it, holding up a hand with his fingers outstretched. He tucked his thumb until only four fingers remained.

A rush of adrenaline propelled Kenzie off the bench, her nerves suddenly wired and alive. She was aware of her every movement as if she could feel Will's gaze on her. The measured pace of her strides. The way her skirt tangled with her legs. The way her hair brushed her shoulders with every step.

The way her heart still pounded too hard.

What was it about this brutally handsome man that made her aware of him on a cellular level?

Kenzie didn't know, but she had a heads-up about his character and after the renovations, he'd be gone, leaving her with a new location as sparkly as his gray eyes and a chance to carry on Madame Estelle's legacy by reaching for the stars.

And a place to start practicing what she preached.

Kenzie was in control here, not her inner child. She knew the difference between the *L* words and wouldn't confuse the two.

CHAPTER FOUR

WHEN WILL HAD watched Kenzie sign the lease nearly three weeks ago, he could not have known that he'd only swapped one problem for another. Angel House might get a shot at the Ramsey Foundation grant—*if* Will lived long enough to get any work done on that side of the building.

Little Ms. Demanding had spent the better part of three weeks parading through her square footage, ordering him around in that soft-hush of a voice, commands always phrased as questions.

Is it possible…

Would you mind…

Not that she'd been overseeing the work. Thank God. But she'd shown up almost every night like clockwork to waltz through the rooms, checking out the day's progress. Always observant. Always complimentary.

Always with a written list of tasks for him that she added to whenever something struck her fancy.

"Would it be much work to replace those fluorescent fixtures for something more conducive to learning?"

"Could we possibly relocate these mirrors to the

ladies' facilities? They're out of place in the media-
tion rooms, but I hate to leave them gathering dust
in the attic."

Her nostalgia might be the end of him.

Tonight was the perfect example. He watched her
check out the new drywall in what she'd already designated as her office. She complimented him on the
work, thanked him for the effort, although the effort
hadn't been his. He'd been pulling crews from job
sites wherever he could spare them. No one minded.
One job was as good as another provided it came attached to a paycheck. Even better when it ran into
overtime.

Suddenly she made a beeline straight across the
room toward the window, and he could tell, even before she opened her mouth, that whatever was on her
mind would mean more work for him. Or his crew,
which was the same thing.

"What are your plans for these windows?"

"Replace the sills and trim," he said. "They're beat,
but the windows themselves are solid. Looks like they
were replaced not all that long ago." For a building
that had been around as long as this one, a few decades didn't qualify as so long ago.

"Any chance of preserving them, Will?" Kenzie ran a hand along the wooden grooves. "They're
lovely, and I don't imagine you can replicate this trim
easily."

He forced his gaze from the pouty mouth that had
exhaled his name to the polished pink fingertips on

the windowsill in question, a sweep of touch as light as her voice.

It took him a moment to comprehend the latest demand.

These windowsills were scored with dings and grooves and scratches. They'd been painted and re-painted through the years until the paint was layered thick and uneven.

He could probably rip out all the wood on every one of Kenzie's windows and replace it in less time than it would take to strip and hand sand the wood from a single one. But she was right about the re-placements. He could substitute the ornate woodwork with a modern manufactured equivalent, pre-cut and plain. The craftsmanship of the original win-dow trim—and the baseboards and crown molding for that matter—didn't exist anymore, not without a custom price tag well beyond his budget.

"You're talking about a lot of work." An *insane* amount of work. "The wood has to be stripped and sanded—"

"You don't think it's practical?"

"Restoring those sills and that trim is the meticu-lous work more suited to a retiree with nothing bet-ter to do all day than coax scrolled woodwork back to life with a detail sander."

Will was not retired. And his back was already against the wall to meet the deadline, and he got fur-ther behind schedule with every second they wasted considering window trim.

Kenzie only inclined her head, red-gold hair threading over her shoulders with the motion. Her expression didn't change, but somehow she seemed to deflate.

Will wasn't sure why he thought that. Her eyes, maybe? They were all hazel with gold specks. But now her gaze looked as if someone had blown out the spark.

Okay, now it was official—he was losing his mind from lack of sleep.

"Is there any way I could help?" she offered. "I'd be happy to do some of the work if you'll show me what to do."

Now he was deflating. Restoring all that scrolled trim meant something to her. And if she coerced him into doing the window trim, she might want to bring back the crown molding, too. And the baseboards. And the quarter-rounds.

The thought made him twitch. He stared at her. The smattering of freckles across her nose was more noticeable than usual in the unsuited-to-teach fluorescent lighting.

It wasn't enough that he needed to renovate this building on a time limit, now she wanted him to train unskilled labor? Okay…time for plan B. Given this woman's career, she should appreciate the art of negotiation.

Because he couldn't look a gift horse in the mouth.

"We can work something out as long as you're flexible on the time frame. There are a lot of windows around here, and I don't want to hold you up from moving in." He needed to get moving on Angel House. "If you're willing to tackle the job one room at a time *after* I get everything under control, I can show you what to do, provide tools. With both of us on the job, we'll bring all those windows back." Before the turn of the next millennia. He hoped. "Does that sound doable?"

"Sounds perfect."

"Do I need to put this agreement in writing?"

"I'll take you at your word." She glanced at the windowsill, her expression glowing again. "I think they'll be worth the wait."

No surprises there. Kenzie had consistently favored the quality of work over speedy resolutions. He'd been involved in residential construction for a lot of years and recognized the symptoms. Will finally had to ask. "I get the sense this building is more than your agency's new address. Do you know someone on the preservation commission or are old buildings a hobby of yours?"

The question seemed to amuse her. A smile played around her mouth, softened around the edges of her expression. "I was a student here. I studied dance from the time I was six years old all the way through college. Lots of memories."

"Of course." He didn't have to look too closely to imagine her as a dancer. She was slender and lean with long, long legs. She wore a fitted skirt that showcased her shapely legs tonight—a similar outfit to the others he'd seen her in.

Suddenly Will could imagine her wearing a skin-tight nothing outfit and doing all sorts of dance-y moves in front of the mirrors in one of the studios. Will knew nothing about dance, beyond the image of female bodies in motion, stretching and swaying erotically around poles.

He had to shake his head to clear the image.

Kenzie's connection to this building shouldn't have been rocket science. Not when he knew she was Hendersonville born and bred, and even looked the part with her graceful form. But former student hadn't once occurred to him. He needed sleep.

Still, he had trouble reconciling this gentle and proper woman with the building's former business. Dance implied motion and abandon. Pole or not, Will simply couldn't see this prim woman spinning around in front of mirrors with all that red hair whipping around her.

Time for this interview to be over. Kenzie had gotten all the minutes he had to give. The night wasn't even close to being over yet, and he hadn't seen Sam since dropping him off at Angel House this morning. "Let's have a look at that checklist of yours."

"Oh, okay." Surprise was all over her breathless words, and she quickly handed him the list. Will kicked shut his toolbox and sat on it to take advantage of the work lights.

Her list was as neat as he would have expected

from a woman who presented as properly as this one did. Items listed in her concise handwriting. Items crossed out with even lines. Items added neatly in different colored ink. From the order of the jobs, he knew she'd copied most from his proposal and added her own, likely as they'd occurred to her.

"Building separated," he said. "Check."

That job had taken the better part of the first week to complete. Will had run the electrical himself, staying every night until the wee hours.

"Air handlers. Check."

He'd spent the entire weekend here with Sam, installing those new handlers on both sides of the building.

"Ductwork is this week's project. If we don't run into any aggravation, we should be done by Thursday."

So he could pull Roger from the subdivision going up on State Road 27 to texture the ceilings around the new vents. He hoped there would be something left of WLR General Contracting and Development by the time he'd completed this project.

If he ever completed this project.

"Masonry repaired outside around the canopies. Not yet." He continued. "We're waiting for shipment on the canopies. Don't want to put in the new frames until they arrive. Rebuild the attic stairs. Check. Replaced the door header and support beams. Check." That job had been a mess. Some old roof leak had compromised the supports and had been repaired in the most half-assed job he'd ever seen. Just good luck that the bathroom ceiling hadn't caved in on a bunch of ballerinas.

"New lighting fixtures. Not until after the ducts and vents are in. Have you chosen the ones you want yet?" He glanced up and found her watching him intently.

"I did. Let me grab the catalog, I flagged the page." Spinning lightly on her heels, she headed toward the doorway where she'd dropped her gear.

Will didn't wait, but kept on with the list. "Painting won't happen until after we get everything done with the ceilings. We're not refinishing the floors until after we get the painting done. We won't replace the baseboards until after we get the floors refinished."

"That makes sense," she said, returning with the catalog in hand.

He was relieved she'd found something from this supplier because he could get delivery within a day rather than wasting more time waiting. He didn't tell Kenzie that.

In fact, the only thing working in their favor right now time-wise was the inspections. He'd muscled his way straight to the supervisor and insisted on not being jerked around because this was a city project. All the work he'd been doing on the council and his proximity to the mayor and city manager had produced all sorts of reassurances. So far the inspectors had shown up exactly when they said they would, which almost never happened. Will knew that firsthand.

"All this other stuff, along with the windowsills and trim can be done after you move in. I consider that fine-tuning, so just trust I'll get around to it. Neither of us can anticipate everything that needs to be done until you're in the building. More stuff will come up, so as it does, add it to your list. I'll work around you for all that stuff. Sound good?"

She nodded. "Sounds good."

"Great. So is there anything else, Kenzie? What's left to get you moved in? I want to set a date."

She appeared to consider that. "Okay. To work I need the reception area with the phones, a mediation room, the large classroom and the first floor public restrooms. My office would be nice, too. Or at least a place to set up my computer equipment if my office isn't ready yet. That should do it."

"Then let's look at the calendar, so you can call the utility companies and schedule service. That way they don't hold you up."

"That's a really good idea."

He was filled with them. The only problem was that he always wound up executing every good idea he came up with. This building was a case in point.

Pulling up the calendar on his smartphone, he held it up to her. "I'll have you ready by the weekend of the eleventh."

"Really? That soon?"

"Really."

"That's Mother's Day weekend."

He shrugged. Maybe he'd luck out and Melinda would want to spend some time with Sam.

"Okay," she said, sounding like the idea was gaining steam. "But the only time I can make the move is over the weekend when I don't have classes. Will that work for you or would you rather I wait for the following weekend?"

No more waiting. "I'll be done with what I have to do, and if I'm not, I'll stay out of your hair."

Kenzie smiled. "Okay, then. The weekend of the eleventh it is."

Will forced a smile in return. One more problem solved. One more piece in place. Provided he could actually get the work done by then, of course.

KENZIE INVITED QUITE a few of her nearest and dearest for moving day but wasn't sure who would turn up since her move competed with a family weekend. Her own mother had joked about returning from Florida in time to work rather than celebrate Mother's Day.

But the promise of adequate compensation in the form of lunch had produced results. A few generous cousins and many friends showed up, so packing the rental truck had been a breeze. By the time Kenzie stood at her new front door on South Main Street, she was surrounded by a small crowd to cheer her on.

"I know this isn't the first time you've hung your

shingle," Geri said, pragmatic as always, "but I'd say quality beats quantity today, wouldn't you?"

Kenzie unfastened the key ring from the belt loop of her jeans, where it hung from a carabiner so she wouldn't misplace it during all the activity of the move. "Absolutely. Have I thanked you for mentioning my agency yet?"

Geri chuckled. "A number of times, in fact, and you are most welcome. The situation sounded perfect. For you and Hendersonville. Glad everything worked out."

"Exactly the way it was meant to." Mom huddled closer and slipped a fond arm around Geri's shoulders. "Madame Estelle will be at peace passing the torch. She was so fond of Kenzie."

That thought made Kenzie smile. "The place looks just like it used to."

She had the City of Hendersonville to thank for making that possible. And WLR General Contracting and Development for the renovations. Will had attended to most of the items on her list. The big ones, anyway. Those he hadn't managed in the allotted time, he'd promised to complete as quickly as possible.

Kenzie was content. She understood the nature of construction, knew it wasn't an exact science, particularly when dealing with a building this age and size. Very much like her work with people. Each one unique. Each one requiring careful and exclusive handling.

Will had done a fine job, and she was appreciative. The frames of every outside window were newly painted, and the glass sparkled in the midday sun. The bright blue canopies flapped in a mountain breeze that kept the temperature comfortable. Even the sidewalk appeared to have been pressure washed so every crack and crevice looked neat.

"Go on, honeybunch," her dad said with a grin, standing beside Mom as he always did. Two peas in a pod, he called them. "Give us the tour of your new place."

A few walls wouldn't dramatically change a building where her parents had, by necessity, spent so much time as Kenzie grew up. But they gamely encouraged her, as always, and she savored the moment while inserting her key in the bolt and flipping the lock. A cheer went up as she opened the door.

"Welcome to the new home of Positive Partings." Kenzie's laughter bubbled up from deep inside.

Her dad held open the door so she could enter. Then everyone paraded in behind her until Positive Partings' new reception area was stuffed with people who engendered the sort of values her agency fostered—support, cooperation, caring.

"Thanks so much for being here, everyone," Kenzie said. "I appreciate every one of you."

She received a few laughing replies then she began the tour by pointing out the new ceiling fixtures that cast an almost natural light on the gleaming floors.

The maple planks had been restored to their former glory, and had much more character than the serviceable linoleum left behind in the strip plaza. The air held the tinge of fresh paint.

Then Kenzie noticed the burst of brilliant color in the midst of all these sparkling upgrades—a floral arrangement perched on the reception counter.

"Well, look at that," Dad said as she made her way across the room with an excited gasp, the fragrance of stargazer lilies quickly overpowering the lingering smell of paint.

There was a card that read *Welcome* in a distinctive scrawl. There was no name, but Kenzie guessed who had sent them—the *only* person who would have sent them. She was surprised by the gesture.

"Congratulations, Kenz." A quick kiss on her cheek accompanied the greeting delivered in a familiar, smoothly articulate voice. "This was a very good choice for the agency. I think you'll be happy here."

"I'm glad you think so." Kenzie glanced up at Nathanial, who had appeared behind her.

Nathanial Wright had always been handsome, and Kenzie was in a position to make that statement since she'd known him most of her life. Her father still told the story of the day she and Nathanial had met. She'd come in from playing outside to inform her parents she'd met a boy from the new family in their cul-de-sac, and his name was The Candle Bright.

Her youthful interpretation of Nathanial Wright,

while not phonetically accurate had proven to be figuratively spot on. Nathanial had grown up to be an ambitious attorney known for burning the candle at both ends.

He'd asked her to marry him at their eighth-grade banquet, and they'd dated occasionally through high school, college and law school. No ring. No pressure. No rush. They had much to accomplish before turning their focus on to family life. They were comfortable friends—and occasional friends with benefits—and she had always been content with their relationship.

Kenzie had started her agency and needed to get Positive Partings solidly established. Nathanial wanted to become a full partner in his firm. They were determined to build their lives on a solid foundation, and that meant having all the big pieces in place. Sometimes careers needed attention. Sometimes life. They also believed it was important to become well-rounded individuals before settling down, so they'd both dated other people occasionally, too. It only made sense.

"Are you as proud of her as we are, Nathanial?" Dad asked.

Nathanial slipped an arm around her shoulders and pressed another kiss on the top of her head. "You bet I am."

"Thank you both." Kenzie inhaled the lilies. Such a kind gesture, really. "But all I did was take up the city on its generous offer. Geri's the one who actually did something."

And Will Russell. She kept that admission to herself.

"You're taking a chance by becoming part of the community," Nathanial said. "I know there are perks, but you're also assuming a big responsibility with this old building. Not everyone would do that. Look at where I work."

Kenzie considered. The partners in Nathanial's law firm had just constructed a two-story building in a prestigious part of town. Brand spanking new and every square foot designed to appeal to new clients in a high tax bracket.

"Point made. Does seem as if Positive Partings and Family Foundations were made for each other. Well, come on, everyone." She motioned to an interior door. "I want to show you around so you know where to put things. I'd like to get the truck unloaded before lunch gets here."

"I ordered from The Deli on Main," Lou announced. "Kenzie handed over her credit card and, since we're all working on a Saturday, I made sure I took care of lunch plus overtime."

A cheer went up, and Kenzie joined in with the laughter. Knowing her administrative assistant, she wouldn't be laughing when the bill arrived. "Hope everyone's hungry."

"And thirsty, Kenz." Nathanial caught her gaze

and winked. "I know Lou didn't forget we're thirsty from all this moving."

"Be prepared to unpack a lot of boxes," Lou said. "Because you won't be allowed to drive. Geri's rounding up car keys. You have to blow below the legal limit to get them back."

"You think I carry a breathalyzer on the weekend?" Geri asked, loud enough to echo off the confines of the newly painted walls. "When I'm not wearing my robes?"

More cheering. This time Kenzie only rolled her eyes because she *really* wouldn't be laughing when the bill came.

If they could get the furniture and boxes into the designated rooms and the remainder of the stuff stored in the attic, she might be able to function on Monday. *If* she worked every hour until then.

Could Mom be convinced that ordering in from her favorite restaurant tomorrow would qualify as a special Mother's Day? Kenzie made a mental note to bounce the idea off her dad. Then the tour began and questions started, along with stories of the building during Madame Estelle's regime—to be expected as Kenzie was still close friends with many of her former dancing troupe.

Consensus was with Mom—Madame Estelle would be pleased with who was moving in and how this building was put to use. There were invariably questions about the other tenant.

"There will be children. Little ones. Angel House

is a school. That's really all I can tell you," she explained. "Lou and I did some preliminary research, but we've been working on such a tight time frame. We've barely had time to pack up everything for the truck today."

She'd hoped to conduct some classes at her old offices to save some work notifying upcoming students, but the logistics hadn't made much sense. Two offices meant making two moves since the business required bulky office furniture and conference tables and chairs. Lots and lots of chairs.

Add daily visits to check on the renovations and trying to anticipate everything that needed to be addressed to minimize the amount of work after she moved in, and she hadn't done much sleeping these past weeks.

"We worked the whole time," Lou added from the rear of the group clustered outside a conference room to inspect the newly erected walls. "This slave driver wouldn't let me cancel anything. Not one session. Not one class. And I had to notify everyone on the schedule about the address change."

"Slave driver is right," Geri said. "Kenzie, I had no idea you were such a tyrant."

"Excuse me." Kenzie raised her hands in entreaty. "This from the woman who keeps me in her chambers so long I have to pack food for two meals?"

There was laughter then they moved onto the new landing and doorway that led into the attic. As everyone shuffled through to get a good look at where the furniture for the two unavailable classrooms would be stored, Kenzie overheard comments about her new neighbor.

"Isn't Angel House a private church school?" someone asked.

"I'm pretty sure it is," was the reply. "I want to know how any private school can be funded by the city. And Catholic to boot. How on earth did they pull that off?"

Kenzie thought she might have the answer to that question but kept it to herself. She wouldn't invite a volatile conversation into her moving day. Among her friends, many of whom were politically active, partisan opinions ran the gamut.

But the simple answer was: Will Russell.

Their newest councilman had an agenda. Most politicians did, so no surprises there. But this general contractor had become a politician specifically to further Family Foundations, and the sort of determination Will had shown suggested a great deal of drive and ambition.

As she half listened to her dad suggest various setups for the furniture in her one functioning conference room, a thought occurred to Kenzie. So what part of Family Foundations addressed Will's private agenda?

That question hadn't occurred to her before.

Positive Partings and Angel House both fell under family support. Divorce reform? Will had already gone through the process twice; how many more divorces was he planning?

Angel House? She'd seen him at the park with his son, who was a perfectly adorable little boy.

Public services? Downtown revitalization? Infrastructure? Economic growth for his business, maybe? Kenzie didn't have a clue.

"Oh, I'm sorry, Daddy," she said, annoyed curiosity had distracted her. "Place the computer work station where?"

"Here, honeybunch." Her dad brushed family and friends aside and marched to the middle of the room. At seventy-two, he was still an energetic man thanks to his passion—eighteen holes of golf daily. "This recessed area. Bet the desk will fit right in. Accessible from both ends of your big table, but you won't deal with glare from the windows."

Kenzie followed her dad and stood beside him, considering. There were several windows in this room, the room she intended to make her main mediation room. There were other rooms for more intimate settings, but this one would be perfect for those complicated sessions involving an entourage with both parties.

Leaning up on tiptoe, she kissed his weathered cheek. "What would I do without you? Who's got the measuring tape?"

"Nathanial to the rescue." The group parted to let Nathanial through, and he took the measurements.

This proved the perfect segue to get everyone

working again, and Kenzie led the procession downstairs to unload the truck.

"Lou and I will direct traffic. We want to get the boxes and furniture into the right rooms to start with, please." Toward that end, Kenzie had made a map labeling the rooms to the corresponding tags on the boxes and furniture.

"Look at you." Geri appeared and peered around Kenzie to view the map with interest. "And they say I'm organized."

"No choice. Since not all of the renovation work is completed, I have to make accommodations. But I can't afford to misplace anything. So—" she held the map aloft "—this is my solution."

They were still in the process of unloading the truck when the catering van arrived.

"Would you mind dealing with them, Nathanial? Neither Lou nor I can pull away."

"Where do you want everything?"

"What do you think—reception area or main conference room? The table is already in."

He thought for a moment, brow furrowed, eyes squinted, a familiar expression. "I vote for reception area. Closer to the break room near your office if we need ice. The fridge is working, right?"

Kenzie nodded. "Good idea. And the flowers are there, too. You can use them as a centerpiece."

"You got it, Kenz." He pulled another familiar face. "Flowers to dress up the keg."

"Lou didn't really?"

"Overtime, remember?" He took off outside to greet the van.

Kenzie watched him go with a smile. A big party to celebrate moving day. Perfect. She'd known Lou would take care of everything. As long as Geri collected car keys and Kenzie could actually pay the bill… She headed upstairs to direct the storing of another conference table.

"Good thing the legs come off," the spouse of a former dance buddy told her. "Otherwise there would be no getting up those attic stairs."

"Don't kill yourselves, guys. If we can't get this stuff out of the way, then we'll make a place for it in one of the unfinished conference rooms."

Will would have to shuffle things around to refinish the floors, but then, the time frame had been his, not hers. She'd do the best she could.

By the time she made her way downstairs again, she found a spread worthy of all the hard work that had been taking place today. Nathanial had created a buffet-style setup with some tables he'd grabbed from the main classroom. There was indeed a half keg sitting in a place of honor on the reception window counter, along with bottled beer in a cooler and even a coffee urn so she would have wide-awake intoxicated guests.

Lou appeared with a sleeve of foam cups for the coffee. "Centerpiece is a nice touch, don't you think?"

"As always, you get everything right down to the finest detail."

"Which is why you pay me the big bucks."

That made them both laugh. One day, maybe. Until then Kenzie made sure Lou always knew how much she was appreciated. "Hopefully no one will regret giving me a hand today."

"Might have been cheaper to hire movers."

Kenzie shook her head. "But not close to being so much fun. Perfect excuse to throw a party and celebrate my good fortune with everyone I care about."

With an exaggerated sigh, Lou sank onto one of the sofas. "If I pass out, wake me when it's time to leave."

Lou could easily sleep as the well-appointed leather piece was comfortable in addition to being sturdy enough to weather constant traffic. Kenzie knew firsthand as she had spent more than her fair share of time dozing between her workdays and conducting the night classes when her schedule got hairy.

"Nathanial told us lunch made it." Her dad and mom emerged with several others in tow. "Need fuel to unpack those boxes."

"Please, help yourselves." Kenzie motioned to the table then glanced at Lou. "Want earplugs? Otherwise I don't think you'll be falling asleep anytime soon."

Lou pushed herself up again with a grunt. "Forget it. I can sleep on my time. I want to drink beer on yours. Before there's none left. And you get over to that table right now and grab something. Otherwise you'll get too distracted to eat—I know you. I ordered the maple-glazed turkey especially for you."

"You're the best." Kenzie blew her a kiss, intending to grab a plate and sit with her parents, but when she saw the cooler filled to overflowing with bottled beer, she had a sudden inspiration.

Grabbing a dark beer and a pale ale, she headed to the door with a quick, "Be right back."

Then she stepped outside into the sunny afternoon and circled her new building. She'd noticed the familiar truck at the opposite end of the parking lot as they'd been unloading furniture. Kenzie knew Will had likely been working for hours already as seemed to be his practice.

Filled with excitement and goodwill, she plunged into the dim interior of the recital hall, bracing herself to find Madame Estelle's stage in pieces and the tiered seating torn up. But Will apparently hadn't started work in here yet.

She didn't give herself any opportunity to think better of what she was doing. She only thought about the floral arrangement that had welcomed her into the building and knew she could do no less than return the gesture. A cool beverage to say a simple, "Thanks."

And maybe, just maybe, she'd make some headway at turning a stupid awareness of a man she didn't want to be aware of into a casual rapport. Nothing she'd done so far was doing the trick.

"Will," she called out into the quiet interior. "Will, are you in here? I saw your truck outside."

The dusty quiet was her only reply.

What to do? What to do?

She had an office filled with people and couldn't be gone long. But the awareness of all the work he'd done to allow her to move in and all that still remained to turn this big empty hall into a bunch of classrooms propelled her forward.

This was one of those moments when she needed to practice what she preached. Regardless of any questions she may have about Will's motives—questions that were not hers to ask—the fact was he had put forth a great deal of effort on her behalf. She could put forth a little of her own to thank him.

Circling the small orchestra pit that had never seen much use save for when Madame Estelle would invite students from the local universities to perform at the request of various music directors, Kenzie climbed the steps to the door that led backstage. She had no idea where Will could be working, and there was a lot of dark ground to cover.

"Will," she called out again, her voice echoing on the empty stage. "Oh, Will. Where are you?"

No response. Emerging into the hallway behind the stage that led to the various dressing rooms, Kenzie caught sight of light spilling out of a room toward the end of the hall. With relief, she headed in that direction.

Will stood on a ladder, reaching up to where exposed wires dangled from the ceiling. The sight of him wearing low-slung jeans and work boots, the casual Henley shirt detailing the shape of his chest caught her off guard.

She'd met him when he'd worn a business suit, and for some reason his councilman image loomed large in her brain.

He twisted wires together then separated and twisted some more without seeming to notice her. With the beer bottles starting to sweat, she stood there, observing everything about him from the way the muscles in his forearms flexed with every flick of his wrist to the earphones dangling from his ears.

Will hadn't heard her, which turned out to be a good thing since the sight of him robbed every bit of *casual* from her thank-you. Suddenly, her heart pounded hard. She was too aware of this man and the fact that she'd come to bridge the distance between professional and personal by inviting him to lunch.

She was *such* an idiot.

"Who are these people?" Will growled, disrupting the quiet as he gave another few sharp twists of his fingers. "Since when do we give in to economic bullying? This is America, Land of the Free. Or at least it used to be. Jerks."

Kenzie stood rooted to the spot, unsure whether to interrupt or retreat before being witness to more commentary in that grumbling-beneath-his-breath tone that made her feel as if she'd intruded on his privacy.

But another throbbing heartbeat and the choice was no longer hers because Will jerked an earbud free with a harsh, "What jerks!" He plucked wire clippers from the ladder tray, turned toward the wires and almost stumbled off the ladder when he saw her.

CHAPTER FIVE

WILL BLINKED TO clear his vision, unsure whether or not he imagined the woman who had materialized unexpectedly.

Kenzie. But as he'd never seen her before. Dressed in jeans and a clingy, short-sleeved shirt that revealed curves he hadn't paid attention to before. Not that he hadn't seen them. But her professional skirts and jackets only hinted at the goods beneath.

She was feminine in a graceful sort of way, slender, lanky almost, with curves he hadn't truly appreciated. Now, like this, he could suddenly see her as a dancer with casual elegance, not the overt sexuality of a pole dancer.

Will wasn't sure why he was thinking about pole dancers around this woman. Wasn't sure he wanted to know. That part of his life was a distant memory, the part where he was a man and not a dad in demand 24/7.

Kenzie was the problem, he decided. She was noticeable. He noticed her freckles, the hair, the green-gold eyes…the curves. The gentle slope of her hips, the trim waist, the roundness of breasts molded by that clingy, soft fabric that left nothing to the imagination.

She was real. Every lean inch of her.

"Hey, Kenzie." There was no mistaking that red hair anyway, even pulled back in a ponytail. That vantage was a new one, too. Her jaw delicately angled, and the neckline of her shirt brought his attention to a lot of creamy skin between her slim neck and the hint of cleavage. No missing that.

"Sorry to disturb you." She gave a tentative half laugh. "Here you are working peacefully and enjoying your music."

He plucked the remaining earbud out of his ear. "I wouldn't go straight to enjoying. I'm listening to the audio of the last council meeting."

"Oh."

She didn't seem to have a reply for that, so he felt obligated to further explain. "I can't seem to sit still long enough to review the minutes, so I listen to them."

Nowadays when he sat still, he usually passed out with exhaustion, but he didn't admit that. Didn't want a vote of no confidence from this woman who still had work for him to do.

Not that she'd voted for him. She'd readily admitted that.

Holding up two cold beers, she seemed to rally. "It's moving day on my side of the building. Everyone's taking a break for lunch. I thought you might be hungry."

That was not what he expected. When Will thought of Kenzie, he heard questions.

"Would it be possible..."

"How difficult would it be..."

Or maybe that was the Kenzie who wore feminine skirts and jackets that downplayed the sleek terrain of her dancer's body.

Will's thoughts had taken an unexpected turn, so he bought himself some time by climbing down the ladder, sacrificing the superior view of her neckline in the process.

"Lunch, huh? That's better than hearing something's broken and needs to be fixed. Nothing needs my attention yet, does it?"

Shaking her head and sending the ponytail flying, she held up the beers. "Wasn't sure what you liked to drink."

He stepped off the ladder and onto level playing field. He was taller than she by a good bit, but not staring down at her in a way that he'd be distracted by the vision she presented in her casual clothes. She really was a lovely woman. Fresh-faced and creamy-skinned and ultra feminine with that silky voice and fiery hair.

He took the dark beer and said, "Thanks. Perfect picker-upper. Getting hot as hell in here."

"You mentioned replacing the air-conditioning units. For some reason I thought you meant you'd replaced both sides."

She clearly listened when he spoke. He would have

to remember that. "I did. There's a lot more ductwork on this side though. Got guys coming in Monday."

"Hmm." Her lips pursed as she paused, then said slowly, "Maybe you should come by then and get another beer before they're gone. Or you're welcome to this one."

He eyed the bottle she held, too. Would he look like a drunk if he took both? "What about you?"

"It's a little early for me. I've got to get everything unpacked and set up this weekend so I'm ready for work on Monday."

Well, that answer was yes. He would look like a drunk. "I'm good, thanks. Sounds like you have a crowd next door."

"A thirsty crowd apparently. Guess I'm working them hard."

That much he didn't doubt. Little Ms. Tyrant whether in a skirt or jeans. "Glad you're getting settled."

"Want to grab some lunch? My administrative assistant ordered from the deli down the street. And the flowers are gorgeous, by the way. That was really thoughtful of you."

He tilted the bottle toward her. "Welcome."

She smiled, and silence fell between them. Will wasn't sure why this conversation felt disjointed and strange. Awkward even. Then he realized she must be waiting for an answer about lunch.

"Thanks for the invite, Kenzie, but I've got a lot to do here today myself." And he couldn't be sure when his cell phone would ring and drag him away. Melinda had wanted to see Sam for Mother's Day and intended to spend quality time with him all weekend, so she was at the house. But Will knew from experience that the length of time she stayed depended purely on the kind of day Sam was having.

Of course, the kind of day Sam would have depended purely on Melinda's ability to deal with him.

The chicken and the egg again.

"Have you eaten yet?" Kenzie surprised him by her persistence.

He shook his head.

"Then let me put together a plate for you and bring it over. I know you've been working nonstop, Will, and I really appreciate all you've done. The very least I can do is feed you."

There really wasn't any nice way to turn her down. Especially when the mention of food had reminded him he hadn't eaten since the banana he'd grabbed on the way out the door before dawn. Guadalupe had told him to start packing lunches. A good idea that would probably make his life easier if he could only remember to do it.

"Thanks. I'll come over and grab something." After all, that would be quicker than closing up this place and heading to the deli for to-go.

"Great." She liked getting her way. He could tell because a smile played around her mouth—a soft, full mouth that made him think of kissing.

Kenzie with the kissing mouth.

That thought made him groan inwardly. Sleep deprivation truly might be the death of him.

Twisting off the top of the bottle, he took an appreciative swig of cold beer as they walked to the entrance that would soon become the drop-off point for the kids at Angel House.

"So how's the work coming over here?" she asked, obviously more comfortable with chatter than the quiet.

As far as Will was concerned, this was a leap for Kenzie, a big one. To his way of thinking they weren't at the chatting stage of their relationship. To date, they'd discussed the building. Period. Kenzie kept distance around her like an invisible wall and surprised him today by breaching it. Because she appreciated the work he'd done. He appreciated her making the move as quickly as she had, so they were even.

But he was glad she liked the flowers.

They headed outside and around the building.

"Look at all these cars," Will said. "You weren't kidding about everyone helping you move. Anyone notice the windowsills yet?"

That got another smile. He was on a roll today. "If they did, they haven't mentioned it to me."

"Then we're good. We'll get there."

"I know," she said earnestly. "I also know how much work there is before school begins. I have to get settled in, so we'll get to the windowsills when we get to the windowsills. Sound good?"

Will appreciated her flexibility. And his first

glimpse of Kenzie the not-always-distant-professional. Maybe she was simply the type of person who took some time warming up.

But he had to reevaluate that opinion once he stepped inside her agency's newly renovated reception area, where a party was clearly in full swing. There were people everywhere. A full spread of food was laid out on a table. Another table was loaded with drinks and cups. Coolers and buckets of ice sat on the floor close by. There was a half keg perched on the reception counter. And here he'd been worried she'd think *he* was a drunk.

"Excuse me, everyone," Kenzie said then repeated in a loud voice that didn't do much to lower the volume of the chatter.

Only a whistle finally pierced the noise. A blond man from the other end of the room yelled in a dull roar, "Yo, pay attention to the lady."

Kenzie inclined her head in appreciation of the man's intervention as the volume dropped. When she had everyone's attention, she said, "Everyone, I want you to meet Will, the man responsible for bringing Madame Estelle's place back to life. He and his company have done all the work."

There was a polite round of applause, and Will raised the beer bottle to acknowledge everyone, wondering how many of these folks recognized him as a councilman, but hadn't voted for him. Or hadn't voted at all. In Will's new line of work, one never stopped campaigning. Constituents were everywhere he went.

He forgot that sometimes. He'd made a good call not going for that second beer.

Then Kenzie ushered him toward the food, introducing him as they worked their way through the crowd.

He met some cousins and some friends, buddies from the dance studio who approved the way he and the city council were utilizing this beloved building.

"Our tax dollars visibly at work," Kenzie pointed out and her friends agreed.

He hadn't expected her support, but appreciated it. If he hadn't been convinced she was pleased with the renovations, he was convinced now. For a woman who hadn't voted for him…

He met her parents who, at first glance, he'd pegged as her grandparents. Thank God he hadn't opened his mouth. But Kenzie had been quick to make introductions, so quick, in fact that he suspected she might have encountered that problem before.

"These are my parents, Will. Carl and Mary James. Dad, Mom, this is Will Russell, not only the renovation contractor but also one of our city councilmen."

Kenzie had obviously inherited her red hair from her father, whose faded hair still held a tinge of red with the gray. His skin was more weathered than his wife's healthy tan, but both appeared to enjoy the outdoors. Retired, if Will guessed right.

"We voted for you," Carl said over a genial handshake. "Know about your work with the Historic Preservation Commission from a friend who sits on the advisory committee. He owns a sporting goods place on Main Street and has been pushing the city to do something with downtown for a long time."

This appeared to be news to Kenzie, who simply fixed a smile on her face and didn't say a word.

"That'd be Steve Berry, right?" Will said.

"That's him. Good guy. Great golfer."

Definitely retired. Probably playing golf every day and loving every minute. "That's what I've heard. Family Foundations has me working closely with the council member who serves as liaison and nonvoting member to the committee. Steve's member-at-large this term if memory serves."

Mary leaned into her husband and gave Will a sweet smile that looked a lot like the one currently plastered on her daughter's face. "Memory does serve. His wife, Marianna, coordinates my bridge club. She says he's not around to help her anymore, and she's filling five tables every week."

"Good thing they have term appointments then."

"I believe Marianna would agree."

"Will's working on the other side of the building today," Kenzie explained. "I wanted him to grab something to eat before everything's gone."

"I think he'll be okay, honeybunch." Carl winked. "If you get him over to that table fast."

"And don't you forget to grab something, too, Kenzie," Mary added.

"Will do." Then Kenzie urged him forward again,

but before he reached the table, Will encountered someone he recognized.

"Judge Parrish." He extended his hand.

She did not look as formidable in her jeans as she did in her robes, but he still would have recognized her anywhere. He'd run into her often enough coming and going through the revolving door that was the mayor's office.

"Good to see you, Will. You've done an amazing job on this place. I can see why Kenzie's so pleased."

"Glad to hear she is."

Will supposed he shouldn't be surprised Kenzie knew the judge when he considered that Judge Parrish was originally the one to mention this agency to Deanne.

They finally reached the food, and he noticed how the flowers he'd sent presided over the table. She seemed genuinely pleased he'd sent them, and Will was glad he'd gotten that right. Anything to keep in her good graces so he could fit in the rest of her work around Angel House's schedule.

Kenzie grabbed two plates, handed him one and instructed him to help himself. Since she hadn't eaten yet, either, his plan to grab some food and run was out the window. But Will didn't mind. He should mind, of course, with everything he needed to accomplish before he sent in the guys to install the new ductwork on Monday. Yet he didn't feel frantic or stressed. Instead, he felt welcomed at this working party, even though he'd met only a few people.

"I can't believe you're getting anything done in here with all these people," he said when she directed him behind the reception counter, the only place left to sit.

She set down her plate and glanced fondly at the group. "They're a handful, all right, but so generous to give up their Saturday. We packed up my old office, loaded the truck and got over here by noon."

"That's why everyone is thirsty." A woman peered over the counter as she filled a disposable cup from the keg.

Kenzie only smiled. "Will, this is my assistant, Lou."

"So, you're the man of the hour," Lou said. "Place looks great. Think the agency will be perfect here once we get everything in place."

"I hope so." Will sat beside Kenzie.

Her parents and the judge appeared again, and they all chatted while Will made quick work of lunch and went back for seconds.

The blond whistler showed up, too. An attorney named Nathanial, who appeared to be on good terms with everyone. Especially Kenzie. The guy was certainly territorial, draping his arm over her shoulder, casually drinking from her bottled water. Her boyfriend?

Of course such a beautiful woman would have one. Will didn't want to think about why he was suddenly so interested in Kenzie's personal life. Their relationship was building and business focused. Period.

But maybe he just felt included in her life right now. The whole situation felt familiar, in fact. Lots of laughter and affection. Wasn't all that long ago he and Melinda had thrown their own parties. Family gatherings on holidays. Dinner parties to schmooze Melinda's clients or his own business associates.

But that had been before they'd decided to take the next step in their long-term relationship, to get married and settle down. That's when life had taken a sharp left turn in a new direction, one that involved autism, divorce and an unexpected career in politics.

KENZIE DROPPED ANOTHER folder into the file drawer of her desk. After the moving party yesterday, she was left alone to organize her office so she could work this week. Only the cases she currently mediated were kept nearby. Most of the information she needed to work was handled digitally, but there were still some hard-copy documents that needed old-fashioned signatures.

Crossing another item off her list, she scanned what was left to do in preparation for Monday's appointments.

Check internet connection.

Get printer and scanner running.

Set up switchboard.

Hang shingle.

The equipment company would move the copier tomorrow afternoon and set up the machine, so Lou would deal with that. Kenzie could temporarily live without the switchboard thanks to other modes of communication—voice mail, cell phones and email—but the shingle was important.

Her parents had gifted her with the gold nameplate when she'd first opened her agency. It had hung beside the door to her offices in the strip plaza since the day she'd first opened for business.

To Kenzie, the shingle symbolized a lot more than a good-luck memento. Wrapped up in one simple nameplate, inscribed in an elegant font, was all the love and support and respect of parents who loved and supported unconditionally but didn't give their respect unless earned.

Her parents were the product of another generation with a different work ethic, a generation that had been big on rewarding effort. Businesses were established by the sweat of hard work and practical choices, of tightening belts when times were tough and making disciplined sacrifices for long-term goals rather than indulging immediate gratification.

They hadn't bought their first home until they'd saved enough money to purchase a starter house in cash. They'd bought only used cars until financially able to afford new cars and didn't believe in paying a bank to lend them money. They believed they shouldn't be spending money unless they had it in their pockets—or accounts—to spend.

Her father had established his title insurance company with her mother running the office by his side, and they'd grown that company successfully over forty-plus years. Not only had they provided quality of life for Kenzie, including a private school education, but they'd looked after their own retirement. When they'd finally sold the company, they were financially secure and able to enjoy their golden years.

They were proud of Kenzie's accomplishments, and she didn't want to begin her first official day in her new location without that shingle hanging beside the front door. Sentimental, true, but Kenzie liked feeling that love and support was with her on this all-important start, so she was motivated to get the equipment up fast, so there'd be some daylight left to install the shingle.

A scanner and printer were essential since she'd scheduled her first meeting for 7:30 a.m. The furniture was already in place thanks to Nathanial, so all she had to do was unpack the boxes, network the equipment and make sure everything worked.

Fortunately, her mother hadn't minded cutting short the Mother's Day festivities. Since her parents had arrived back in town from their winter home in Punta Gorda specifically to help Kenzie move, they hadn't yet settled in from the trip.

Both had looked tired at the celebratory lunch and more than content to get home and rest after a long drive and moving day. Kenzie was tired, too. With any luck tonight would be an early one, so she could start the week somewhat clearheaded.

Fortunately both her new internet connection and equipment cooperated and she was ready to tackle the shingle with plenty of daylight to spare. She should have asked her father to install it before returning the rental truck yesterday, but she'd gotten derailed by her inspiration to provide Will a meal. How hard could hanging a shingle be? She was all sorts of handy. She'd hung everything in her house from new drapery hardware to mirrors.

But when Kenzie tried to track down her toolbox, she couldn't find it anywhere. The last person she'd seen with it yesterday had been Nathanial, who had been using the drill to reassemble table legs.

One phone call solved the mystery.

"Damn, Kenz. It must still be on my backseat," Nathanial said. "I had it when I got ambushed by Fiona and Jess in the parking lot."

Fiona and Jess were identical twin sisters and friends of Kenzie's from the earliest years with Madame Estelle. They'd alternated having crushes on Nathanial all through middle school, vying for his attention unsuccessfully until Kenzie had officially claimed him for herself in the eighth grade. To this very day neither could resist the chance to bask in his blond-haired, blued-eyed, president-of-the-student-government gorgeousness and reminisce about the old days.

"I meant to bring it inside with those books I promised you," Nathanial explained. "But I couldn't shake them without jumping in my car and physically leaving."

Kenzie smiled. Fiona and Jess in tandem had always had the ability to overwhelm Nathanial. Truth be told, they could overwhelm Kenzie when they got going. "Where are you now?"

"Command performance at Sarah and Sean's for Mother's Day."

That ended her plan to retrieve the toolbox since his older sister Sarah and her husband lived in Charlotte, two hours away. "Her first Mother's Day. How special. She feeling all right?"

"Okay for just having a baby I guess. Can't stop smiling but looks pretty wiped. I wouldn't say that to her face, of course. Little Sophie is pretty cute. Doesn't do much but sleep."

"I think that's normal. Probably good for Sarah because it sounds like she needs to rest up. Well, no big deal. Say hi to everyone and give Mom and Sarah hugs."

"Will do. Sure you don't mind waiting until tomorrow? I'll drop everything off on my way into the office in the morning."

"No problem. Have fun and get home safely."

"Will do. Sorry I bailed on you today. Not enough hours in the day, and this case is kicking my butt."

Kenzie sank back in her chair and yawned. She needed coffee. "Nathanial, please. You went above and beyond this week helping me. I appreciate everything you've done. Enjoy your day. I'm trying to get out of here myself."

"Get done what you need to and leave the rest. It will be there waiting tomorrow."

"Sound advice."

"That you need to hear even if you don't ever listen."

"Ha! Takes one to know one."

He chuckled. "Go home, Kenz. See you in the morning."

"I'll be here. Hugs."

"Hugs back at you," he replied with their usual goodbye.

And as she disconnected the call, Kenzie continued to smile. Nathanial had that effect on her. They were a solid part of each other's lives. Nathanial had always been there through every up and down, through every decision and accomplishment, through every disappointment and heartache. He was a man who shared the same views about life and love, and she believed she'd been as reliable a part of his life, too.

He was right about one thing—all these tasks would wait until she got around to them.

But she was still set on the shingle. She didn't have the heart to ask her dad to make the drive over when he was probably napping. Then a thought occurred to her, and she pushed away from the desk and went to her newly installed door that led directly to the parking lot. Sure enough Will's truck sat in the closest spot to Angel House. Did she dare trouble the man again?

She debated for the grand total of two seconds.

The door was unlocked, so she slipped in and headed down the hallway of rooms that had once

been the preschool studios for jazz, acro and ballet.
She wondered what Angel House would do with these
rooms—make them offices or classrooms?

Kenzie turned the corner into the open area that
led backstage of the recital hall then stopped short
when she saw the young boy sitting on the floor in
front of a laptop.

"Oh, hello," she said, surprised.

Will's son. He looked even more like his dad up
close, except for his eyes, which were deep blue.

Sam didn't seem to hear her. He seemed completely
absorbed in the laptop. A computer game, perhaps.

"Hello," she said again.

The little boy glanced up but didn't make eye contact. He didn't respond to her at all. Not a greeting,
not a smile, not even the slightest hint of recognition
she'd addressed him. But he kept pressing keys and
working the mouse pad with intensity.

Kenzie wasn't sure what to make of that, but felt
uncomfortable ignoring him, so she tried again. "I'm
sorry to disturb you, but I'm looking for your dad."

He didn't look up again, but she did get a response.
His brow drew tight beneath the glossy black bangs,
not exactly annoyance. Or was it?

Okay...

She wouldn't have expected such antisocial behavior from the child of such a socially adept man. He'd
been every bit of charming and gracious yesterday
to her family and friends, and Kenzie would have

expected nothing less from a man who had successfully entered the political arena.

But in all fairness, she didn't know this little guy
and didn't have children herself. She did know children of divorce carried their own special burden, precisely the awareness she tried to impart divorcing
parents.

"I'm going to find your dad," she said. "Nice meeting you."

His brow furrowed more deeply, but Kenzie didn't
get a chance to consider what to make of Will's son's
uncommunicative behavior before movement in the
open doorway caught her attention.

She glanced inside to find Will on his back on one
of those wheeled dollies, hanging half out of an opening in the wall. A panel that looked as if it had once
covered the cutout had been propped nearby, and she
realized that's why his son was sitting where he was
in the hallway within eyeshot of his dad.

That was about all Kenzie noticed though, because
Will scooted the dolly then, and a little more of him
vanished into the wall. What was still visible was
quite a sight, though.

Long, long legs that ended in sturdy work boots.
Knees bent to draw her attention to the way the jeans
hugged his thighs and hips. With his knees parted,
there was simply no avoiding the sight of his crotch
and the expanse of toned tummy that made her own
tummy swoop drunkenly.

What was it about this man that so appealed to her,

a man who had already gone through two wives? He was handsome to be sure, but Kenzie knew her share of handsome men and hadn't ever been engaged in a power struggle with her inner child over one before.

As if she didn't have enough on her plate right now.

"Excuse me, Will." She refused to let her stupid reactions interfere with her actions. "I don't want to disturb you."

But she did disturb him, judging by the sound of clattering metal—some tool hitting the floor.

His thighs flexed as he set the dolly in motion with one strong pull. He slid out of that wall cubby, emerging in a fluid motion, a breathtaking expanse of muscled chest in tight T-shirt, broad, broad shoulders then the thick cords of his neck, and that chiseled face with those quick dimples and eyes that managed to see right through her.

"Hello, Kenzie." His gruff voice filtered through her in a physical way.

She barely managed to whisper, "Hello, Will."

Maybe it was the sight of him from this angle, all stretched out before her in one completely attractive package. Whatever the excuse, her foolish inner child had taken over her thought processes and left him to assume control of the conversation as she stared at him like a deer in the headlights.

"What can I do for you, Kenzie?"

Foolish, foolish inner child. "I need to hang my shingle. May I borrow some tools?"

"Sure, what do you need?"

"A drill and a hammer, please. I already have anchors and nails."

"Help yourself." He pointed to a massive industrial tool cart that was easily waist-high.

Then he scooted the dolly away from the wall so he could sit up and glance toward his son.

"I met your son." She headed for the tool cart, exhaling a relieved sigh to escape his high-beam gaze. "He's adorable. I thought I heard you call him Sam that morning in the park. Did I get that right?"

"You did. His name's Sam."

"How old is he?"

She heard the dolly wheels clatter again, but didn't turn around. Instead, she occupied herself with locating a hammer. The drill hung from a hook on the outside of the cart as if it had been recently used.

"He just turned six."

"I was right, then. That's what I guessed." She was babbling now to fill up the quiet. All this to hang a shingle? Oh, and to avoid getting caught staring at Will.

Yesterday, she'd had the distraction of playing hostess and lots of people to help rein in her stupidity. Not so today. It was the being alone with him that intensified her reaction, she decided. And except for yesterday and the day they'd signed the lease in the mayor's office, she'd usually been alone with him. Another piece of the puzzle in place.

"Where are you hanging that shingle? On the door?"

"Next to it. Under the porch light probably."

"That bit won't work, Kenzie. You need a masonry bit. They're in that big orange case there. I've got every size so you should find what you need."

"Oh, okay."

She found the case, and it appeared that Will did, indeed, have every size known to man. She must have looked confused because the next thing she knew he towered over her shoulder, so close she could feel the warmth of his body.

Her chest tightened around her next breath, but as he had her sandwiched between the tool cart and his big self, there was no slipping away without some dramatic maneuver that would draw notice. She did not want to appear anything but casual.

"What size do you need?" His throaty voice was close enough to send shivers through her.

"I'm not sure."

"Where's the thing you're hanging?"

"My place."

"If you'll be working awhile," he said. "I'll come over and hang it. I just got Sam settled in front of his game, so I'll come when he takes a break."

That admission provided a welcome distraction from the way her insides vibrated softly in the wake of his voice.

But she was surprised that Will didn't want to disturb his son. She hadn't pegged him as one of those divorced fathers who overcompensated by allowing his child to call all the shots. If that was the case, he was doing his son a disservice. Poor kid was in for a tough time if he grew up thinking people would cater to his every desire.

"I don't want to be a bother, Will. I can figure out how to drill a hole in brick. I've hung lots of things in my house."

A flicker of movement in her periphery drew her around to stare into his face. Against her better judgment, of course.

Something about the sudden granitelike expression suggested he might be assessing all the things that could go wrong if she screwed up, things he'd be called upon to repair.

"You're leaving right now?" he asked.

She shook her head.

"Then let me come. Won't be too long, and it'll take me only a couple of minutes to install, tops."

"You're sure you don't mind? I'd have done it already if Nathanial hadn't forgotten my toolbox in his car."

That brought Will back a step so he could look at her full in the face. "Nathanial? The blond attorney?"

She nodded, miraculously able to breathe again with the added space between them.

"Boyfriend?"

"Sometimes."

"Right now?"

"Not at the moment." The admission was out of her mouth before she had a chance to decide whether or not she wanted to answer such personal questions. She supposed his curiosity was natural, though, considering she'd dragged him over to eat and introduced everyone yesterday.

And he was still curious. She could see it all over his expression, but he just asked, "Do you want me to come over?"

"Only if you're sure you don't mind."

He shook his head, and Kenzie got the sense that he was suddenly as eager to end this exchange as she was. This fact seemed to be borne out when he walked to the doorway and gave a thumbs-up to his son. Whatever response he received brought a small smile to his face.

"No, I don't mind. I'll do it as soon as Sam takes a break. I've got to feed him, anyway."

Kenzie knew she shouldn't open her mouth, but her unruly inner child got the better of her. "You're welcome to feed him and yourself from my fridge. Lots of leftovers from yesterday."

That surprised him, she could tell by his expression. Surprised her, too, truth be told.

"Still have any of those chicken strips and carrots left?" he asked.

She nodded.

"That could work. Okay, then. Thanks." The dimples flashed.

Kenzie headed toward Will and the door. "Come over when it's convenient for you, then. I appreciate the help."

"Won't be too long."

Kenzie got to the door where Will still stood and

glanced through at the adorable boy still engaged in his game. "He's six, you said? Is he starting kindergarten this year, or has he started school already?"

Will's gaze fixed on his son, and the dimples vanished, replaced by a thoughtful expression. "He's been in a program for almost two years now. When he graduates from that, he'll start school—probably the private school at the church that started Angel House. That's my hope, anyway."

There was so much in his expression that he didn't bother to hide that Kenzie could only issue a vague, "Oh."

Because suddenly the pieces started falling into place, all the little things she'd noticed, all the questions about why Will would fight his beautiful and ultraprofessional wife for custody of their son in court and win primary custody.

"A program?" she asked, curiosity getting the better of her. "Like a preschool?"

His crystal gaze fixed on her, one glance that stole her breath again. "An ABA program. Applied Behavior Analysis. That's why Angel House needs more classrooms. Lot of kids around need the program."

So many things clashed in her head at that exact moment. A special-needs school. Will's private agenda with Family Foundations. So private in fact that he was willing to renovate this property himself. Primary physical custody. A young boy who didn't acknowledge her.

Looked like she had her answer about Will's personal interest in creating Family Foundations.

But Kenzie couldn't pull it all together that fast, not when Will awaited a reply, not when she felt compelled to make it a reply that counted.

"He's a beautiful boy, Will," was all she could think to say. "And he's very handsome. Like his dad." Then she headed through the door, whispering, "Bye, Sam. Nice meeting you."

She wasn't sure what else to do because she didn't know the first thing about autism, didn't know what was allowed and what wasn't. Didn't know why she had asked such a personal question in the first place.

The only thing Kenzie knew was that nowhere in the initial consultation and preliminary information Will's ex-wife had provided had she mentioned anything about her son's special needs.

CHAPTER SIX

WILL RUFFLED SAM'S hair to get his son's attention. "Computer time's up, buddy."

Sam protested. He hadn't found his words yet, as Deanne called crossing the language barrier, but there was no mistaking that growl of frustration even if Will hadn't recognized the mutiny in his son's demeanor. Will held up a laminated checklist on a clipboard. Sam's schedule. They laid out every minute of the day in dry-erase ink, whatever color Sam chose each morning.

Today was a green day.

"Remember?" Will handed Sam the marker. "Check."

Sam's scowl didn't fade but he did place a big check mark next to the word *computer*. The word *eat* had originally come next, but Will had added in another direction.

Meet.

He'd needed the lead time to give Sam a heads-up about changing the schedule.

"What comes next?" he asked and waited.

It took a while. Sam really wanted to be in front

of the computer, but he finally shifted his gaze to the next item on the list.

"Good job, buddy." Will ruffled Sam's hair again. "Meet a new friend. Then eat."

Will waited while Sam slipped the marker into the holder that kept it attached to the schedule. As a tool, the schedule wasn't any good without the marker, and both accompanied Sam from the minute he opened his eyes in the morning to the minute he shut them at night. Good days were the ones they could walk through scheduling a few steps ahead without lots of additions or changes. Days when too many unexpected things happened could get hairy.

Sam was antsy from all the sitting, so Will took his time shutting down the laptop and packing it up, giving Sam a chance to run up and down the hallway. Back and forth, his footsteps echoing rhythmically in the emptiness. The new Angel House in its unfinished state would be any kid's dream. Lots of space to run unobstructed by furniture. Lots of empty rooms to explore.

Will grabbed the drill and a few things he'd need to hang Kenzie's shingle and stuffed them into Sam's backpack, which he slung over his shoulder. He tucked Sam's schedule under his arm.

"Time to go." He extended his hand to Sam and waited.

They dropped off the laptop in the truck and made their way to Kenzie's side of the building.

Will had known he'd taken Kenzie off guard with

his explanation about Sam. People would never know Sam was a child with autism by looking at him. But she'd rallied by the time he had arrived with his son and his drill in tow. When she appeared in the doorway, she greeted them with a welcoming smile.

"Hi," was all she said, allowing him to lead the conversation.

"This is my son, Sam," he said before leaning over to meet his son's gaze. "Ms. Kenzie is our new friend."

Will whipped out a card from his pocket and showed it to Sam. This card was the size of a small index card with instructions on it and was one of a set that went with him wherever he went. Guadalupe kept a set, too. One for Sam, and another for Rafael, who'd found his language and was now expanding his vocabulary with the help of aids like these cards.

This card had an actual photo of a smiling Sam, a prompt for how to respond when Sam met a new person.

Make eye contact.

Smile.

Sam smiled. One out of two wasn't bad. Not when Kenzie waited patiently with her calm firmly in place, as if she had all day and did not mind the delay one bit. Will liked that about her.

She smiled in reply, a big, bright smile that illuminated her features and communicated everything she didn't say. He liked her smile, too.

And he was impressed. She either had experience

with autism or possessed an abundance of common sense. He had no clue which, but very much appreciated her patience right now. So many people got uncomfortable when they dealt with Sam and let nerves dictate the encounter. Too many would get chatty, which could be so confusing to his son, a really smart kid who didn't process sensory information the way most people did.

Handing Sam the marker, Will held out the clipboard with the schedule. Sam checked off another item on their list. Will pointed to the picture of an apple.

"Now we eat. Then you can spin." He met Sam's gaze and knew his son was good with that. Will glanced at Kenzie, found her watching them with a soft expression in her eyes. "I need a place to sit him down and eat. You may regret offering to feed us."

"Not at all, Will," she said genially. "Just tell me what needs to happen, and we'll make it happen."

This woman might be a stranger to his private life, to Sam, but she was a compassionate one. She bridged the distance between their short professional relationship and this understanding of his family circumstances easily.

Will knew when he saw the paper cups, plates and silverware stacked on the table in her break room that she was already prepared. She'd readied what she could in anticipation of their visit. There was three of everything, so Will guessed she planned to eat with them.

So many people avoided dealing with Sam when they couldn't engage him in expected ways. Not necessarily unkindness, just uncertainty, and sometimes fear. People could be *scared* of his son, this smart and funny boy who loved to laugh and play ball and give hugs, simply because they didn't understand him.

Will had taken a long time to accept that truth, the frustration, the anger, the ache.

But Kenzie was rolling with the situation. Brave? Or naive? Will didn't know, but he appreciated her effort as she retrieved containers from the fridge.

"What about you, Will? I have sandwiches. Turkey? Ham? There's still some potato salad, too."

"Sounds great. Turkey would be good. Although ham works, too." Food was food. He wasn't picky nowadays. At least until he tackled gluten-free again.

After directing Sam to the table, Will watched Kenzie, all brisk efficiency and effortless grace as she separated plates and set out sandwiches. She stood at the sink with her back to them, red hair tumbling over her shoulders, still somewhat unfamiliar to him in her jeans and sneakers.

"Anything to drink?" she asked.

"Water's good for both of us. You?"

"Me, too." She reached for the cups, but Will was already there, taking them to the dispenser.

He caught a sight of her smile in profile, and decided he liked this glimpse of the woman he'd seen this weekend. Not so distant. Approachable.

He had no idea what had changed, didn't doubt

she'd still keep him busy with her never-ending requests, but he understood that she appreciated all his work around here, enough to want to thank him however she could. Food worked. For him, and Sam.

Setting the cups on the table, he prepared Sam's plate, chopping chicken into thin strips with a plastic knife so they resembled the shape of the carrot sticks.

"Anything else?" she asked.

He shook his head, and Kenzie sat, slipping napkins beside their plates while Will tackled the backpack, forced to pull out the drill before tracking down the plastic container that protected Sam's apple from bruising.

"Rectangle day, buddy. First rectangles then the circle." He held up the apple. "Sam's on an apple kick lately," Will explained, taking his seat. "That's all he wants to eat."

"Couldn't pick a better place to live if you like apples."

Will laughed. "You're right there."

Hendersonville was so renowned for its apples that people came from all over to attend the annual apple festival on Labor Day weekend. Angel House's booths were their largest fund-raiser of the year, and parents staffed booths from sunup to sundown. The booths provided everything from cultural foods to crafts. This year they were adding a 50/50 draw in the bingo tent.

The thought occurred to Will that city council would likely make some sort of appearance with the mayor that day, too. He made a mental note to ask at the next council meeting. Advance notice was always good for arranging Sam's care. Particularly as Will was already committed to grill in Angel House's American booth.

"So how's the unpacking coming along?" he asked. "Besides the shingle, I mean."

Kenzie set the sandwich on her plate—she'd gone for the turkey, too—and met his gaze. "Accomplished a lot. Although I'm not close to done, I am ready to work in the morning, and that's what I was hoping for."

"Looked like you had a lot of help."

An animated expression that dispelled some of her calm crossed her features. "Right? Any excuse for a party. I thought about hiring movers, but given the time frame I was working with…well, the thought of trying to find everything that someone else packed gave me nightmares. I'm a bit of a control freak."

She shrugged sheepishly as if admitting something that wasn't readily apparent to anyone who had dealt with her and her lists and her intense attention to detail.

"Really?" He feigned innocence.

She eyed him as if gauging whether or not he was serious. "Just a little."

"Running a business, right?"

"You know. At the end of the day, everything comes right back to you. You're the key decision-maker."

"True." He didn't think she'd decided whether

or not he was serious, but she'd latched on to his reasoning with both hands.

Sam made quick work of the chicken but left the carrots untouched. Sliding his chair back, Will reached to the counter and grabbed a few carrots from the container. He dropped them onto his plate. "Mm, carrots. My favorite."

Kenzie surprised him by reaching toward his plate. "Carrots are my favorite, too. Do you mind?"

"Help yourself."

She plucked up a carrot stick and nibbled appreciatively.

Will ate a carrot, too, suddenly so grateful for her participation. He knew this feeling intimately, felt it every single time someone interacted with Sam in a positive way. Deanne. Therapists. Aides. Teachers. Guadalupe. The other parents at support group.

People who weren't scared of his son.

Every positive interaction managed to dispel the weight of feeling as if he was the only one interacting positively with Sam, the only one who saw the possibility of a normal future. Will barely noticed it anymore, not like he did at first anyway, but the feeling was always there, underlying everything, most especially noticeable when he got an unexpected breather.

Sam got the hint and was soon munching away like a rabbit. He liked carrots. Today. And they were gluten free.

And Kenzie noticed, a smile playing around the

corners of her mouth as she brought the cup to her lips and sipped.

She made things easy, Will realized, an entirely unexpected and ironic realization about a woman who had been running him ragged with her never-ending list.

"So tell me about my new neighbors, Will," she said. "Angel House is a school."

"Yes and no. It does have a school but probably not in the sense you're thinking of. It's a resource center."

A Sanctuary for Families Facing Autism.

"There are classes for kids and parents," he continued, giving the layperson's overview of services. "Angel House provides just about everything a family needs to deal with the disorder. There's a lot involved with helping parents, a lot more than most people realize. Angel House has it all."

Except enough money. Angel House never had that.

"Wow. I keep meaning to look into it for my own information, but I haven't found the time."

"This came up pretty suddenly." He gestured to the room around them.

The delicate line of her eyebrows furrowed. "Seventy-two hours was a challenge. I'm not going to lie."

"Sorry about that. We're on a time limit."

"You mentioned that. For the school year, right?"

He nodded. "Can't move the kids once the school year begins. That would be unsettling for students in a normal school setting. Angel House's kids already have problems transitioning. And if we have to push the move back until next year, Angel House will miss out on a big, private foundation grant."

"Sounds important."

"It is." Kenzie had no idea, and Will didn't share exactly how important that grant was.

Leaning back in her chair, she tucked a strand of hair behind her ear, clearly considering. "Okay, so Angel House outgrew its current location at the church. Is that right?"

Will nodded. "And not for the first time. The program started in some empty classrooms in the grade school, but didn't last long there. So the parish donated a house that sits on the property behind the school. That's when it officially became known as Angel House."

"How does a resource center work? Do people pay for the services like private education? Is it sliding scale?"

Will knew exactly what she was asking—to understand the relationship between the church and school and city funds.

Back to that religious designation.

"It's a not-for-profit, Kenzie. The church continues to contribute to the program, since it started as a parish ministry, but Angel House has grown way beyond their means. The director is a positive genius at fund-raising. She's the one who heard about your agency from Judge Parrish."

Kenzie inclined her head but her gaze flicked to Sam. "I think someone's ready for his apple."

"Here you go, buddy." Will grabbed the apple from the counter and handed it to Sam, who crunched into it, clearly content. "Good job."

Will removed the empty plate and tossed it in the trash before sitting down again.

Kenzie was silent while finishing her sandwich. "So that's why Family Foundations is so important, isn't it? To get Angel House funding, like with that grant you mentioned?"

He nodded.

"And I understand Family Foundations is your brainchild. Is that right?"

He nodded again, buying time by taking the last bites of his own sandwich. Then he cleared both their plates and tossed them. Will suspected he knew what conclusion she'd draw given the questions she'd asked during their first meeting.

There was no sugarcoating the truth, but he found he didn't like the idea of her thinking of him as a self-serving jerk who was using the city to further own private agenda.

He didn't like the idea at all.

"You've got to understand, Kenzie," he said simply and sank into the chair to wait for Sam to finish eating. "There's a need. An impossibly huge need that even Family Foundations and Angel House combined don't come close to touching."

She frowned. "The federal government provides

services. I deal with families all the time that have to negotiate handling those services after a divorce. Which parent chooses the services or has the right to defer them or stop them entirely."

"Your dad was in title insurance, right?"

Her gold-flecked eyes widened. "Oh, he got you, didn't he?"

"Enjoyed talking business." Will forced a smile to ease up the mood. "I want you to think about gap insurance. The federal government provides services for school, from three years of age when kids can go to preschool all the way through to their early twenties when they'd normally graduate college."

"Where's the gap part?"

"What happens if a kid isn't ready for school at three?"

"Will, they have exceptional centers for children who need more support. That much I know because I've dealt with the situation in mediation."

"But Sam doesn't need that kind of support. Think about it, Kenzie. Exceptional centers deal with kids who are physically and emotionally disabled. Kids who can't function on their own or aren't able to learn. That's not Sam's situation. It's not the situation for a majority of kids with autism. They have a problem processing sensory information and language and need to be taught the things that you and I do automatically. They can learn. They simply need help and time."

He met Kenzie's gaze, knew she was giving him

a chance to convince her. "They don't get that help in an exceptional center. In fact, research has proven they need to be mainstreamed with higher-functioning kids so they learn to emulate the behaviors. Sam is entirely capable of learning in a normal classroom setting. He's a smart kid. But first we have to give him the skills he needs to get him in that classroom."

"So you're saying federal services aren't adequate?"

"That's exactly what I'm saying. There's an entire population of kids who aren't being served right now. You would be shocked to learn how long it can take to even get a child diagnosed properly. That's where Angel House, and other places like it, fit in. Autism awareness is getting more media attention as the medical community understands more about the disorder, but until the insurance companies and government at whatever level—city, state or federal—catch up and provide services, these kids aren't getting the help they need."

"Except from places like Angel House."

Not a question this time. Progress. "Right. Angel House provides training to help parents deal effectively with their kids. They provide access to therapists and staffing specialists and health professionals who can come up with personalized behavior plans. They help parents maneuver the system to pay for all these services that the government and health insurance doesn't cover. They provide assistance."

In so many ways. Not the least of which was through support groups with other parents, so they didn't feel isolated or despairing in those interminable times before their kids showed some discernible step in a forward direction.

They provided hope.

"Once Sam masters these skills and finds his language, he'll be ready for a mainstream classroom. That's when government services will help. That's the gap part, and it's a matter of time really. Kids move at their own paces, but that's the good part. Kids keep moving. The learning never stops. They become higher and higher functioning, and they don't ever lose anything they learn."

Will extended a hand to Sam. "Put the apple there. Let's not eat the seeds. They don't taste so good."

That got a smile from Kenzie. "I appreciate you helping me understand all this."

Will shrugged, grateful for the interruption, for a chance to check the emotions that could so easily get out of hand. This was his private agenda because the situation was personal. He needed help for his son.

"Ready, Sam." Grabbing the clipboard, he held out the schedule, was aware of Kenzie's gaze on them as Sam checked off another item on the list.

"Spin?" she asked, someone else who appreciated lists.

"To get the wiggles out."

"Oh. I've got lots of room."

Will managed a smile. "Would you mind if he commandeers the studio with the unfinished floor?

It's close to where I'll be working, and he'll have plenty of room to run around."

"Of course. Come on, Sam. Right this way." She spun lightly on her toes and headed out of the break room.

Will caught Sam's hand, and his smile that had felt forced came more easily as they followed Kenzie down the hall, watching the red waves bounce on her shoulders with her light steps.

Sam was smiling, too.

KENZIE THOUGHT SHE heard a noise. Leaving her office, she headed into the reception area and found Will. She hadn't seen him in a week. As usual, he seemed to suck up all the space with his tall presence and the masculinity that was such a physical part of him no matter what role he played. Father. Handyman. Councilman. Tonight, he combined personas, dressed professionally in a business suit and carrying a toolbox.

"Hello," she said, surprised.

The dimples didn't flash in reply. In fact, the gaze he leveled her way was all disapproval. "This is a big place, Kenzie. You need a bell or something to give you a heads-up when someone comes in. I'll bring something to hook up the next time I come."

He glanced at the door in question with a frown, as if debating whether or not to continue. He did. "Better yet, why don't you lock the door when you're here at night?"

She nodded, embarrassed he'd called her on her oversight and appreciative of his concern. A strange blend of too much emotion for a man she hadn't expected to see tonight. He was simply being thoughtful, she knew, a gentleman, but his concern for her *felt* like so much more.

"I wasn't thinking," she admitted, squelching all the craziness that flared inside her at their every interaction. "I do usually lock up when I don't have a class."

"Good. I know we're in Hendersonville, but…" He let the comment trail off. He'd made his point. "So no class tonight. Now's an okay time?"

"For what?" she asked.

He set the toolbox on the floor beside the coffee table. "I got your email about the outlet in the new wall."

Leaning against the doorway, she folded her arms over her chest and eyed him in surprise. "Wow. That's some kind of service. I only sent that email an hour ago. It really wasn't urgent. I'm sorry if I gave that impression."

Sorry because she knew how much work he had to do. A WLR General Contracting and Development truck had been in the parking lot every day this week when she'd arrived for work. And she showed up early. That truck hadn't left until after six o'clock each night, during Kenzie's break before her night classes began at seven. Sometimes another truck or two showed up during the day.

Will's crew had unloaded materials to install the new ducts for Angel House, a seemingly monumental task considering the size of the building.

He waved a dismissive hand. "No, you didn't make it sound urgent. You told me to come whenever it was convenient."

"Then if it's convenient for you, it works for me."

"I wouldn't go right to convenient." Kneeling, he unlatched the toolbox and glanced over his shoulder at her with a wry expression. "That outlet you said you needed in the new wall is already there."

Now it was her turn to frown. "Then why are you here? To bring me a map so I can find it because it must be invisible?"

With the sun fading beyond the windows and the overhead lights off inside, Will's grin flashed white in the dim interior. "It is invisible. Unless you have x-ray vision."

"Which you apparently have."

"No. What I have is an idiot drywaller. He's new and young. The nephew of one of my subcontractors, who happens to be a good friend and the guy who got me started in this business a million years ago."

She nodded, waiting for him to pull the pieces together, enjoying the sight of him huddled over his toolbox, the jacket stretching across his broad back, the lines of his pants pulling up on strong thighs.

Jeez, she was one hot mess.

"The minute I read your message, I knew what he did." Will grabbed his toolbox and stood. She was back to staring up at him again as he gestured to the door. "Mind if I go back?"

She pushed away from the doorway and swept an arm toward the hall beyond. "Please."

He took off toward the rear mediation room, one of the two that were up and running, along a path he knew very well by now, leaving her to follow if she chose.

Kenzie did. "So what did he do?" she asked, hurrying along behind him.

He glanced at her with an expression that clearly wasn't thrilled. "Kid got some training in high school but doesn't have any work experience, except for the jobs he's been on with Bob. But Bob's on a job with liability concerns right now, so I'm letting the kid help out so he can learn his way around a construction site. *Thought* I could trust him to hang drywall if he was supervised by my electrician, who does have experience and lots of it. I was wrong."

Oh, yes. There was absolutely no missing his irritation. It was all over his scowling expression. Seeping in his voice. But she liked that he helped out his friend. That said something nice about him. That he cared.

Ambitious charmer? Bullying ex-husband? Caring dad? Concerned friend? Attractive man she should not be so aware of. No wonder her head was spinning. "I appreciate you rushing over. I figured I'd make do with a new surge strip and an extension cord."

He came to such a sudden stop that Kenzie almost crashed into him. Glancing up automatically, she found herself so close she had to crane her head back to meet his gaze.

"Exposed electrical wires under your drywall? *Not* a good idea."

"Oh." How did one tiny exclamation sound so breathless?

Because the view from this vantage stole her breath? His face seemed a bit disjointed as she got an up-close shot of individual features. The faintly stubbly cheeks. The chiseled angle of his jaw. The mouth that suddenly looked so soft and full with his lips slightly parted... Kenzie mentally shaking herself. She was the idiot here. Right along with the drywaller.

Then he flipped on the light and the moment was over.

"Won't take long." He strode across the room to the wall separating her from Angel House. "I brought another outlet cover, too, so you'll be all set."

He crouched and ran his hand along the lower wall.

"I appreciate this, Will. I would have had to rig something with an extension cord for tomorrow's meetings because leaving the room during a session really isn't an option."

That admission appeared to catch his attention because he stopped what he was doing and looked up at her. "People argue?"

With two divorces behind him, Will likely understood the process pretty well himself.

"Let's just say leaving the room leaves too much out of my control. Couples are here to collaborate, but divorce is generally emotional. A few unguided moments can undo all my hard work." And cause her even more work to get a couple back on track.

"Sounds like mediation takes some doing."

"It's an art form. Definitely."

He smiled at that then went back to running his hand along the wall. She did appreciate Will's timing because she hoped to conclude negotiations with one of her couples here in the morning, which meant lots of printing. Doctor and Mrs. Tagliara had been married fifteen years and were successfully dividing assets and properties between them to move on with their lives.

They had four minor children, but Dr. Tagliara had demonstrated an understanding that as primary breadwinner, he was responsible to his wife to continue the support until their children were raised and she could reenter the workforce.

Sadly, not all men were so conscientious and not all couples were willing to collaborate, despite their choice to work with Positive Partings. The Spencers were a case in point.

While Kenzie would be in session with the Tagliaras, she had scheduled Lou to review preliminary information in the other mediation room with the Spencers. He wanted to collaborate. She wanted to make him suffer for initiating the divorce.

Kenzie had some work to do there.

"Here we are." Will gave the wall a solid pat. "Right where it's supposed to be."

He opened the toolbox then stood to shrug out of his jacket.

She quickly covered the distance and helped him pull out of the sleeves. "Let me."

"Thanks."

Smoothing the lines of the silky fabric, she hung the jacket on the back of a chair so it wouldn't wrinkle. He didn't seem to care, but she did. Like an idiot. Because she stood there feeling all sparkly inside. A *complete* idiot.

Will cut away the drywall with a utility knife to reveal the electrical receptacle hidden beneath.

"Wow," she said to distract herself from everything going on inside her.

She had the tools to rein in her emotions, to make constructive choices, but keeping them under control proved a struggle. Was there really any wonder why her classes were always full?

He set the chunk of drywall aside. "I'd like to say stupid things like this don't ever happen, but I'd be lying. Sorry is about all I can say."

"I'm just glad you realized what happened. It wasn't really noticeable." A thought occurred to her. "How did you know, Will?"

"I know where the outlets go, Kenzie," he said wryly. "You said it wasn't there, and it should be. Simple. I oversee the work my people do. That's my job."

When he wasn't actually doing the work himself,

which he did a lot. She kept that to herself, but she knew this sort of work ethic intimately, the kind her parents would approve of.

"Well, I appreciate you doing your job so thoroughly and taking care of the problem." *Before* the building burned down or whatever happened when live wires were exposed under the drywall.

"I suppose if this is the worst obstacle we face, then I shouldn't complain." He appeared to be checking wires, making sure everything was in order.

"So how's Sam?" she asked.

"An okay day, from what Guadalupe tells me. Haven't seen him since I dropped him off this morning."

"Who's Guadalupe?"

"Sam's sitter. His Spanish nanny. If he ever finds his words, I'm hoping he'll be bilingual." The comment was lighthearted, but there was so much in there.

Finds his words. Did that mean Sam didn't speak at all? He certainly hadn't spoken during their time together. She'd noticed, hadn't been sure if he'd just been quiet because he'd been around a new person.

She hadn't asked. Wouldn't.

But she remembered Sam, the energetic child who had spun circles in the dance studio to get the wiggles out, as Will had called it, until most people would have fallen on their faces with dizziness or motion sickness.

Sam had really seemed to enjoy the open space to move around unhindered.

A born dancer, Madame Estelle would have noticed and encouraged his interest. She was always on the lookout for boys to study dance because there were never enough for the male roles in theatrical performances.

She wondered what Will would have thought of that. She'd had friends whose fathers wouldn't consider letting their sons dance. Nathanial's had been one of them. Pop Wright had very clear boundaries about what constituted acceptable male and female activities. Nathanial had broken his arm in the third grade, and Pop Wright had exercised executive privilege and vetoed a pink cast.

Kenzie supposed Will had a different yardstick for what comprised normal childhood activities. Computer games and spinning were two that she knew of. And ball in the park. Then again, maybe not so different after all.

He lived such a challenging situation, and without help from Sam's mother. Why? Sam's mother had seemed so genuine in her determination to keep him, and Kenzie was usually a fair judge of character—an essential tool in her work. There was so much more to this story than she knew.

The mystery of this man continued to deepen. As if the waters weren't muddy enough with her crazy awareness of him, the newfound knowledge that he was a dad raising Sam alone made it harder for her to remember her initial reservations about him.

That must be hard as a single parent. Tough enough for a mother. What about a father who wasn't inherently wired to nurture and think for everyone around him?

Yet when she thought of Will with his son…in the park playing ball, during dinner made up of party leftovers, directing him from computer games to pirouettes in the studio, Kenzie melted at the sight of this big, oh, so masculine man and his charming smiles and gentle ways.

"Damn it." Will growled. The plate fell off with a clatter. A screw skittered over the newly refinished floor and he lunged for it before it could get away.

"May I help?" She hurried over. Didn't take a rocket scientist to figure out what the trouble was.

Big man with big hands. Teeny-tiny screw.

However, she did question why she'd instinctively assumed that a general contractor would need *her* help to screw on an outlet cover. But before she could come up with an answer she was willing to live with, Kenzie had reached him and was scooting down at his direction. She accepted the screw he dropped into her hand. They crouched close together, as if trying to occupy the very same space to tackle this daunting job.

He lined up the cover plate over the receptacle. "If you can get the screw in there and aligned, I'll do the rest."

His voice sounded throatier with their heads bent close, so close she might have rested hers against his shoulder.

She'd never had trouble with fine motor skills, but suddenly Kenzie's efforts felt heavy-handed and forced as if accomplishing the task was cause for breathless anticipation.

Coaxing the screw into the small hole, she swiveled it gently to find the groove. "There."

His motions were so much surer as he pressed the plate against the wall and twisted the screwdriver a few times.

"There you are. Thanks." His words hummed through her, a trick of proximity, because their thighs were nearly aligned.

She could sense the warmth of his body through this barest touch. Or maybe that was simply her imagination. But the gaze he fixed on her, clear as crystal and equally direct, suggested she wasn't the only one to notice their proximity.

"Excuse me," said a voice as cool as springwater. A familiar voice that prompted Kenzie to tear her gaze away.

Nathanial. His greeting was her first clue something wasn't right. Her second was when she looked at him. Distance shielded his expression, was evident all over his handsome face.

"Nathanial." She sprang to her feet, suddenly jumpy and swamped with guilt as if she'd been caught red-handed.

She *had* been caught, a tiny voice inside chided. Caught in the throes of guilty pleasure, being aware of another man and reacting—didn't matter that it was against her will—in a way that was all excitement and inner child. So opposite from the steady slow burn of her adult relationship with Nathanial. Whether or not they were currently together.

"You remember Will Russell?" she managed to say while crossing the distance between them and kissing Nathanial's cool cheek in greeting.

"I remember," Nathanial said. "Our newest councilman."

Kenzie could tell he wasn't sure what he'd walked in on and did not like what he'd seen one bit. She knew him so well.

Will stood and crossed the distance, too, extending his hand. "Hey," was all he said, but his unsmiling expression seemed to emphasize his point about needing a bell on the door because anyone could just stroll in off the street.

Kenzie wasn't sure why she had that impression, when she didn't know Will at all. But suddenly she felt as if all the air had been sucked out of the room as she stood sandwiched between these two men, both dressed to the nines in their pricey suits. The moment became surreal.

Somehow Will managed to dwarf Nathanial, who was a pretty sizeable man. But Will's raw masculinity cast Nathanial's polished good looks in such a different light.

Nathanial was all goldenly handsome and always impeccably dressed. Will was quite the opposite with his glossy hair and five o'clock shadow, not even able to make a full day without stubble darkening where dimples should have been.

Day and night.

And such a fanciful thought for a woman unused to being fanciful. She was losing her mind, Kenzie decided. The haste of this move had finally robbed her of judgment. But why? She'd never had trouble with stress or pressure before. Her healthy coping skills always saw her through in the end.

"Will came by to deal with my outlet issue." She explained, when the explanation was obvious, given the tools on the floor beside a hunk of drywall.

"And I still need to deal with the ceiling tiles." Will fixed that clear gaze on her with all his attention, as if Nathanial wasn't even there. "I'll be replacing them myself. What nights are you having classes next week?"

The question was completely innocuous, entirely practical on every level, but Kenzie wished Will had chosen any other time to ask. "Monday through Wednesday. Nothing scheduled for Thursday and Friday."

"Then I'll see if I can get by to work on the empty classrooms Monday through Wednesday and save the big classroom for Thursday and Friday," he said, moving toward the chair where his jacket hung. "Probably take me two nights in there. Work for you?"

"Of course," she said, smiling up at Nathanial, who arched an eyebrow, assuring her he hadn't missed how flustered she was and was curious about why.

Will Russell.

The only answer to that question. Darn man.

Just the act of getting his jacket implied he'd taken it off and that came attached with all sorts of implications that had nothing to do with reality. But Kenzie didn't seem to be dealing in reality right now. She was dealing in adrenaline, a physical response to turmoil that was entirely internal.

Will tossed his jacket over his shoulder, retrieved his tools, then flashed that grin at her. "See you around."

Then he inclined his head at Nathanial. "Wright."

"Russell," Nathanial replied.

"I'll lock the door on my way out," Will said, then he was gone, leaving Kenzie staring after him, alone with her dear Nathanial and no longer able to deny her stupid reactions were getting entirely out of hand.

CHAPTER SEVEN

WILL LOCKED THE door to Kenzie's place and stepped into the night. A car drove past, tires chewing up the road as it sped too fast down Main Street. The porch light cast a glow into the twilight, onto the shingle that read Positive Partings.

A misnomer, he decided, because there was nothing positive about the way he was parting right now.

Inhaling deeply, he allowed the brisk air to cool his agitation from the encounter that had made him bristle. What was it about Nathanial Wright that rubbed Will the wrong way?

He didn't like the answer. He didn't like it on so many levels that he bristled some more.

Bypassing the door that led from the parking lot into Angel House, Will went to his truck. He couldn't bring himself to go in tonight. Just the thought of work heightened his agitation.

Work didn't stretch his brain anymore, hadn't in a long time. How could he? He'd been working construction since he'd been fourteen and old enough to figure out his mom struggled to pay the bills. Autism, politics…another story entirely. He had learning curves there that challenged him, distracted him.

If he went inside that building to inspect ductwork and walk the demolition that would start tomorrow, he'd be trapped inside his head to obsess on the way he felt.

Suddenly Will wanted to be anywhere but here tonight.

Or in his own head.

Didn't matter that he had five hundred things to do in the two hours until he needed to pick up his son from Guadalupe's.

Tossing the toolbox in the passenger side, Will circled the truck and got behind the wheel. He'd been going nonstop since Kenzie had signed on to Family Foundations. He'd barely seen his son, who was the entire point of all this work.

Right now Will wanted to focus on walking through Sam's bedtime routine, checking off scheduled items one by one as he worked through the steps that would get him into bed to read a story—his reward for completing the tasks he found so distasteful.

Brushing his teeth had once topped that list, but climbing into bed when he'd rather be swinging in the backyard or tear-assing around the house or tackling his favorite game on the computer had been a close second.

Once these daily tasks had been a battlefield for power struggles. Now they were performed perfunctorily, barely noticed by Sam, who had grasped the pattern of events that needed to take place before bed.

Daily tasks that were also a tangible reminder of all the progress he'd made.

Sometimes Will really needed that reminder.

Like tonight.

Shoving the truck into gear, he drove out of the parking lot, ignoring the sight of Kenzie's midsize, midpriced sedan in a neutral color that wouldn't easily show dirt. Exactly the sort of car he would have guessed her to drive. Practical. Economical. But Will couldn't miss the pricey BMW parked beside it. Subtly showy like the man who drove it.

And why did Will even care about Nathanial Wright?

Will didn't. Not beyond the fact that Nathanial had intruded on a close moment when sparks had been flying. Will and Kenzie had been so close he could smell the scent of her hair, something citrusy and fresh.

Not beyond the fact that Kenzie had practically tripped over herself reassuring her *not*-at-the-moment boyfriend that nothing noteworthy had been going on.

Which meant she'd been as caught up in those flying sparks as much as Will had been.

And Will didn't care about Nathanial Wright beyond the fact that the man had gone out of his way to get territorial, putting an arm around Kenzie to warn Will his redheaded *not*-at-the-moment date was off-limits.

Which meant Nathanial had noticed something was up with Kenzie, too.

Will wasn't sure what bugged him most—that sparks had been flying and he'd only just noticed? He wasn't sure why that should surprise him. Not only was he overworked, overtired and overwhelmed most of the time, but he hadn't dated a woman since Melinda.

Once women had come easily to him, the same way everyone else had. Of course, he didn't seem to have a clue how to keep a woman around for the long haul. Nowadays he was so distracted, his brain clogged with a thousand things, that he'd been enjoying interactions with Kenzie and hadn't even noticed.

But when he thought back on the past weeks, he hadn't missed an opportunity to be around her, not from the first time he'd run into her in the park. He'd seized every chance to make an impression, to talk to her, right down to dropping everything after a meeting with the council to rush over here tonight after he'd picked up her email.

No, he didn't want those improperly covered wires to create a problem, but he could have at least changed out of his suit.

Will had been going through the motions automatically and hadn't once considered what he was doing. Why?

That question wasn't so hard to answer.

He didn't need more complications in his life right now.

He'd sworn off women the day he'd been granted custody of Sam. He had a son who needed him, and

Will wasn't stupid. How many divorces did he need to go through before admitting he wasn't doing something right?

Exactly two.

He had no clue if he wasn't choosing his wives correctly or if he was terminally flawed so no woman could stand to be around him for long. He did know that he'd done things very differently with Melinda than he had with his first wife, Trish, his high school girlfriend.

And wound up with the exact same outcome—asking a judge to dissolve the marriage.

He didn't have time to figure out what the problem was. He didn't have time to miss sex, either, so no problem there. Wheeling into traffic, he cut off an SUV that was speeding.

Guilt tugged at him. Not for the lady he'd just forced to brake. She'd needed to slow down. But he had a good two hours to work. He could have at least inspected the ducts that had been installed today. Not that he thought there would be a problem. He'd had a good crew of guys on the job.

Then again, he'd thought he could trust his electrician to oversee the kid with the drywall, too.

Will waited until he met the pace of the traffic before grabbing his cell phone. Speed dial. More waiting.

Then Bob's gruff voice came on. "Normal folks are sitting down to dinner after a hard day's work."

"*Not* talking normal here. We're talking you or me.

And I know you're not sitting down to dinner after a hard day's work."

"What? You don't think I did a hard day's work?" A gruff chuckle followed the question.

Bob Atteberry had been a part of Will's life as far back as he could remember. A friend of Will's father, they'd been navy buddies first then union buddies and poker buddies. Bob had been a frequent visitor at the house when Will's parents had still been married.

After Will's father had decided a wife and three sons required more effort than he was willing to expend, he'd gone AWOL from family life. That's where the friendship ended. Bob hadn't approved of the way his buddy had selfishly shirked his responsibilities, leaving his family behind to struggle.

Bob simply never left their lives. He was good people, as Mom was so fond of saying. He was always around for fishing or ball games or slipping Mom some money so Santa could show up on Christmas or giving Will his first job on a construction site.

In turn, Bob, who didn't have a family of his own, was always included in holiday feasts, where Mom would cook his favorite foods and pack up enough leftovers to last a week.

"You work hard enough, Bob," Will admitted. "But you're not sitting down to eat. You're wolfing a sandwich over the sink."

A disgruntled snort came over the line, but Bob didn't bother denying anything. Guilty as charged. "What do you want, city honcho?"

"You might want to mention to your nephew what can happen when we hang drywall over electrical receptacles. Explain to him what a utility knife can be used for."

"He didn't." Not a question. "Idiot."

"Funny, that's what I said. Not to him, though. He's a good kid and eager to learn. I'm reserving opinion on his attention span for the time being, if you don't mind."

Another grunt. "I won't remind you then about some of the boneheaded things you pulled."

"Good, don't. I do not need to be reminded." Particularly tonight when he was already feeling stupid enough about a very lovely redhead who smelled faintly of tangerines.

"How's the building going other than the drywall?"

"Not fast enough. Starting to dismantle that big hall tomorrow."

"Shit, that's a job. Not putting my nephew on it, I hope."

"To haul debris, maybe."

There was a beat of silence. "Sounds like you've got an awful lot of work ahead. You stand a chance in hell of meeting that deadline?"

Will watched the numbers on the pedestrian walkway count down. *5. 4. 3. 2. 1.* The traffic light turned green and he hit the gas and was on his way again. "If everything goes smoothly and nothing unexpected comes up."

"Yeah, like that ever happens."

"Don't piss in my cereal, Bob."

"Well, I hope you don't die trying."

Will could practically see the burly, grizzle-haired foreman rolling his eyes. "I'm not going anywhere if I've got a choice in the matter."

"Listen, kid. You know I'm available when you need me. I can get some of the other guys, too. I know they'll help. You've passed around your fair share of jobs through the years, and that counts for something. So just say the word."

The edginess that was making every nerve feel raw eased up a bit. "Thanks, Bob."

"All right, then. I'll give my nephew a utility knife and tell him what to do with it."

"Sounds good. I've got plenty to keep him busy."

"You call, Will. I'm serious."

Will found himself smiling. "Count on it."

"Good. Say hi to your mom."

That was that. Not even a goodbye. But Bob didn't have to say goodbye because he made a habit of saying hello when he was needed. *Good people,* just like Mom always said.

Will was breathing easier when he finally pulled into Guadalupe's driveway. He wasn't going to think about why sparks were flying between him and Kenzie because he didn't need any more damned distractions. Obviously Kenzie wasn't interested in distractions, either, because as Will thought more about it, he had to wonder where all her careful distance fit in. When had the sparks started melting through that invisible wall she'd had around her? That wall had been firmly in place until he'd sent the flowers, at least.

Flowers. Where in hell had that idea come from? Last time he'd sent a woman flowers he'd been asking her on a date. But it had seemed like the perfect thing to do at the time.

Because he *wasn't* thinking.

He pulled in behind the van Guadalupe and her daughter shared to drive Rafael around. Today's work gear and the notes from the council meeting cluttered the backseat in the extended cab, so he made a place for Sam to sit then went to get his son.

He knew the instant the door opened and he saw Gabriella's expression that something was up. "Today a good day?"

A lovely woman who wasn't any taller than her mother even if she was considerably smaller, Gabriella leveled big doe eyes his way. "Mom said it wasn't the worst."

Translated: not the worst meant not the best. He braced himself. "Anything happen?"

As if on cue, a familiar cry rose on crescendo from the rear of the house.

Gabriella stepped aside and held the door open so Will could enter. "Sam's mom dropped in. She had a meeting nearby and brought him and Rafael gifts."

"Did she call first?"

Gabriella shook her head, so careful to keep opinions off her face.

Will sighed, a dull throb starting in his temples. A nice gesture well meant by a loving mother but just didn't seem to get that she couldn't strong-arm normal interactions on her son. Will tried not to respond negatively. Vocally, at least.

"I'm sorry, Gabriella."

She gave a little smile, both sad and knowing. "Go on in, Will. Mom could use backup. Jorge has Rafael."

Backup. Translated, it meant a meltdown, and not a tantrum. And when one of the kids got worked up, the other was usually right behind him. Will hoped Jorge had whisked Rafael away fast.

"Good. Thanks."

The playroom had once been an office, but had been cleared out and set up similarly to a classroom at Angel House. A place without distractions, where Guadalupe could get the boys on task then easily clear the deck when the time came to transition them to the next activity, whether it was eating or playing or practicing their latest skills.

Will had barely cracked the playroom door when he saw Guadalupe standing alone, whispering Sam's name in a calm voice that belied the way she wrung her hands anxiously.

That told Will everything he needed to know. She was well trained to handle the behaviors that could crop up during the course of a day, and the fact that she'd backed off meant she was keeping an eye on

Sam to make sure he didn't get hurt, but was also allowing him to wind down on his own.

He slipped inside and shut the door quickly. He found Sam red-cheeked and sweaty as he flapped his arms and prowled the perimeter of the room at a run, around and around and around. His little jaw was rigid from the way he ground his teeth and his gaze fixed on the ground in front of him, unfocused. He didn't seem to notice Will had even entered.

He let out a shriek that made Guadalupe startle and wring her hands even more. But another revolution and he let out that same shriek when he passed by the window again.

"They had a really nice visit." Guadalupe met Will's gaze with a strained expression. "Melinda bought both boys beautiful gifts. They loved them and played for a long time."

"Sam got upset when she left?"

Guadalupe nodded.

Of course he had. Bringing gifts seemed to be the only way she knew how to mother her son. And Sam wanted her attention, just like any six-year-old would. But she always sailed out the door again, leaving behind a little boy who didn't know how to express his anxiety and disappointment in any productive way.

Deanne swore Sam would learn to manage his reactions and if Rafael was any indication, she could be believed. But Sam simply wasn't there yet.

"Gabriella said Melinda just showed up. I'm sorry. I've told her to call first," Will said in a low voice.

Sam shrieked at the top of his lungs, a frustrated growl that said everything he couldn't express with words. And his frustration thrust a knife into Will's heart as it always did.

Guadalupe waved a dismissive hand. "Don't worry. I know you have. I've told her, also. She was between clients. I made her wait until he finished his snack. I hoped maybe it would help."

"Good for you. I'll talk to her again."

Guadalupe shrugged. Sam yelled. Will's head throbbed harder.

That time to transition was absolutely essential for Sam to smoothly end one task and start the next. But Melinda couldn't seem to grasp that she couldn't simply pop in and out at her convenience—not without considerable fallout.

Will took a deep breath and knelt down, close enough that he could have reached out and touched Sam on a pass. He didn't try to make contact.

"Hey, buddy," he said softly. "What's the problem?"

Like Guadalupe had, Will kept calmly repeating Sam's name, closing in slowly, nonthreateningly, giving Sam a chance to recognize Will's presence.

Guadalupe slipped out of the room, and luck was with them tonight because Sam didn't get any worse and eventually wound down. Not too bad, all things considered. Any time Will could wait Sam out and didn't have to intervene because he was out of control and at risk of hurting himself was good. Letting

Sam expel those frustrations without anyone adding to them was good.

Now Sam was drenched with sweat and completely exhausted.

"Come on, buddy. Let's go home."

Sam could barely keep his eyes open, but he wrestled weakly in Will's arms.

Guadalupe had returned and knew exactly what Sam wanted. She retrieved the big Transformer-type robot with the adjustable arms and legs, a pricey toy from some upscale toy store like FAO Schwartz. Sure enough Sam wrapped an arm around the robot and stopped fighting sleep.

Guadalupe smiled. "He's coming along, Will. He'll be talking soon. You trust me."

Will managed a smile. He hoped she was right. But between the pounding head and the raw nerves, he couldn't say he felt encouraged more than angry at Melinda's unnecessary selfishness.

Not that meltdowns didn't happen for all kinds of reasons. They did. But a lot of the time, giving Sam a heads-up about what was coming then allowing him enough time to finish up whatever he was doing made all the difference in the world at keeping his stress level down.

It was such a simple thing. Not easy necessarily because waiting took patience and time. But so, so simple.

Will said his goodbyes and carried his exhausted

son to the truck. Did he need to take Melinda back to court to get her to comply with one simple request?

He'd considered telling Guadalupe not to allow Melinda to see Sam when she showed up unannounced, but he didn't want to place that sort of responsibility on Guadalupe, putting her in an uncomfortable situation. Melinda had a right to see Sam. More importantly, she wanted to see Sam. Sam wanted to see his mother. And Will wanted them to see each other.

One simple request. Was it really so much to ask?

No, Will didn't need any more complications right now.

Not one.

KENZIE MET NATHANIAL'S gaze as he opened her car door. He'd hung around to help her set up the equipment in the mediation room, but he hadn't mentioned anything about Will until this very moment, when he stared at her with blue eyes uncharacteristically serious.

"I don't like this guy, Kenz. That's twice I've met him, and every red flag I have is flying."

Adrenaline had stopped pumping through her a while ago. Maybe the activity of setting up equipment had made her feel more in control. Nathanial's presence had definitely helped smooth away the raw edges of her mood, a calming presence as he usually was. Or maybe, as much as she hated to admit it, she'd simply settled down because Will had left.

How could she deny that adrenaline went from zero to sixty with one flash of his dimples?

"Will is not my cup of tea, Nathanial." That much was the truth. "You above everyone should know that."

"What exactly about him isn't your cup? That he owns his own business? That he's active in politics? Or that he made your dreams come true by installing you in Madame Estelle's building for a low-income rent?"

She usually appreciated Nathanial's straight-to-the-point presentation. Not tonight.

"Maybe it's the part where he's been divorced—not once, but twice. Or the part where he has primary physical custody of his son in addition to his own business and a seat on council. I'm thinking the guy doesn't do much dating even if he was my cup of tea." All entirely true.

"Divorced *twice?*" Nathanial pulled a face. "And they gave him custody? That speaks for itself, don't you think? Who voted this guy into office, anyway?"

Kenzie shrugged, suddenly unwilling to admit she hadn't voted for Will. The image of a sweet little boy with big eyes and a happy smile flashed in her mind. There were special circumstances about why Will had gotten custody of his son. Kenzie might not know the whole story, but she had met both Sam's parents and had seen Will with his son.

She understood his loyalty to Angel House. Loyalty that had spurred him to run for city council to further his private agenda. He may have won the seat because of the cause he served. Or simply on the strength of his charm. Given her own experiences with the man, Kenzie would believe that. Easily. But clearly winning that seat had been meant to be.

There were definitely special circumstances about the custody arrangement. *Definitely.*

But Kenzie kept her mouth shut and didn't attempt to explain. Nathanial was her best friend in the world, and she'd always shared freely with him, but right now she felt protective of Will, and Sam. She didn't want to open them up to judgment. Any judgment, especially since Nathanial had already decided he didn't like Will.

"I appreciate your concern, and your opinion," she said softly. "But don't worry about me." Slipping her hand over his where it still sat poised on her open window, she gave a reassuring squeeze.

Nathanial didn't look reassured. Not one bit. He leveled an unwavering gaze. "I hear what you're saying."

Which implied he didn't believe her.

She supposed that shouldn't surprise her, either. He could see what she wasn't sharing. And was worried. Normally, he would be the one she hashed through her feelings with, the one who would listen to her think out loud or rant or do whatever she needed to do to make some sense of the way she felt.

She wanted to talk, *needed* to talk after tonight, but the idea of discussing her reaction to Will with

Nathanial made her feel vulnerable, as if she'd open up herself to be stepped on.

Which was so unfair to Nathanial. True, he'd never been one to sugarcoat his opinion, but he was a wonderful, caring man who loved her. Kenzie was the problem. And the way she felt.

She was the *biggest fool*.

But Nathanial didn't offer to talk, which cued her that he wasn't available. They played this little game whenever they weren't in full relationship mode.

Nathanial hadn't mentioned he was dating anyone, though, and he would have. They were friends before anything else. That was her favorite part of their relationship. They usually shared everything. She'd cried in his arms after Jack had ended their relationship when he shipped off for his second tour in Iraq.

Nathanial had railed until 4:00 a.m. after a fight with ex Charlotte that had resulted in the demise of their relationship. She'd been casually seeing someone else and hadn't wanted to break up with Nathanial until forced to make a decision. He'd felt betrayed and hurt, which had manifested as an anger the likes of which Kenzie hadn't seen before or since.

They could share their feelings this way because they had forever plans. But those plans wouldn't start until they established their careers and were ready to settle down to begin the next phase of life, to commit completely and start a family, because they both wanted one.

That only made sense.

Nathanial bent into the open window and pressed a soft kiss to her forehead. "Drive safely," was all he said. Then he hopped into his car and waited for her to pull out, ever the gentleman.

Kenzie drove on autopilot, heading toward their part of town. They didn't live far from each other. But Nathanial turned off Main Street as if heading in the direction of his office. She wondered if he was preparing for a big case and felt selfish for not asking. She was so wrapped up in her own emotions right now, trying to manage them and failing miserably.

Kenzie needed to talk. Her thoughts were spinning again now that she didn't have Nathanial or work to distract her. The situation was ridiculous.

As she sat through the unnecessarily long traffic light at the intersection of Blossom and Sixth, she texted her other best friends in the world, Fiona and Jess.

SOS. Can you guys meet at Kevin's?

Kevin's bistro was one of Hendersonville's best-kept secrets, and the locals liked it that way. And while Kenzie had no appetite whatsoever, a glass of wine would work in a big way. Jess responded almost instantly. Kenzie glanced at her phone at the next traffic light.

Sorry! No can do! Any time tomorrow.

"Bummer," she said aloud. Didn't matter whether or not Fiona could make it now. Fiona and Jess were a package deal. If she shared her angst with Fiona first, Jess would feel left out and vice versa. She would share anything with either of them, but she could only share when they were together, an unspoken rule, which made their friendship a bit of a balancing act.

She was nearly home when Fiona finally replied.

Got a function. Won't get out of here until ten.

Kenzie waited until she pulled into her driveway before replying.

Too late. Any time free tomorrow?

No. Saturday?

Which effectively took care of talking with her other two best friends for the moment. Kenzie suggested lunch and asked Fiona to check the time with Jess then received the reply:

Kk. Let you know ;-)

And that was that. Grabbing her laptop case, Kenzie headed inside, accepting that she was alone with her thoughts tonight.

She changed into more comfortable clothes. She called her parents to see how their day had been and resisted the urge to discuss the situation with her mother. Mom was a wonderful listener and would offer practical advice if asked, but she was also not as young as she used to be. She and Dad sat down after dinner and dozed in their chairs through all their favorite programs. To spring this on her at this time of night…

So Kenzie opened the bottle of Malbec that she'd been hoarding since Nathanial had given it to her on Valentine's Day. She'd hoped to share it with him, but lately they seemed to get together everywhere but here, so she poured a glass, even though she knew she'd never finish the bottle herself before it turned.

No sooner did she settle into her comfy chair in the living room with a stack of pending cases to review when her cell rang. She glanced at the display.

"Geri, what a nice surprise. What's up?"

"Am I catching you at an okay time?"

"Couldn't be better. I hope you're not still working though. It's almost eight o'clock." Kenzie tucked her legs underneath her and reached for her glass.

"I'm home, but do we ever stop working? I mean, really stop. Put everything out of our heads and not think about anything work-related at all."

"Given that I just sat down for the first time today, and I brought a stack of folders of potential clients to review, I'm going to answer no."

Geri chuckled. "Me, either. I think we need to get lives."

Which was Geri's polite way of telling Kenzie to

get a life. Geri already had one. Two wonderful, successful children who were married and lived within driving distance. No grandchildren yet, but they were likely in the works, so little ones shouldn't be in the too-distant future.

But Geri's husband had died two years ago from a heart attack, far too young. Geri had been dealing with the unexpectedness of his passing and coping with her grief since then. She got a free pass for not having much else outside of work. All her plans to grow old with her husband had been derailed. She would eventually figure out what the future held for her, but she wouldn't rush. She'd fill her life with the people she loved and work.

But as far as Geri was concerned Kenzie hadn't started her life yet, and she'd never been shy about sharing that opinion, going so far as to ask Nathanial why he was waiting to pop the big question at last year's Independence Day picnic.

And suddenly Kenzie was struck by the similarities between them. She filled her life with the people she loved and work, too. That was a good thing, right?

"This is the first chance I've had all day to give you a call." Geri launched into the summary of a case that had led her to a mediator from another county she thought Kenzie might be interested in. "I want you to check her out. I was impressed by her work on a tough case. She's not technically practicing collaborative mediation, but it was close enough that I thought you'd be interested in what she's doing. I know you're always on the hunt for qualified professionals."

"Especially now I have room to start my training program, thanks to you. I appreciate how you always keep your eyes open."

"We'll never push divorce reform in this state without the professionals willing to crusade for the cause. You know that as well as I do."

"I do. Feels like nothing is really happening yet."

A sharply exhaled breath hissed over the line. "Kenzie, how can you even say that? You've accomplished so much even before you started the agency. *We've* accomplished a lot with our family court here in Henderson County."

"True, thank you for the pep talk. I am excited." She laughed. "Well, I will be, when my classrooms are functioning."

"How's that going, by the way? You settling in?"

Kenzie sipped the Malbec, savored the deliciously dry and full-bodied wine in her mouth before swallowing. Nathanial was the best. Chocolate for Valentine's Day? Not for Kenzie. She'd take a blooming plant for her garden and a bottle of wine any day. Only good wine, though. "I think so."

"You sound undecided. Want to talk?"

Kenzie smiled into the beautiful space she'd created in her living room with huge circles of soft light from the beaded lamps and all the paned windows and live ferns and an airy rattan sofa with the big cushions that matched this chair.

And here she thought she'd be alone with her thoughts tonight. Things worked out exactly the way they were meant to. Kenzie needed to remember that. "Something divine must be at work right now because you're a little angel."

Hearty laughter. "I know what that means. What's on your mind, dear girl. I have lots of opinions. Always glad to share."

"And I value your opinions, Geri. You know I do."

"Always said you were a smart girl."

Which meant something since Geri had been around for as long as Kenzie could remember. So she explained what had been going on with her and Will. There was no embarrassment to admit when she was in over her head. Not with Geri, who knew everything about Kenzie and had daughters of her own.

By the time Kenzie had finished explaining about her run-in with Nathanial and Will tonight, she was halfway through her glass of wine and Geri was on the other end of the line saying, "Mmm-hmm. I understand the problem."

"I'm thrilled to hear that," Kenzie said. "Any idea about a solution? I could use one of those right now."

"Do you hear yourself, Kenzie? I mean really hear what you're saying?"

"What?"

"You're micromanaging your physical reactions. Or trying to. I really don't think you can do that, which is probably why it's not working."

"Of course I'm micromanaging them, Geri. If I don't, who will? They're *my* reactions."

Silence. Then a deep sigh. "That's not exactly what I meant. I get that you're choosing what to do with your feelings, and I agree. But it seems that if you're having this strong of a reaction to Will, maybe you should be analyzing why instead of attempting to ignore how you feel when that's not working."

"I'm not sure knowing why matters."

"But don't you think it's possible that something might be there, something special between the two of you? Why else would you be having such a physical reaction to the man?"

Something between her and Will? It took Kenzie a moment to wrap her brain around what Geri suggested.

"No," Kenzie finally said. Then repeated more decidedly. "No, Geri. *No.* There can't be anything between me and Will, special or otherwise. Absolutely not."

"Why?"

"Because he's not the kind of man I want a future with."

"I didn't say you had to marry him."

Kenzie shook her head. "What are you saying then?"

"Um, you date, right?"

"The man's been divorced twice."

"And?"

"The man's been divorced twice."

"Oh, you have criteria. Got it. Will Russell is unsuitable." Geri chuckled. "Does that mean you found out what the deal was with his son? Why did he get primary physical custody? I'd be interested in hearing."

"I have no idea." Kenzie realized that she didn't mind sharing revelations about Sam with Geri. "My guess is that it has something to do with his son's special needs."

"That makes the situation tough. What's he dealing with?"

"Autism."

"What a shame. The mother involved at all?"

Kenzie turned to stare out the picture window into the darkness beyond, shadowed by the bright interior light. She might not be able to see them, but her gardenia bushes were there, scenting the night with their heavenly fragrance.

"I think so, but I'm not sure how much," Kenzie said. "Will mentioned his son on moving day. Got the impression he was with his mother for Mother's Day."

"That's good. Can't be easy taking care of his son alone."

"No, I imagine not." She remembered their ball game in the park. Their dinner at Kenzie's. Putting the big dance studio to use so Sam could get the wiggles out, as Will had called it.

"I have to be honest, Kenzie. I'm not hearing too much unsuitable about Will yet. Two divorces. Is that all you have?"

"Two divorces means we have a man with some relationship issues. I don't have any idea what they are, of course, but I promise you he has them. He could be choosing his partners poorly, but I don't think that's the case because I've met one of his ex-wives." Of course, she'd lost custody of her son, so maybe Kenzie was the one who shouldn't be forming opinions.

She *definitely* shouldn't be forming opinions.

"You mentioned that. So what do you think it is? Dealing with an autistic child is tough, Kenzie. Couldn't stress have played a big factor?"

"I'd imagine it could. But what about the first divorce? No autism there to my knowledge. My guess is inadequate relationship skills."

"Speculation."

"Agreed," Kenzie said. "But enough circumstantial evidence to suggest he has some issues."

"We don't convict on circumstantial evidence, and you won't have hard facts unless you get to know the man personally."

"Point taken. But I'm not interested in his issues, Geri. I don't have time to date at the moment, and he's not the sort of man I'd consider a future with."

"Then you're back to square one with your reactions." Before Kenzie got a chance to reply, Geri said impatiently, "Okay, okay. So what sort of man do you want a future with?"

Kenzie glanced at the credenza that housed a flat-screen television, on so seldom she couldn't be sure it still worked. Beside it sat a framed photo of Nathanial and her, arms raised, faces contorted with laughing shrieks as they plunged into the spray of Thunder Mountain Railroad, a roller coaster at Disney World. In the dual frame was another photo. Nathanial wore a crown in this one and she wore a pink princess hat.

Mementos from their trip to Florida two years ago. Right before she started the agency. The answer was easy.

"Nathanial."

A snort. "I swear you two give me whiplash. I didn't know you were dating right now. You're always together. Always. But I never know if you're *together* together."

"We're not."

"You're killing me here, Kenzie. You do know you're *not* together together more than you're together, right?"

She chuckled. "Oh, my. I'm not even going to try to wrap my brain around that. It's really not all that complicated, Geri. Nathanial and I weren't interested in getting married right out of high school. Both our parents gave us the same advice: live a little. There'll be plenty of time for mortgages and responsibilities. Don't skip steps, otherwise, down the road we'll wake up and wonder what we missed."

"Sound advice. But you're almost thirty. If you still haven't gotten all the pieces in place yet with Nathanial, then your problem with Will is solved. Get together with Will for a while. Stop engaging in a power struggle with your feelings."

Get together? Geri hadn't actually said to sleep with the man, had she?

Of course *not*.

Kenzie was the one who made the leap from Geri's suggestion to date into bed. Because her inner child was out of control and they were locked in a power struggle.

Geri was right about that.

Kenzie knew full well that no one ever won a power struggle. She wasn't going to be able to bully or muscle her inner child into giving up. She had to be much smarter than that. She downed the last of the wine in her glass. "I should be practicing what I preach."

"But you are, my friend. Sounds to me as though you've analyzed your reaction to death."

"But it's not going away." It was getting *worse*.

The laughter on the other end of the line annoyed Kenzie enough to propel her from the chair. Action as distraction. She headed straight into the kitchen to refill her glass.

"Your reaction is only getting worse because you're not dealing with it. You're acknowledging that your attraction to this man exists and that's it. Is it really so hard to grasp? You teach this stuff."

Kenzie poured the fragrant wine. Only a quarter of a glass. Then, on second thought, she added another healthy splash. "Even if I was inclined to give in to my petulant inner child, which I'm not, I don't see that involving myself with a man when neither of us has the time will solve anything. Will has a child who needs him even more than a normal six-year-old needs his parents. Plural. There are supposed to be two."

There was a thoughtful silence on the other end.

Kenzie returned to the living room and sat in her chair again.

"You know, Kenzie," Geri finally said. "I recognize you have issues with Will because of his divorces, but it seems to me that there's more to the man that might be worth taking another look at. I mean, he seems to be moving heaven and earth to help his son. The city council. Family Foundations."

She paused, and Kenzie took another fortifying sip before Geri continued.

"Sally deals with all kinds of folks as mayor, and she thinks highly of Will. If she didn't, I would have never passed along your name. Seems to me you might want to step back and take a look at the forest instead of looking at only one tree."

Kenzie understood what Geri was saying, but her choice of metaphor raised another question.

How was Kenzie supposed to handle the forest when she could barely handle one tree?

CHAPTER EIGHT

Melinda Patterson.

Will frowned at the nameplate outside the office door. Although why he should be surprised was a mystery. He'd known Melinda had gone back to her maiden name, the one she'd used professionally throughout their marriage. The legality had actually been ruled on by the judge in the divorce.

Maybe seeing her name brought up the memory of the years they'd dated, before marriage and kids.

The *good times,* as it turned out.

Or maybe seeing her maiden name emphasized the separation between mother and son.

He hadn't been to Melinda's office since before she'd decided to work from home to accommodate all of Sam's doctor's appointments and therapy sessions. She hadn't been willing to give up her job entirely, and the company had been more than willing to take what they could get from her.

She'd worked for Blue Ridge Productions, LLC, since an internship in college and had branded the company so they'd earned a recognizable and reliable name among the directors and producers who wanted to film in the region. Her company scouted locations all over the Blue Ridge and Smokey Mountains and the surrounding areas, pulled permits and generally took care of all the accommodations so a production company could come to town and shoot without wasting time and money.

The job was a perfect fit for Melinda, who was both motivated and social. Lots of parties. Lots of travel. Right up her alley. His once, too, when they'd been together. He wasn't surprised Blue Ridge Productions had moved heaven and earth to keep her. Will himself had learned an awful lot about his own business from her. She was *that* good.

The administrative assistant motioned him forward with a polite, "She's expecting you, Mr. Russell."

Will was glad that they'd given Melinda the corner office she'd always loved, with windows on two walls that overlooked a conservation lot with a pond and against the backdrop of the Blue Ridge Mountains that featured so prominently in her work.

He rapped on the door, then entered. He'd only come here today because she'd been pressed for time, and he didn't want to address the issue about dropping in on Sam over the phone. She obviously didn't get the importance of giving Guadalupe a heads-up. A face-to-face conversation would help Will read her, so he could figure out how to get her to understand. He needed her cooperation, not an argument. And

Sam didn't deserve to have a simple, but important, direction ignored.

Funny how the sight of her behind her desk, reading glasses on her head, pushing the sleek blond hair back from her face, seemed so familiar, reminiscent of the years before their marriage when they'd been a solid couple, enjoying life, laying a strong foundation for the future.

So he'd thought. Melinda, too, by all accounts.

"Hey, Will," she said. "Come on in. Give me two seconds. Just let me send this email."

"No problem." He sat in a chair in front of the desk, resisted the urge to grab his own phone and check his messages. Always business with them. Instead, he glanced out the windows at the view and took in the peace of the scene.

"So what's up that we need to discuss but I don't need to worry about?" she asked on one long breath, repeating almost verbatim what he'd told her when he'd suggested they get together to talk.

She'd turned away from the computer, folding her hands in front of her and giving him her undivided attention.

He'd considered how to begin this conversation, mentally tried out several approaches to sidestep a bad start because the minute Melinda felt cornered, she got defensive and the conversation was over. The productive part, anyway.

Then he got annoyed. Never a good thing.

"Sam's still dragging around your latest gift everywhere he goes. Rafael, too, from what Guadalupe says. She takes them outside and tells them to go annihilate the universe."

Melinda flashed her trademark high-beam smile. "I knew he'd like it the minute I saw it. I had my fingers crossed about Rafael, because he's a little older."

"Guadalupe appreciated you thinking of him."

"Of course. He and Sam are like brothers. I wouldn't ever show up with something for one and not the other."

There it was. The opening he'd been hoping for. "Speaking of, I wanted to mention that it works out best for Sam if you call before you drop by."

There was a beat of silence. "I know that, Will."

He went the stupid route. "Oh, I didn't realize you'd called that day."

Her smile faded, replaced by the first hint of ice in her expression. "Did Guadalupe complain because I dropped by?"

Melinda didn't admit to not calling which confirmed everything Will already knew. "No, of course not. She would never. You know that. She knows how much Sam enjoys spending time with you."

"That's good, because I'm his mother."

Will leaned back in the chair, affected a casual posture that he didn't come close to feeling. Tired more accurately described how he felt. Unhappy that he was here once again having a discussion with his ex-wife that they'd already had—several times. "I know that, Melinda."

"Then what's the problem? What did you want to discuss?"

"The importance of giving whoever's caring for Sam a chance to prepare him for visits."

She exhaled heavily, obviously as tired as he was—with this conversation, anyway. "I know I should have called, but I was in the area scouting a site. I wound up getting done early and had to choose whether or not to miss an unexpected chance to visit. I wanted him to have his gift since he's been spending so much time at Guadalupe's while you've been working on the new building."

Which might be acceptable if exactly the same thing hadn't happened before. Often. Whenever it suited Melinda, in fact. He didn't point that out. He knew these situations arose whenever she started feeling guilty because Sam didn't live with her and would only resent Will calling her out on her lack of consideration. "By the time I got there to pick Sam up, he was having a meltdown."

Shaking her head, she said firmly, "Not from seeing his mother, he wasn't."

"Melinda, he gets stressed. When Guadalupe doesn't let him know you're coming until you're there, he doesn't get the time he needs to anticipate your visit. By the time he wraps his head around it, you're leaving, then he's disappointed because he doesn't want you to go. All those feelings happening that fast stress him out. Then he acts out. You know all this."

Exactly the wrong thing to say because her expression suddenly seemed sculpted from ice.

"Yes, Will. I do." Her tone was equally frigid. "So I don't need you telling me what I already know. Are you trying to make me feel bad because I chose not to miss visiting my son so I could take the time to make a phone call? If that's the case, you didn't need to make a special trip over here because you can make me feel like a crummy mother quite well over the phone."

The throbbing in his temples kicked up a notch. Great. And he still had a good eight hours left of this day. "Melinda, why would I do that? I don't think you're a crummy mother, and I certainly never said that I did."

Rising in a smooth motion, she turned her back to him. He recognized the move for exactly what it was—buying herself time to get her emotions under control so she could restrategize.

"I know you love Sam," he said. "I know you want what's best for him. Sam loves spending time with you. You're his mother, for God's sake, Melinda. Of course he wants to be with you. I just thought maybe you didn't realize—"

"Oh, I realize all right. I realize exactly what you're doing. The same thing you always do." She spun on him, gaze teary and voice tremulous.

Now he was stressing her out. Exactly what he hadn't wanted.

"I appreciate you dropping by to upset me before I have to walk into a really important meeting. Thank you so much. I know you're the superhero daddy, Will. Mr. Custody Councilman, fighting for his son's right for a good school. And I know I pale by comparison—"

"This isn't about me. Or you, for that matter. It's about Sam, and what's best for him." And Will resented the fact that he was dancing around on eggshells only to wind up exactly where he didn't want to be—arguing with her.

"I wanted to see my son and bring him and his friend gifts. The judge told me I could see Sam whenever I want. He encouraged me to drop by since our son doesn't live with his mother."

"A phone call, Melinda. Is it really so difficult to make one phone call?"

"I already explained but you don't seem to be listening. If I'd have taken the time to call and wait until Guadalupe gave me permission to see my son, I would have missed the chance to see him. But there's no reasoning with you. You're a total control freak. I tried collaborating with you, and you turned around and fought me for custody. I try coparenting with you, and you're still not happy. What will make you happy? When I don't have any contact with my son at all? That's not going to happen. Ever."

There were so many things Will could have latched

on to in that little outburst. *Him* a control freak? Melinda needing permission to see her son? But Will bypassed them all because he was too busy latching on to one unexpected piece of information.

"I tried collaborating with you."

Suddenly Will remembered why Positive Partings had sounded so familiar. Melinda had contacted the agency when their divorce proceedings started.

And he suspected he now knew exactly why Kenzie hadn't voted for him.

WILL HEARD THE tranquil sound of Kenzie's voice from a distance as he crouched on a catwalk in a crawl space in the attic. He hadn't been to this side of the building in weeks. Not since the night before remembering Melinda had consulted with Kenzie. He simply hadn't wanted to deal with one more thing, not even something as simple as speculation about Kenzie's opinion of him. He shouldn't be obsessing about what she thought of him. Ceiling tiles and her list. That's all he should be thinking about.

They didn't build buildings like this anymore, meant to endure, with space to access the electrical and plumbing. Construction to today's specs, with focus on efficiency of space and energy use, meant one burst pipe could bring half the building to a standstill dealing with the damage.

He hadn't expected Kenzie to be teaching upstairs tonight, using the smaller of the two classrooms currently available. He didn't want to disturb her, but he couldn't wait to deal with these ceiling tiles any longer, either. He'd told her he'd replace them, then he'd dropped completely out of sight as he and his crew gutted the hall and built Angel House's new classrooms.

Deanne had toured the redesigned space this morning. There was still a ton of work to do with painting and carpet and fixtures before they could install the classroom equipment, but she'd seen past what still needed to be done as he'd known she would. She'd had tears in her eyes when she'd hugged him.

Sometimes the most unexpected things kept him going. And he'd needed those things, especially after confrontations like the last one he'd had with Melinda.

Superhero Daddy. How about practical parent who was looking out for Sam? That worked. The kid deserved one parent who would since his mother didn't seem capable.

Just the thought angered him.

Taking a deep breath, he tried to concentrate on what he had accomplished for his son. What had recently been seven thousand square feet of open space and tiered seating had turned into seven separate classrooms uniquely designed to meet the needs of Angel House's students, from the air flow to the lighting and everything in between.

Windows and observation panels had been constructed to minimize distractions yet still give students things to learn from to engage their attention and grow their skills. The room scale may be smaller than an average classroom, but not one of the seven was a sterile environment.

No, each classroom possessed unique qualities of scale, light, color and mood. The rooms served various functions, mimicking the variations of a normal home. Kitchens differed from bedrooms, bathrooms from living rooms.

These variations of space were one of the ways Angel House helped kids learn in a natural environment, teaching them to generalize and transition from one setting to another. To teach things that most kids did instinctively.

But not kids with autism.

Not Sam.

Crawling through the narrow space, Will pulled along a flat of ceiling tiles behind him. Pushing the toolbox in front of him, he winced when the corner nailed some old metal ductwork and rang a resounding echo.

Damn. He hoped Kenzie hadn't heard that.

Oh, well. Wasn't much he could do but try to keep the noise down. He didn't want her to think the work she needed done was being sacrificed for the work on Angel House, which was exactly what had been happening. There were only so many hours in a day, so he hadn't crossed off one thing from her never-ending list recently.

Of course, a lot of that had to do with the fact that he didn't want complications right now, didn't need distractions. He'd enjoyed three weeks Kenzie-free because she was a feminine, redheaded distraction, no matter how he cut it.

But Will had pushed his luck to the furthest limit and needed to accomplish something before Kenzie lost faith. With Sam away at summer camp for a full seven days, the timing couldn't be better. Will could work all day and not have to worry about getting to Guadalupe's house before Sam's bedtime.

Summer camp had been a gift from Deanne, as she'd arranged to get Sam into the program. She sat on the board to oversee the autism program and had promised Will Sam would not only be well cared for but would have a great time. Will took her at her word and was grateful for this new experience. He hadn't been away from Sam overnight since Melinda had left home, long before the divorce.

He received a nightly phone call to report on Sam's activities during the day, and so far so good. In the meantime, Will had been putting the extra hours to use.

Maneuvering through the narrow passage, he attempted to be quiet when replacing the tiles. Not always possible with decades-old ceiling tiles that had frequently melded onto the framework. In one area, he had to cut away the frame entirely, so the work was slow going.

But as he made his way across the span of the classroom, Kenzie's voice grew ever clearer with each tile he replaced until finally he could make out what she was saying.

"Once the divorce is finalized, your former spouse becomes your parenting partner. Successfully parenting together after a divorce means respecting each other's boundaries."

Boundaries, hmm? Could Melinda respect his boundaries when he wasn't even sure what they were? Will didn't know. He couldn't remember hearing anything about boundaries when he'd sat through this class. Yet he'd put in his time and money to get the paperwork he needed to finalize the divorce.

But Will liked the sound of Kenzie's voice and found himself listening. He wasn't so much paying attention to what she said as he was being lured into the gentle cadence of her voice, a soft-spoken elocution that enticed like a drug.

But he did catch some things that made sense.

"You must appreciate another person's strengths and recognize their limitations," she was saying. "This is absolutely essential because once you choose to identify your parenting partner's behavior you can also choose how to react when situations invariably come up."

Wedging a screwdriver into the dry panel, he pried it loose from the grid. A shower of crunchy particles sprinkled down over the newly refinished plank floor. One more mess to clean.

"What idiot thought a drop ceiling was a good idea

for this old building?" he whispered on the edge of a breath.

But Will already knew the answer. There had been a renovation done decades ago. Probably in the early seventies from the looks of the materials. The drop ceiling would have been a quick fix to cover the HVAC ductwork and wiring from the sprinkler system. Of course, they'd sacrificed the magnificent height in the room for the benefit of the plenum space. The crown molding was still intact. Good thing Kenzie hadn't seen it or she would have asked him if it was possible to rip down all the grids so she could have soaring ceilings again.

Of course, the first floor didn't have this access. He'd have to check Kenzie's class schedule so he could get into those rooms to remove the panels from the other side.

"Use this situation as an example," she was saying. "Your child has an after-school program he needs to arrive at promptly on time. But it's your parenting partner's visitation day and he works a job that makes it hard to pinpoint exactly when he can leave work. Maybe he's a dentist and leaving depends on when he finishes up his last patient. Or an attorney who's in the courtroom and can't leave until the judge dismisses."

No doubt Nathanial inspired that example. Will tugged so hard the panel snapped off a corner, sending another spray of dry fiber raining down.

"You can rely on your parenting partner to do

something that's problematic. This will likely introduce tension into the situation because if he runs late, there's going to be fallout. Your child is going to be upset that he missed out on his program. He's likely to be disappointed in the parent who's responsible for making him miss his program. The parent who ran late will likely feel inadequate because he disappointed his child and defensive around you because he didn't live up to his end of the bargain. You'll probably wind up feeling hurt for your child and resentful toward your parenting partner for not arriving on time. I mean, picking up your child from school on time. Is that really so much to ask? In one word—*tension.*"

There was a pause before she continued. "Successful parenting partners respect limitations. A productive way to handle that situation might be to acknowledge your parenting partner will have a problem picking up your child on time. You could offer to get him to his program and swap the pickup responsibilities for another day when the schedule's more fluid. Now your child gets where he needs to be on time and is happy. Your parenting partner still gets quality drive time with his child and doesn't feel as if he's shirking his responsibility or that you're controlling the situation. You feel as if you have a partner to rely upon with the parenting responsibilities who will return the favor when you need him to. See the difference? We've eliminated the tension. Yes, question."

"What happens when your parenting partner won't

parent productively?" a woman asked. "You offer to pick your child up, but he refuses then doesn't show up at all."

Deadbeat dad. Will knew about those.

"In that situation you might place yourself on standby," Kenzie suggested. "So if your parenting partner doesn't show, then you can step in."

"But if he knows I'll always step in and pick up his slack, then he'll never be responsible."

"That's quite possible," Kenzie agreed.

"Then wouldn't it be better not to step in and let him deal with the consequences of his actions with our son?"

"It may be. You're in the best position to answer that question," Kenzie said. "But I'd suggest asking yourself whether your goal is attempting to get your former spouse to become an effective parenting partner or to get your son to his after-school program."

The mom with the deadbeat ex gave a brittle laugh. "My ex isn't capable of being an effective parenting anything."

"Sounds as if it's even more important for you to be the responsible parent, then."

"I want to know how it's fair for me to be constantly picking up his slack with our son?"

Will wanted to know that, too.

"I didn't say it was fair," Kenzie said matter-of-factly. "But if we reproduced with an irresponsible partner then all we can do is deal with the situation. This is when adults step back to look at what's best for their children. If one parent chooses to act irresponsibly, then the responsibility falls on the other parent to balance the situation as best they can."

That made Will smile. Kenzie's calm-voiced delivery had a way of softening the edges of even a brutal truth. He couldn't help but wonder what the woman with the deadbeat ex thought of that no-nonsense response.

Especially when Kenzie added, "The situation may not be fair, but at least you had a choice. You chose your former spouse. Your child didn't get to choose either of his parents, but he's dependent on you both to provide what he needs. If that means you run interference and conduct damage control, so be it. It's our jobs to teach our children coping skills so they learn to deal constructively with all the unfair situations that invariably come up in life."

Will exhaled a low whistle. Kenzie did not mince words, but she did effectively shut down that discussion and move on to address her next topic. And as he continued removing panels from the grid, chiseling away the crusty remains from the T-bars so the new panel fit in snugly, he considered what Kenzie had said.

She might not have sugarcoated her opinion, but her response was both simple and true. Will's own mother had been in a similar situation, and she'd responded much in the way Kenzie had suggested. As a responsible parent who put the interests of her sons first and foremost. She hadn't been able to effect a change with Will's deadbeat dad, but she did populate her sons' world with some good male role models from her own father and brothers to friends like Bob.

Will and his younger brothers had learned to fish with their grandfather and to hunt with Uncle Jeremy and train for marathons with Uncle Brent. Bob had given Will a career by teaching him how to fix things around the house. With Mom working two jobs most of the time, they'd hated spending money unnecessarily. Bob had always made himself available. Replacing faucets and bathroom fixtures. Replacing the hot water heater. Caulking leaking windows. Fixing the washing machine.

If Bob could fix it, he did. Otherwise, he always knew someone who could for a fair price. And he'd always enlisted Will's help, since he was the man of the family.

Now that Will thought about it, he suspected Bob had been giving Will responsibility to empower him, one of those coping skills Kenzie had mentioned.

He worked automatically and was so entrenched in his thoughts that he barely noticed crawling past the wall dividing one room from the next. He'd already pried up a panel before realizing he was over Kenzie's classroom.

He only realized his error because the sight of her jarred him into the moment.

She stared up at him through the open grid, green-gold eyes twinkling with barely concealed amusement, and said, "Hello."

The three weeks that had passed since he'd seen her suddenly felt like a lifetime. She wore her hair up with tendrils escaping to wisp around her slender neck, the delicate line of her jaw at total odds with the no-nonsense practicality pouring out of her mouth.

He'd seen her in jeans and business casual but tonight she'd traded the flowy skirts for a fitted one that ended above the knee and revealed long, shapely legs and skin as creamy as her face.

"Hello," he finally managed to respond, realizing he needed to conduct some damage control of his own. "Sorry to disturb you."

The amusement retreated behind that familiar distant expression, as if she'd suddenly shut the window and pulled down the blinds. She set the marker she held onto the tray of the dry-erase board, folded her arms over her chest and waited.

For him to disappear again?

Instead, Will leaned through the empty grid, hanging on to the catwalk support and hoping like hell it held his weight so he didn't land on his head and really disturb the class.

"I apologize, folks." Will waved at everyone.

"No sweat, man," a young guy said from the back of the room. He couldn't have been much older than Will had been the first time he'd gotten married. "Court-ordered class."

That said everything that needed saying.

"Hey, aren't you that politician?" a woman asked, not specifying exactly which politician she meant.

She wore a familiar uniform from a local grocery store. "I voted for you."

"Appreciate it." Will flashed her a smile. He certainly hadn't intended to be seen, especially since he was up here dressed in jeans, sweating because he was roasting his ass off up in the attic crawl space. "Always good to meet voters. Can't make solid decisions for our city unless you share what's on your mind."

"When are you going to fix the potholes on my street?" A middle-aged man gave a gruff laugh.

Will had faced that question before. It was a campaign classic. "What part of town?"

"East end."

He shook his head. "Sorry. Not on this year's schedule. But if it's a big street, you can call Public Works. As long as the city maintains your street, they'll fix it."

"Who else would maintain my street?" the gruff guy asked.

Will shook his head. "Could be the state or privately owned. There's a map on the Public Works website. Check it out if you're not sure. The City of Hendersonville prides itself on its street maintenance. Think we fixed something like twelve hundred potholes last year."

"Think they missed one." The gruff old guy gave a snort. "What happens if my street isn't city maintained?"

"You're going to spend some bucks balancing and aligning your car," the young guy offered.

"No joke," the old guy replied.

"Public Works will report it to the North Carolina Department of Transportation. Then it's up to them." Will grinned. "Remember that the next time you're driving around craters on North Church Street or MLK."

"Who maintains Main Street?" Kenzie asked.

Will shifted around to face her again, and raked his gaze over the sight she made half sitting on the desk with her arms folded over her chest. The skirt fitted her body so he could see the curve of her hip and the long line of her thigh. Her pose showed off those curvy bits that were usually hidden. He realized that the blood rushing to his head from hanging here was making him so stupid.

"The city."

She inclined her head, sending those wispy red strands waving around her cheeks and neck. "Good to know."

Then she met his gaze with those big, gold-flecked eyes and asked deadpan, "Done hijacking the class yet?"

Will didn't bother with a reply. "Time to go, folks. Don't forget to vote in the next election. It's important."

Then he pulled himself up through the grid and backed away as quietly as possible. Once he was safely out of sight, Will sat back, balancing himself on the narrow catwalk and wiping the sweat from his brow.

He stared blankly into the dim crawl space, wishing he had a rewind button. If he didn't want more complications in his life, then why had he just made an absolute idiot of himself?

That answer came as easily as it was surprising.

Despite having a young son, too many jobs and not enough hours in the day, he was still a man. Wow. Imagine that.

KENZIE SHOWED THE last of the students out the side door to the parking lot.

"Good night," she said. "Drive safely."

Good luck, she added silently.

When she got right down to essentials, Kenzie wanted to give students one new tool to take home, one revelation or skill or inspiration to help them navigate divorce in a way that protected the family unit for their children. She believed in that goal with her heart and soul. A family could take many forms, and did, but children needed and deserved a solid unit.

Giving a final wave as the last student disappeared into her car, she pulled shut the door. Kenzie usually left this task to the off-duty police officer, but tonight she wanted to see if a truck with WLR General Contracting and Developers emblazoned on the side sat in the parking lot.

Will's truck was parked exactly where it had been every night she'd been here. She suspected his truck was here even on nights she wasn't. He'd obviously been busy because until tonight Kenzie hadn't seen him for weeks.

The man had popped through her ceiling and started campaigning with her students. In the middle of a class, no less.

Ruthless charmer, indeed.

"Sure you don't want me to wait until you lock up? It's late." The officer held the door so she could enter. He was one of a group who rotated as rent-a-cop during classes.

"Thanks, but Lou was out today, and I've got a session at the crack of dawn. I'd rather print everything I need tonight than drag myself in here even earlier in the morning. It's going to take a while."

He glanced through the panel in the door. "Well, I don't feel so bad about leaving you alone here as I did at your old office. Parking lot is well lit. Got good cops on this beat, too. Pay attention when you go to your car. I don't think your neighbor will hear you if you need help."

"I don't think so, either. Big place."

"The parking lot is open so you can see in all directions."

She smiled. "I'll pay attention. Promise."

After handing him an envelope with his moonlighting fee, Kenzie let him out the door, the new chimes Will had sent a worker to install while he'd been AWOL ringing cheerily, and loudly, as the officer departed. She locked the door and headed to her office, wondering if Will still crawled around inside her attic. Squelching her curiosity with effort, Kenzie organized the paperwork needed for tomorrow's session.

Mediating the Spencers had proven a challenge. They'd moved past voluntary collaboration into court-appointed mediation, which always added a level of resistance because people generally didn't like to be told what to do. That was human nature. And especially when it had to do with something as personal as their families and hard-earned assets.

Mrs. Spencer resented that Mr. Spencer wanted to end their marriage after fourteen years and two children, who were still relatively young. It didn't help that they were in that gray period where alimony wasn't likely, and Mrs. Spencer felt as if she would be left to maneuver the teenage years alone and face the difficult task of getting her children into good colleges without her husband's support.

She would be forced back into the job market to make a living. Not only was the economy difficult right now, but as a registered nurse, Mrs. Spencer would be required to work twelve-hour shifts, which created problems with car pools and after-school activities.

All because Mr. Spencer had decided to value wild monkey sex—Mrs. Spencer's words—with his massage therapist more than his wife and children.

Despite that questionable choice, Mr. Spencer was attempting to handle the divorce responsibly. Guilt, most likely, for placing his wants and needs above those of his family. Of course, that was Kenzie's read on the situation based upon surface observation. The only people who ever knew what really took place in a marriage were the people in it.

But she also knew that riding the guilt wave wouldn't last forever. The more Mrs. Spencer resisted negotiation, the more ammunition she gave Mr. Spencer to feel justified in tossing up his hands and saying, "I did the best I could."

Kenzie had been mediating long enough to gauge the escalation of frustration. Mr. Spencer was nearly there. Somehow she needed to help Mrs. Spencer refocus her resentment and fear on to the best interests of her children and the needs of her family. So far they'd only accomplished grudging baby steps before Mrs. Spencer remembered how angry she was again.

Kenzie considered the problem while the printer whirred steadily, spitting out the list of assets they'd successfully negotiated so far. She'd recap their successes before addressing the issues that had been tabled for further discussion.

Five copies. One each for Mrs. Spencer and her attorney. One each for Mr. Spencer and his attorney. One copy for Kenzie.

Sinking into her chair, she placed her feet up on the desk and reviewed the tabled discussions. Kenzie needed to get Mrs. Spencer to recognize the good position she was actually in because North Carolina was a state of equitable distribution. A judge would consider that Mrs. Spencer had given up her career to rear children and keep the books for Mr. Spencer's plumbing business, which involved payroll, accounts payable and receivable. Her contribution to the family and increasing the value of her husband's business would factor a great deal in the division of assets.

That was not the case in community property states.

They'd already addressed a number of the bigger issues such as physical custody, visitation and housing, to name a few, but they hadn't made much headway because Kenzie couldn't give Mrs. Spencer the only thing she wanted—her life to remain unchanged.

Rubbing her temples, Kenzie rested her head back and closed her eyes, reviewing the situation with the hope of finding some detail that might break through Mrs. Spencer's resentment.

The next thing Kenzie knew the whirring of the printer had faded to silence. She must have dozed because her eyelids were heavy and, blinking to clear her gaze, she sensed a presence. She glanced up and saw him.

Will.

He stood in the doorway of her office as if he belonged there, as if leaning against the doorjamb with his arms folded over his broad chest was exactly where he should be. He watched her. Kenzie only knew she could feel his gaze through her lingering slumber as a caress.

No, that couldn't be right.

A voice in her head argued against the potency of the moment, but Kenzie knew what she felt, an awareness that closed the distance, made a simple glance feel alive.

Or maybe she only reacted to his presence. She hadn't seen him in so long, three weeks suddenly seemed a lifetime.

The absence should have let the memory of him to fade. But it hadn't. No, absence had only given rise to her imagination, to a thousand tiny expectations every time she drove into the parking lot wondering whether she'd find his truck, every time she finished up with a client or a class to wonder whether he'd show up *finally* to continue work, every time she turned a corner because he had a key to come and go as he pleased, a key he wouldn't turn over until renovations were complete.

And he had finally come. Tonight. Earlier. *Now.*

The natural glow from the lamps she favored above the glare of fluorescent lighting played tricks with her still-drowsy gaze, softened Will's features in an unfamiliar way, cast shadows on the clear eyes that sparked such incredible turmoil inside her.

She was being ridiculous. Even half-asleep she knew it. Especially when a thought niggled at the edges of her awareness, a thought that urged how much easier it would be to let her inner child run the show. This power struggle was exhausting.

She empathized with her students, realized how much she complicated their lives—and her own— with her beliefs and her classes and her coping skills. Letting her inner child run rampant then dealing with the fallout seemed so much easier than battling her inner child for control. So much easier to go with the powerful emotion sparked by this man than to constantly remind herself he was off-limits for almost every adult reason she could think of.

Suddenly Kenzie felt as tired as Will looked.

And once she could see past her reaction to him, she recognized that he looked exhausted.

"You're working late tonight." Her words were a whisper in the stillness, intruding on the dreamy quality of the moment.

On the inherent danger of moments like this one when the boundaries were blurred and reason prowled the edges of thought, unable to get anyone's attention.

But her words didn't shatter the moment in the way she'd counted on. Not when the light caught his hair when he nodded, a gleam that drew her attention to the way it had started to curl at his nape. Sam's hair. Will needed a trim.

And definitely not when he replied in that gently gruff voice. "You, too."

Except that she hadn't been working. She'd been sleeping.

And he'd been watching.

"I didn't want to disturb you," he said. "You looked so peaceful."

Was that longing she heard in his voice, as if he didn't find peace all that much himself?

"I should be problem-solving, not sleeping." She gave a nervous laugh, reality rearing its head. There was no denying that what she'd once thought of as

Will's ruthless ambition suddenly looked a lot like determination. Or had it been determination all along?

Kenzie believed it had, based on what she'd seen with her own eyes, not the impressions she'd had of Will and secondhand accounts. That realization was a dangerous transition, proved she hadn't been keeping her distance as much as she'd intended.

She'd been dealing with her reaction by rationalizing, reasoning, attempting to control.

But beneath the logic and sensibility, her opinion had been subtly shifting. Until his exhaustion looked like determination, and Will didn't feel nearly as dangerous as he should.

"What exactly about him isn't your cup?" Nathanial's question replayed in her memory.

In this moment, when Kenzie gazed into Will's quiet expression, saw the shadows beneath his eyes, she couldn't come up with one single thing.

"I just wanted to apologize for crashing your class tonight," he said. "Totally unintentional. I was on a roll and not paying attention."

"Oh, no problem. I'm sure you made the students' night. No one wants to be there listening to me preach for four hours."

The corners of his mouth tipped up in a smile. A dimple peeked from its hiding place beneath his five o'clock shadow.

Nearly eleven o'clock shadow now.

"Didn't sound like preaching from where I was sitting."

"Hanging you mean?"

The dimple made an appearance for real. "Yeah."

"You've been here late a lot of nights recently," she said, desperate for this conversation to drown out the voice in her head, an awareness of this man the quiet only amplified.

"Sam's at camp. Putting the time to work."

"How fun for him."

Will nodded, his smile thoughtful now, somehow gentle in the soft light. He had such an expressive mouth…she wondered how he kissed. He was such an interesting blend of opposites, a big man who managed to be gentle, a ruthlessly charming man who managed to be vulnerable, an ambitious local politician who could work miracles with his hands.

Maybe she was seeing him reflected against his interactions with Sam. Or maybe he made her think of kissing because she loved kissing in all its forms, from the exquisite tenderness of shared breaths to the wild hunger of needy exploration.

And now she was thinking about kissing him.

Kenzie was in so, so much trouble here.

"How much longer are you going to be?" he asked, thoughtful as always, a gentleman. "I just dropped by to apologize. And now I'm heading out. We can walk out together."

This time, when offered a gentlemanly escort to her car, Kenzie accepted.

CHAPTER NINE

AN UNUSUALLY EMPTY HOUSE, a few hours of sleep and a frenzied day spent rushing from one job site to the next didn't do a damn thing to help Will shake the memory of last night.

He didn't even need to close his eyes to see Kenzie the way she'd looked, fast asleep at her desk with her chin resting against her chest and wisps of her hair playing about her face.

Her hair hadn't come anywhere close to covering her legs though, which she'd propped on the desk for his viewing pleasure. Gravity had kindly worked its magic on her skirt so he'd gotten a prime shot of those dancer legs, which is exactly how he thought of them—long, lean and shapely. He saw more thigh than this proper miss would have revealed—to him, anyway.

Maybe not to her not-at-the-moment attorney.

Just the thought soured Will's mood. Kenzie was making him remember what he'd forgotten in the crush of his busy life.

He was a man who hadn't been with a woman in a long time.

Okay, well, he hadn't so much forgotten as he had

been too busy and preoccupied to notice anything that could be ignored. Sam. Work. Angel House. City council. Family. Friends even still made it onto the list for holidays and play dates for Sam whenever they found time. He'd pack up Sam and off they'd go to Charlie and Nicole's or Greg and Ashley's to watch a game or grill outdoors so the kids could swim.

But hell no to anything even resembling a woman or a date. There hadn't been room in his life to even think about someone let alone meet someone and invest the one thing he didn't have into a relationship—time.

To date, sex hadn't made the list and wouldn't as long as it could be ignored. He wished he could somehow figure out that part of his life, because he hadn't been wrong about Kenzie. She was aware of him the way he was of her. No question.

So how long could he go without sex? As he'd already broken his personal record, Will supposed he'd go back to ignoring the situation. Any possibility of sex would be even easier to ignore once Sam got home to keep him focused on what was important in his life.

Glancing at the dashboard clock, he cursed.

Hunger was making him irritable, but he had to abandon his plan of picking up a to-go dinner from the deli to make up for the lunch he hadn't had. Well, the protein bar and bag of peanuts he kept in the glove compartment didn't count. Deanne had wanted to meet at the new building at five, and it was already 4:50 p.m.

Will would rather starve than complain, though. Not when he'd been enjoying the break from dealing with food—the planning of meals, the buying groceries, the meal preparation. A never-ending job on top of all the others. And he still had to tackle gluten free. He had an entirely new appreciation for his mother and Melinda, who had once fed houses filled with hungry guys. And whatever Melinda's difficulties with handling Sam's situation now, she'd always made sure there was plenty of food when they'd been together.

Kenzie's car was parked where it always was. Amazing how one stupid, midpriced sedan could spike his pulse. He was ignoring that. His crew was still there, too, working on the plumbing and fixtures in the new classrooms from the last phone call with his foreman an hour ago.

Deanne's SUV was there already, too.

Will wound up burning another ten minutes in conversation with his foreman about an unexpected problem with an inspector. It was always something in this business. Rip down a wall to find the wiring fried. Get the inspectors to actually show up when they said they would and they weren't happy with something.

Deanne finally hunted him down as he was wrapping up his conversation. She smiled and waved, looking as she always did—focused and frazzled around the edges and somehow amused by it all. She always said she'd never have made it through a day without finding humor in it. She managed to share that gift with everyone around her.

But her smile seemed forced today.

"Hey, you. Come on." He gave Deanne a hug and led her out of the hallway-in-progress where the framed walls didn't provide any privacy. He wanted to get out the way of his crew, who had to wrap up their day before six otherwise Will would be looking at overtime and a payroll he couldn't afford to write checks for.

He led her into a room that would eventually be one of the offices; which one hadn't been decided yet. "I'll give you a key if you want to drop by to see how much work we're getting done every day."

"Like I have that kind of time." Deanne pulled a face as she half sat on a rung of the painter's ladder—the only piece of furniture in the room. "I just needed to be here, to be reassured. I wouldn't have even bothered you if I'd realized the crew would still be here."

"What's up?"

She exhaled sharply and waved a dismissive hand. "I'm being ridiculous. I cut a check for the printer. I had to change the address on the agendas and all the promotional materials for the apple festival, and by the time I finished signing my name I was almost hyperventilating."

With money tight, Will understood why writing any check could create anxiety. He experienced his own fair share of that when he looked at his supply bills and the payroll increase for the crew he kept yanking off paying jobs to work on Angel House.

But he didn't think that's what was bothering Deanne.

"We're moving along okay. On schedule." *For the most part.* Not even he could have anticipated the structural problem with the space the architect had allotted to move several of the mechanical systems into. Not at least until they'd demolished walls. He didn't share that with Deanne. It was need-to-know information that would only add to her stress.

"I know, Will." She sounded apologetic and annoyed at the same time. "I'm being so selfish. I needed to walk around here and see everything for myself. I needed to hear you tell me we're going to make it, and that I didn't just throw away a lot of money that would have been put to better use giving all our wonderful employees at least a little severance pay."

"Deanne," he said on a long breath. Selfish was one thing this woman had never been in Will's acquaintance. But he also lived the life Deanne did and could hear everything she wasn't saying to him.

Something had rocked her boat. Could be as simple as a tough few days with her daughter, who had outgrown her during the past year, shooting up like teens did and now towering over her mother. Add the accompanying hormones and her daughter had hit a transition point and the need for a new skillset that would take time to learn.

Or it could be something complicated such as stress weighing on her and her husband, their biggest support system for each another. That part could be really tough. Will knew the toll autism took on a marriage. He'd lost his to it.

But no matter what had Deanne's faith wavering today, the reason was personal, hers to share or not as she chose.

That was an unspoken rule with Angel House parents. They supported one another, no questions asked. *Always.*

Sometimes the parents in the support group were all each other had when no one in their lives understood the unique challenges, and the unique joys, of having a child with autism. Not family. Not friends. Not the strangers in the stores who could be well-meaning or really unkind when they witnessed a meltdown for reasons they didn't understand.

When kids looked normal, they were expected to act that way, too. People could even be cruel.

"It's all good." Will knelt in front of her and took her hands in his. "We're making it happen."

She nodded, clenched his hands tightly.

"We haven't gone through all this work to *not* move into this building. I didn't exactly remodel this place, Deanne. I renovated the space to fit our needs exactly. No one's going to want it after I'm through."

He smiled. "Besides, we've got a really long lease and great rent."

She inclined her head, dark hair falling forward but not hiding eyes that glinted and her struggle to maintain a composed expression. She was fighting, trying to keep her emotions from taking over.

Talking to help her through the moment, he said, "If the Ramsey Foundation grant doesn't come through, then something else will. You know what I'm talking about. A door closes and a window opens. That whole thing."

Silence was his only reply for a long moment then she took a deep, steadying breath. "We do what we can do, and that's all we can do, right?"

"Right."

There was more silence between them, a healing silence. He suspected she was looking for humor to get her through whatever was happening in her world, whatever had frayed her nerves.

Finally she met his gaze. "You've moved heaven and earth to make this place happen, Will. You know how much everyone appreciates everything you've done and are still doing?"

"We do what we can do."

That's when her expression melted and she smiled softly. He witnessed the effort, hoped that whatever had her worried today would resolve quickly, but she'd found her humor again.

"We do what we can do." A reminder. "And trust that God's got a plan."

"Yep," Will agreed. "So you do your thing at Angel House, and let me worry about this place for the moment. That a deal?"

"Deal." She tightened her grip on his hands. "So what do you have going on around here tonight? I know you're not heading home yet."

"I wish." Will laughed. "Well, not really. House is quiet without Sam around, to be honest."

"I'll bet. Crazy, isn't it?"

"What?"

"How life might not happen as we expect, but somehow things turn out exactly the way they're supposed to. Different maybe, but better in so many ways."

Will let out a low whistle. "Different is right. Maybe we just learn to appreciate things more, the simple things that get lost in the shuffle. What do you think?"

"Could be." Finally, a sincere smile. "Thanks."

He had no reply because one wasn't necessary. They were there for each other. Period. That was what Angel House taught its parents. To care. To have faith. To trust that everything would work out for the best. To let the heartaches fuel appreciation for the victories. To find humor in the uniqueness of the journey. For that last one alone, Will owed Deanne more than he would ever get a chance to repay.

He walked her through the building, pointing out a few more things that had been done since her tour yesterday morning.

Then he escorted Deanne to her car. "I'll send the key over sometime this week."

"You don't have to trouble—"

"I'll send it with someone who's headed in that direction." Which would likely be him on the way to City Hall. "Rekeyed the whole building when we replaced the doors, and should have thought of it then. You come whenever and start bringing your stuff."

That made her laugh. "You are a total doll. Enjoy your free time. I might be able to finagle a few extra days of camp for Sam but that'll be it. The program age group shifts next week."

"*You're* the doll. I really needed this extra time to get things under control here." If that's what he could call it.

He opened her car door when the lock clicked and shut it behind her. With a wave she drove off.

Will glanced at Kenzie's side of the lot. Her car was still there. He wouldn't have minded avoiding her tonight. In general he found ignoring the unattended aspects of his life easier when he wasn't around Kenzie James.

After falling asleep at her desk last night, he was surprised she hadn't headed home early—and wished she had. But she was probably like everyone else around here with too much to do and not enough time to do it. Deanne wasn't the only one on the verge of hyperventilating.

Which wiped out avoidance as one of his choices tonight. He couldn't dodge work. Not if he planned to keep his promises to Deanne and Kenzie. Which brought to mind another promise. Will stopped at his truck to grab his toolbox and sanding equipment.

After knocking on the side door, he rang the bell. When he still didn't get an answer, he let himself in with the key, unwilling to waste any more time trying to be polite. For all he knew she could be dozing at her desk again. He didn't think she was in class since there were no cars around.

He made a tour of the administrative offices but didn't find her. Maybe he could finish up the classroom with the missing ceiling panel, compliments of last night's stupidity.

"WHERE ARE YOU, Nathanial?" Kenzie asked when the call rolled to voice mail yet again.

She frowned at the display and disconnected without leaving a message. She'd already left two, one last night and another earlier today, when she thought the judge might break for lunch. She'd sent her good-morning text message wishing him a successful day as she always did when he was in court. She hadn't expected a reply to the text because she always tried to be his last encouraging thought before he closed the door on his personal life to focus on what took place in the courtroom. A very high-stress and surprising world by all accounts.

"Not even a text, Nathanial, really?" she said aloud, but there was no one in her office to reply.

Just Kenzie and her thoughts—exactly what she didn't want to be alone with right now.

Which was the problem. Nathanial was probably crazy busy. The urgency was entirely hers, and she factored that in every time she began to get impatient.

Dragging a fingertip across her touch-screen display, she decided not to wait. She would send him another text. Then she stopped herself before typing the first word of a message. Reason argued he would have replied already if he'd been available. Desperation was transforming her into a shrew.

Did she really want to make that choice?

Setting down the phone, she slid it across her desk until it was out of easy reach.

No, she did not want to become a shrew, but she also thought the most important man in her life besides her father should be available when she needed him.

That wasn't entirely fair, since he usually was.

Then again, she was pretty low-maintenance.

Okay, okay. To be fair to Nathanial, he was entrenched in a big case at the moment. It wasn't his fault she was needy right now, simply unfortunate timing.

That acknowledgment didn't change the fact she was needy.

There was only one way to purge this fascination with Will, and that was to involve herself with the man who was her life partner. They hadn't been friends with benefits, as they'd called it, since that last trip to Florida. She didn't know what Nathanial had going on right now, but he'd always been there for her in every way.

Except today.

Kenzie stood and prowled the edges of the room, glancing out at her view of Main Street. The sun had started to set, lengthening the shadows from the direction of the courthouse. The streetlamps wouldn't cycle on for another half hour at least.

She was agitated and edgy and needed a distraction. Of all the nights not to have a class scheduled… That left unpacking another room since she was already prepped for tomorrow's meetings. But renovations made her think of Will, so no help there. It wouldn't kill her to go home and take care of everything she'd been ignoring because of this move.

Just the thought of being alone in her head right now brought on a mild wave of panic.

Which left friends.

Beelining for her desk, Kenzie sent a bulk text to Fiona and Jess.

Kevin's tonight, PLEASE!

She depressed the Send button and envisioned sitting around a table in the busy bistro, talking nonstop and sipping wine, with all the distractions of diners coming in and out for Kevin's anticipated nightly specials.

The phone vibrated. Not a text but a call. Kenzie answered it before she even knew who it was.

"Okay, Kenzie. You haven't had two SOSes in the past five years, now all of a sudden I'm getting two in a month. What on earth is going on?"

Fiona.

"Just drowning in the sludge of my thoughts tonight," she said lamely because that's exactly how she felt. *Lame.*

"I know the sound of man trouble," Fiona said sagely. "What on earth is going on with you and Nathanial?"

Funny how she jumped straight to Nathanial and asked exactly the question that Kenzie had been avoiding. But why would she think anything else. Who else would be in her life but Nathanial? How long had it been since Kenzie had another date?

"No, no. It's nothing like that. I've got some other stuff going on, and Nathanial isn't available because he's in court."

"Hmm. Sounds like a problem to me. Just saying."

"Fiona," Kenzie warned. She was *not* in the mood for a lecture. "I don't need any more things to worry about tonight, thank you. I needed to vent."

"Cody and I have tickets for that fund-raiser at Mission Children's Hospital tonight. I'm on my way to meet him now, but I'll bag. I'm sure he'll understand—"

"Absolutely not. You do not cancel your plans to rescue me."

"Oh, God, Kenzie. This sounds serious. I don't mind. Cody is way more excited about hearing Dr. Yovino speak than I am. Trust me."

"I appreciate that, but go have fun. I'm glad someone has a cocktail dress in her night."

"How am I supposed to have fun when I'm going to worry about you?"

"No worrying. I am fine. I mean it."

"Tomorrow night? I get off work at eight. We can meet up at Kevin's then. Sound good?"

"Sounds great. I'll look forward to hearing about Dr. Yovino's presentation," she added to sound up-beat.

The pediatric cardiologist had been active and visible in gaining recognition for the Mission Foundation and all their various causes. Surely he'd be an interesting speaker. And then there'd be the pricey dinner and probably dancing... Fiona had a life, and a man. And they were doing things together. Like a normal couple who didn't work all the time.

That was the problem with her and Nathanial— they'd prioritized wrong. Their relationship should be first, work second....

"All right, then. I'll text you during dinner to find out how you're doing."

"Have fun."

"See you tomorrow night."

Kenzie disconnected the call. See, she had friends who cared, and the call did make her feel a little better. She checked her texts to see if Jess had responded, but no luck. Probably still at work.

Kenzie considered calling Geri, but she already knew what Geri would say.

"If you thought the problem would go away on its own then think again because it doesn't work that way, and I already weighed in on the solution."

Geri *had* delivered a verdict. Fiona would encourage Kenzie to pour out her heart while Jess would come up with an abundance of ideas to tackle the problem. Nathanial was the one who would make Kenzie feel better by being there.

They could pick one of the ongoing home improvement projects at Kenzie's house to work on, chatting companionably while they worked. Or they could head to Nathanial's house and blow off the world by popping in any Jason Statham movie, which were Nathanial's favorites. Or *The Matrix.* He could watch those over and over again. Not the last of the trilogy, though. He didn't even own that one, deeming it an unworthy conclusion to the series.

Whatever they did, things would feel right in her world again, and this overwhelming urge to pour her heart out would subside. Which was good since she couldn't share this problem with him, anyway.

That thought stopped her cold.

Why wouldn't she share her feelings with Nathanial? Because he'd warned her against getting involved with Will?

Kenzie considered that as she headed back to the

window. The streetlamps were still dark, but a car cruised past with its lights on. What on earth was she doing? Why did waking up to Will last night suddenly throw her into such a tizzy when she wasn't the tizzy type?

Ugh!

She'd spoken with her parents before dinner, but made another call just to hear a voice. "Hey, Mom. I forgot to ask how bridge went today."

"That's sweet of you, Kenzie. We made five tables happen."

There was a sigh in that statement, so Kenzie asked, "Trouble with your group?"

Mom launched into a tale about the amount of work she put in coordinating the tables, who could sit with whom and who bickered when they were together. By the time she'd worked her way through all the confirmation phone calls and buffet issues to all the trouble one cancellation caused and people's thoughtlessness about not making their own replacements, Kenzie was nicely distracted and pretty convinced the need to rant was a genetic thing in the James family.

"Your father told me I should resign and let someone else take over," Mom said.

Kenzie had been about to suggest the very same thing, but guessed by Mom's tone that her reaction to Dad's suggestion hadn't been favorable. Instead, Kenzie said, "Is it possible to ask for some help?"

"*I'm* the help. Marianna coordinates the group all

winter while your father and I are in Florida, so I give her a break when we're home."

"Sounds like you both need some more backup."

"Hmm. I'm sure Marianna would agree, but I'm not sure the sort of help we'd get would be very productive. The last time we asked the ladies to step up, the club didn't meet for months. I hate to see the group disband entirely. Some of us have been playing together for nearly thirty years."

"Is eliminating a table or two a possibility?" Kenzie asked as a beep sounded in her ear. She glanced at the display.

Jess.

"Got another call coming in, Mom. I need to take it. I'll call you in the morning. Sweet dreams."

"Thanks for listening, Kenzie."

"Love you." Someone got to rant tonight. That was something.

Clicking over the call, she hoped against hope Jess would accept her invitation. "Hey. Thanks for getting back with me."

"What's up? Your text sounded urgent."

How a text could *sound* urgent was up for debate. "Need some girl time."

There would be a problem getting together with Jess, but Fiona had already declined. Kenzie would risk it. She was that desperate. As long as they filled Fiona in on the details she'd missed, they might minimize the fallout.

"I'm so sorry. I can't. I'm covering for Professor Wheaton tonight, and class won't let out until ten."

"Good for you." It was a wonderful opportunity for Jess, who was an adjunct at a private college north of town.

"Yeah, I'm excited. But I'm surprised you didn't have a class yourself."

"No, no class tonight I'm afraid." Everyone had a life but her. When had this happened? She prided herself on maintaining balance in her life, on *practicing what she preached,* but right now she'd been abandoned by everyone who mattered.

"Listen, Kenzie. I don't know what's up, but I know something is. Why don't we meet up for Tara's tribal dance class tomorrow night and then hit Kevin's after? Solid plans. Don't worry about Fee. If she can make it, she'll be there. If not, it's just you and me."

"Fiona said she'd be available after eight. I just spoke with her."

"Perfect, then. What about you?"

It took Kenzie a moment to recall her calendar. That was never a good sign. "I'm okay. No class tomorrow night."

"Great! Then it's a date."

"Looking forward to it."

Kenzie disconnected, grateful she had something to look forward to even if it didn't solve tonight's problem. And she did have friends who cared, even if they did have lives.

And she didn't.

Why didn't she have a life? And why hadn't she noticed until right now?

Self-reflection was not going to work tonight. She needed to redirect, distract herself. Then it hit her.

Thanks to Jess, Kenzie knew exactly what would make her feel better. She probably felt as if she was coming unglued at the seams because her workout routine had fallen to the wayside with all the relocating and renovations.

An oversight that would end this very second.

WAS THAT MUSIC?

Will paused in the middle of bolting a T-bar to the track in the original ceiling and strained to hear. He'd had to replace the grid in this room, wouldn't get around to inserting the panels until he was done.

Once again he appreciated the contractor who'd created this crawl space, which was coming in handy for all kinds of reasons.

They'd left the barre and mirrors untouched in this room, had refinished the floors and painted the walls. He hadn't known why and hadn't asked, had only been relieved that Kenzie could mark one room as complete on her list.

The Kenzie of the never-ending lists.

But below him now was Kenzie as he'd never seen her before, hair pulled back in a ponytail, exposing her face in an unfamiliar way, every delicate line pronounced, the slender length of her neck unhindered by the distracting waves of red hair that teased her shoulders with every move.

She wore only some skintight black thing that seemed to have been poured on the way it clung to every inch of her slender curves. Her arms were bare and a pair of tiny pink gym shorts rode low on her hips, ornamentation because they didn't cover much of anything. In fact they really only drew his gaze to the tight curve of her bottom peeping out above long, long thighs. He'd died and gone to heaven. Reason gnawed through the physical haze of the moment, or tried to. That adult Kenzie had talked about warned his inner child that if he wound up in city lock-up, he'd be leaving Sam at Melinda's mercy. He lay on the catwalk, barely breathing, the worst sort of Peeping Tom. He refused to wind up a report on the eleven o'clock news.

This just breaking...city councilman Will Russell has been arrested on charges of alleged voyeurism...

He meant to slip the panel back in place, sure she wouldn't hear him over the music, but then Kenzie bent forward, stretching her splayed hands toward the floor, flashing him with her tight backside. His hand stopped of its own accord, his blood suddenly crashing through his veins, his attention entirely focused on her amazing agility as she conducted a series of moves designed to stretch various muscles and expose her for his viewing pleasure.

There was no possible way that any normal man could watch a beautiful woman move this way and not think of sex. And not only was he a normal man, he was suddenly a horny one who had been ignoring that part of his life for a very long time.

Every shred of integrity urged him to pull the panel into place. A moment of immediate gratification and he wouldn't be able to look himself in the mirror in the morning. Not to mention the risk…

Then Kenzie moved to the barre, first hanging from it as she crouched low in front of the mirrors then hooking a trim ankle and beginning a series of moves that brought every part of her body into play. Will knew exactly why this room had remained virtually untouched.

Her private studio.

Where he was an uninvited guest.

But every poised motion of her hands, fingers outstretched, made him imagine her fingertips lightly brushing his skin.

Every graceful sweep of her bare arms made him imagine how she might slip them around him to pull him close.

Every plunging stretch of those long, long legs made him think how they might wrap around him and lock his body against hers with a grip surprisingly strong, with skin so sleek.

He lay rooted to the spot, barely breathing, the sight of her in motion pummeling his reason into a befuddled daze. His body dominated the battle of wills between reason and need right now. Hot blood slugged toward his crotch with every sharp throb of

his heart. In this moment he was nothing but awareness and need, a sensation so acutely physical, he
could barely breathe.

Then Kenzie moved away from the barre with a
series of practiced spins that whirled her into the
center of the room.

And she began to dance.

Reason finally broke through the lusty ranks of
sensation that had immobilized him. The memory
of her telling him she'd once been a student with the
building's former owner came to him. Will had envisioned kids about Sam's age parading on the big
stage in the hall in tutus.

Will had been so wrong.

Kenzie danced.

Her body moved with the practiced grace of a
dancer. A real one. His experience was limited, but
Melinda had once forced him to sit through a ballet in Charlotte, entertaining some studio executives
who liked that sort of thing. Will had barely been
able to keep his eyes open during the performance,
lulled to sleep by the sedative strains of the orchestra, the numbing movement on stage. He hadn't been
invited again.

But watching Kenzie reminded him of those dancers, of the effortlessly precise movements that displayed her beautiful body in all its exquisite glory. He
couldn't have cared less about the dance he'd seen in
Charlotte, but Kenzie's body in motion reached deep
inside him, touched him on so many levels. Her body

in motion reflected all the gentle passion that made her so uniquely who she was, a woman who was impacting him far more than he could allow her.

Pursuing Kenzie wasn't a choice he could make. Giving in to the way he felt right now wasn't an option, and wouldn't be.

Reason finally won the battle. With a deep breath and a final longing glance, Will eased the panel into place.

CHAPTER TEN

THE BISTRO, OR KEVIN'S, as it was locally known, was the commercial version of an Italian kitchen—all about food and friendship. Guests gathered at the bar, which stocked everything from pricey port to craft beers. The wine cellar routinely earned starred reviews. Guests sat at tables with red-checkered tablecloths inside the dining room or outside on the patio during mild weather to enjoy a sunset over the mountains.

Everyone who walked through the door was a friend of the owner and chef, Kevin, who presided over his establishment through a cutout in the wall where he called out greetings and made small talk with every guest who walked through his door. He personally sent out orders through that cutout, ensuring every dish lived up to expectation. He had a few traditional items on the menu, but most came to eat Kevin's daily special, which was always different and always delicious.

Fiona hadn't been able to make the dance class, only dinner, so as a result, Kenzie and Jess looked like train wrecks compared to Fiona in her business wear.

Twins Fiona and Jess were so identical with their honey-gold hair and warm brown eyes that most people couldn't tell them apart. Back in the days when they'd all danced, Fiona and Jess had been the performance darlings, drawing attention because of their appearance. They'd been known to style their hair and dress alike to confuse people.

Until high school, anyway. Then the pendulum had swung back and they'd made concerted efforts to express their individuality so no one could possibly confuse them. As long as one knew Fiona was the more conventional, type-A-personality twin and Jess the intellectual, avant-garde twin.

Nathanial still mixed them up, but only because he never hung around long enough to tell them apart. Kenzie had never had the problem. She wasn't sure why. They did look alike. Both were striking with their gloriously golden skin, but they were still individuals. Their expressions differentiated them, maybe.

Fiona was the elder by twenty minutes and the big sister in all ways. More take-charge, and definitely the more nurturing of the two, while Jess had a mischievous grin and a quick wit that made her the life of the party.

They greeted Kevin and bypassed the bar for a table, where they ordered a bottle of wine and caught up. They discussed Fiona's fund-raiser of the previous night,

Jess's solo run teaching Wheaton's class and Kenzie's first scheduled presentation of her new curriculum.

Finally, Fiona couldn't stand it. After refilling the glasses, she got down to the real business. "Are we done with all this chitchat yet? It's not as if we haven't seen each other since our last class reunion or something. Anything else, anyone? Anything? Because I want to know what's going on."

"Ditto," Jess said. "You've got the floor, Kenzie."

All the turmoil that had been simmering inside her for days didn't take more than that invitation to erupt verbally. She outlined exactly what had been going on since the day she'd met Will then finally concluded, "Something is wrong with me."

Her audience didn't appear as shell-shocked by all the erupting emotion as Kenzie felt. They exchanged a glance that didn't include her. The exchange was even more than a twin thing, a couple thing that meant two people were intimately connected.

Kenzie's own parents interacted that way. Together so long they could practically read each other's mind. She was like that with Nathanial. One glimpse of his expression, and she knew exactly what he was thinking. His tone of voice alone could cue her about what was coming next.

"Why does something have to be wrong?" Fiona asked. "So you're attracted to the guy. What's wrong with that?"

Hadn't she heard a word Kenzie had said? "The

being attracted part *isn't* the problem. The not being able to control being attracted is."

"Correct me if I'm mistaken," Jess said. "But I thought that was the fundamental nature of chemistry. It's physical. It brings people together who should be together."

"Um, obviously not." Kenzie hissed then lowered her voice to a conspiratorial whisper when a server passed the table. "I'm not supposed to be with this guy. While I admit my opinion of him has grown a great deal from my first impression, he's still not relationship material by any stretch."

Fiona swirled the wine in her glass thoughtfully. "You don't have to marry him, Kenzie."

"Which is good, since he'd be going for round three."

"Then have sex, get him out of your system and move on." Jess pulled a face as if to say, *"What's the problem?"*

Kenzie dropped her face into her hands. Maybe the whole ranting idea hadn't been a good one after all. She didn't feel any better. More confused if anything.

"Oh, please, you two. You're beginning to sound like Geri."

"You shared all this with Geri before us?" Fiona looked as if she might choke. "Well, that's nice. Are we, like, the very last to know?"

"Not for lack of trying. You were too busy to get together, remember?" They had lives. Balanced lives that involved more than work. Geri's life wasn't quite so balanced, but she did pretty well considering.

Jess had yet to weigh in, was still staring wide-eyed when Kenzie finally lifted her head.

"Geri told you to have *sex?*" She blinked a few times for good measure. "Who knew? She always seems so stern and no-nonsense. Must be the black robes."

"Like, when have you seen Geri in court?" Fiona scoffed.

Kenzie shook her head. "No sex, you two. Not an option."

"Why not?" Jess asked. "You and Nathanial aren't together."

"And I liked Will when I met him at the agency," Fiona added. "Which was a good thing since I voted for him."

Had everyone in town voted for the man? Her parents. Fiona. Kenzie seized the perfect segue from the sex conversation with both hands. "You voted for him? Why?"

Fiona shook her head as if to clear it. "You've seen the man and you can still ask me that question?"

"I'm telling Cody," Jess said.

Fiona scowled. "Do not tell Cody."

These two were even more of a comedy skit than usual, which was saying something. "Do not tell me you voted for the man because you thought he was attractive."

"There's no *thought* to it. He is attractive. I have twenty-twenty vision."

This nation was in big, big trouble. "Oh, Fiona." She exhaled in disgust. "Seriously."

"Okay, not really. But I do think he's attractive. You and I have the same taste, Kenzie. Always have." She glanced sidelong at her twin. "Do not tell Cody. I voted for Will because he called my house and told me all about his plans if he got elected. He was really pleasant, and I like the idea of someone in office having a plan."

The very calls that Kenzie had avoided. Would her impression of the man have been influenced if she'd picked up the phone, listened to his campaign spiel? The voice mail messages hadn't conveyed the gravel and silk of his voice.

Or had Kenzie's mind been closed because of her impression of him based only on bits and pieces of information?

"Family Foundations is quite a plan. I know all about it," Jess informed them. "The political science, cultural affairs and religion departments have all been watching with interest to see if the new councilman gets any backlash."

Now this was news. "Really, Jess? How come?"

"That school you're supposed to share the building with. It's a private school with religious affiliations."

"Family Foundations wants to cover all the community demographics from what Will told me. Angel House addresses special needs."

Jess nodded. "I know, but people get really touchy about private institutions and government funding.

Trust me. I work for a private college, and you have no idea how many haters there are. Everyone's got internet access nowadays and wants to share opinions. That school that's supposed to move next to you isn't only private, but it's religious."

"You keep saying *supposed to be* moving next to me. I thought this was a done deal."

"All I know is what's been going around the college," Jess said. "Professor Davis said she's holding her breath to see when the special interest groups start rearing their ugly heads. She says it's bound to happen, and she should know since she's the dean of political science and very knowledgeable about current political events."

"Oh, wow. I don't like the sound of that at all."

"Don't worry, Kenzie." Fiona smiled reassuringly. "I'm sure Will can find someone else to put in the building if that happens. Someone who's not a strip joint. Sounds like you have an in with him."

But Kenzie wasn't thinking about how a new neighbor would reflect on Positive Partings. She was envisioning a glossy-haired little boy who wasn't crazy about carrots. "You'll keep me posted if you hear anything new, won't you, Jess?"

"Yeah, sure. But I agree with Fee. I don't think you have anything to worry about. Positive Partings doesn't touch on any hot issues. Well, I suppose divorce is a hot issue. How about noncontroversial? Better choice of words."

"And this is exactly what I'm talking about," Fiona said sternly. "Do you hear yourself?"

"What?" Kenzie asked, surprised.

Fiona and Jess slanted knowing glances at each other.

"You're right back to worrying about work again." Fiona was the one to break the news. "You need to do something other than work, Kenzie. One could get the impression you've got nothing better to do while you're sitting around waiting on Nathanial."

"Just tell her how you feel, Fee." Jess scowled as she raised her glass in a toast.

"Oh, my. That was direct."

Jess snorted with laughter. "You think?"

Fiona pulled a face. "I'm sorry to be the one to break it to you, but give it some thought. I say this with love."

"I thought you two liked Nathanial." Kenzie sank back in her chair, attempting to wrap her brain around this much *love*.

One thing she did know was to say Fiona and Jess *liked* Nathanial was a mild understatement. Neither of them would ever breach the boundaries of friendship, Kenzie knew, not even back in middle school when hormones had been raging, but long-distance lusting had never been off-limits. It had even become a running joke through the years.

Well, Nathanial had never found it very amusing.

"I do like him," Fiona said. "Don't you like him, Jess?"

"Of course I do. He's family after all these years.

But you snooze you lose." Jess spread her hands in entreaty. "Oh, well. Nathanial can't expect you to sit around and wait forever."

"Is that what you think of us?" Kenzie asked.

They both nodded simultaneously, making Kenzie's eyes cross. "That's not how it is. Not at all."

Jess shrugged and Fiona said neutrally, "If you say so."

Everyone reached for their glasses in the ensuing silence, a feat since Kevin's was hopping and loud on the slowest of nights. Kenzie sipped her wine, savored the disconnect from reality. The intensity of the moment was fading. The urgency of her feelings didn't feel quite so urgent, and all the activity inside Kevin's, all the sights and sounds seemed sharper.

When had drinking become an acceptable coping skill?

"How long has it been since we ordered?" she asked.

"Not that long." Jess hopped up from the table and went to the bar. Fiona watched her go and asked, "You want an unsolicited opinion?"

Kenzie suffered a moment's hesitation. Would she really want to hear this? Probably not. "Solicited. I wanted to get together, remember?"

"Then be happy, Kenzie. I know you love Nathanial. You always have. I know he loves you. Jess and I love him, too. You know that. We've always loved him."

Was she missing the point in there? Had there been one?

She didn't get a chance to ask because Jess returned with a server in her wake, who set a plate of bread and a bowl of olive oil herb dip in the middle of the table.

"Thanks." Jess pushed the plate toward Kenzie.

Fiona did have a point. "I want you to consider that Nathanial's the best friend. Not the hero."

"Isn't that a line from a movie?" Jess laughed and handed Kenzie a piece of bread.

"The Holiday." Fiona smiled. "I made Cody watch it with me last weekend. He wanted to die a little inside, but I did watch *Ironman* with him. Fair's fair."

"Like, how hard is it to watch Robert Downey, Jr.?" Jess rolled her eyes. "Seriously, Kenzie. Maybe you need to look at what you want for the future. Seems to me like you and Nathanial are more apart than together as a couple. I'm just saying."

Nathanial *not* the hero. That came at Kenzie sideways. She stalled, swiping the chunk of bread in the herbed oil. "I've never seen that movie. I don't know what you're talking about. Explain the difference between the best friend and the hero?"

"Well, it's actually the best friend and the leading lady," Jess corrected.

"Then how does this apply to me and Nathanial?"

"It works both ways. Best friend is a nongendered term and leading lady, leading man—same thing."

Kenzie blinked. She seemed to be having more trouble than usual following these two tonight. "Did I mention I've never seen this movie?"

"I can't believe you've never seen it. *Jude Law.*" Fiona brought her hands to her head and leaned back in a dramatic swoon. "*Jude Law.* The man had a cow. What else can I say?"

"A cow?"

Fiona nodded dreamily and gave a squeaky little sigh. "A cow. He was a weeper."

"Okay. I suppose if I'd have seen the movie, right?" Then maybe Kenzie might have a clue what Fiona referred to. "Since I haven't, maybe you can explain to me why a best friend can't be a hero."

Fiona and Jess faced each other, their skeptical expressions comically similar. What wasn't so funny was the way they excluded Kenzie with that glance.

"She definitely needs to see the movie," Fiona said.

Jess turned to Kenzie. "She's right. You do."

"Okay, in all my free time, which, incidentally, is probably why I haven't seen it already."

"Fee's point exactly, don't you think?"

Fiona nodded. "I'm simply saying that maybe this is why you're freaking yourself out about Will. That's the real question, don't you think?"

"What question exactly?" Kenzie asked. The wine was going right to her head tonight. She reached for more bread.

"You've dated before when you and Nathanial weren't together," Jess clarified. "So why is this time any different? That's the question you need to ask yourself."

Okay, Kenzie understood. But she already knew

the answer. The difference was that she'd never been so attracted to a man who was so totally *not* what she was looking for in her life.

MOVEMENT IN THE large, first-floor classroom pointed Will in the right direction, and he found Kenzie there, decorating a long table at the back of the room. A white tablecloth covered what appeared to be a folding table and a centerpiece of bright flowers perched in the middle, while plates, cups and plastic tableware sat in stacks at both ends. She was creating decorative fans out of the napkins, with her back to the door.

"Guess I won't be replacing ceiling panels in here tonight," he said, to make his presence known and avoid feeling like any more of a lurker than he already did.

She startled and spun toward him with a surprised smile. "Will."

Her greeting was quick and breathless, and if Will needed any more proof she was as aware of him as he was of her, the color rising in her cheeks was definitive.

"How's Sam?" she asked. "Still at camp or is he home now?"

"Still at camp. Having a good time from what I'm told."

"That's great." She held her hands poised over the napkins, as if she wasn't sure what to do with them, and watched him like a deer in the headlights.

Not that he'd ever actually seen a deer in the head-lights. But he did recognize the look. The other night she'd had sleep dulling the edges. Not tonight.

"Throwing another party?" he asked.

"Of a sort. What gave it away? The flowers?"

He lugged his equipment inside the room and set it on the floor. "Silverware. Means there's food. What's the occasion?"

She finally abandoned her efforts with the napkins and backed away from the table. "I'm pitching my new curriculum to some of the top-shelf profession-als in my network tomorrow."

"Sounds important." He hadn't realized her agency had top-shelf professionals. Showed him what he knew.

She shrugged lightly, making her blouse pull across her chest in a very appealing way. "Figured I'd keep them in the loop on what's happening."

"You didn't want to wait until the renovations are done? Place will clean up even better with new ceil-ings and refinished windowsills. Not to mention func-tioning rooms."

"I don't want to wait. Not at the rate we're going, anyway."

He deserved that. "You mean me."

She frowned. "No. I'm going to help with the win-dowsills, remember?"

"I haven't shown you how."

Her gaze dropped to his toolbox. "Or loaned me the tools."

"Brought everything tonight as a matter of fact."

"No worries, Will," she said lightly. "I've been so busy getting organized, the trim and sills have dropped from the priority list. My shingle's outside, thanks to you, so I'm good. I'll tour everyone through the place and they'll be even more impressed when it's finished."

"Sounds like a plan." A good one for him. He really didn't need another deadline and more pressure.

Still, he didn't like the thought of touring people through the building when there were still rooms with unfinished floors, missing baseboards and crown molding. Somehow it felt as if she'd be displaying this old place half-dressed.

"This is more of a practice run for me, so I can work on my presentation. I've invited attorneys and mediators I've worked with forever. Geri will be here, too. And Congressman Fleming."

He wouldn't have pegged her as such a party girl, but she sure seemed to like hosting. "So you're pitching a curriculum? For your classes? Do I understand that right?"

She nodded, kneeling in front of the box that held supplies, more plates and cups. She presented him with quite the display of graceful motion and slender curves in the process.

Her blouse might cover everything from her neck to her elbows, but the fabric was sheer nothingness that molded to the lines of her body. Her skirt, another fitted one—his favorite kind, he decided—detailed the length of her thighs, displayed the subtly flexing muscles of her calves and trim ankles poised on matching pumps.

She withdrew a thermal bag, chattering about her five-year plan. "I'm ahead of schedule because of Family Foundations."

"I'm glad to hear that. But what exactly is the five-year goal?"

"To standardize the curriculum for the divorcing parent classes in North Carolina."

He gave a low whistle. "Sounds like a big goal."

Placing the bag on the table, she flashed a bright smile. "It is. But it's an important one. Otherwise, there's really no point in requiring parents to attend these classes. They show up, kill four hours and leave with their certificates to satisfy the court, but they don't always learn anything. You must have attended one of these classes, Will. Do you mind if I ask what you remember about it?"

He searched his memory for one thing he could tell her so he could impress her, but he finally spread his hands in entreaty and admitted, "It was a time killer. But in my defense, my class didn't sound a thing like yours did the other night. Well, from what I heard anyway when I came through your ceiling."

That made her chuckle. "Precisely my point."

She started lifting out foam boxes and setting them on the table. "Are you hungry by any chance? I promised to call the caterer before they close at six to tell them what I want for brunch. They brought all these samples, and I'm running on too much coffee and a protein shake. I don't want to rudely eat in front of you."

His turn to laugh. "Who knew we had so much in common?"

She arched a skeptical eyebrow.

"The protein bar and bag of peanuts wore off a while ago."

"Oh." She waved at the table and starting flipping open boxes. "Please grab a plate and help yourself. I'd appreciate your opinion to help me decide. These are all samples, but they always send so much."

He had no comment, was trying to figure out if she kept trying to feed him because he always looked hungry.

"Looks like we've got a vegetable frittata and some sort of meat strata." She leaned over the box and inhaled tentatively. "Sausage, I think. Mmm. This one's eggs Benedict. My favorite. This looks like eggs Florentine. I'm sure this is spinach."

Or maybe she just liked to eat and share her hobby. Will didn't know, but he'd like to. Too much. He'd guess she wasn't a big sausage fan. Heading to the table, he grabbed a plate. Sharing dinner with Kenzie was exactly what he shouldn't be doing right now. But better he eat here than waste more time leaving to get something. A lame rationalization at best.

Didn't matter if he was wasting time he didn't have when there was so much to do. He filled a plate with everything but Kenzie's favorite eggs Benedict and sat at one of the classroom tables.

She set her plate at the other end of the same table. "Water okay for you?"

"Yeah, thanks."

She disappeared through the door on light steps that echoed down the hallway, leaving him wondering what in hell he was doing here when he'd already decided that he didn't need any reminders of the parts of his life he was ignoring.

Kenzie made him remember those parts.

But there was no possible way Will could avoid this encounter. And it was more than not wanting to appear rude. He could have made an excuse. Told her, "Thanks, but no thanks." She knew better than anyone how much work he had to do. But Will lacked both the desire and the discipline.

It felt too good to talk to her, to notice her, to react.

To be a man for a few minutes.

Not a dad or an Angel House support parent or a contractor with a business and a lot of jobs pending and employees who counted on him or a councilman with responsibilities and decisions that he didn't have time for.

He was powerless to resist this unexpected chance to be just *Will,* a man enjoying a conversation with a beautiful woman. And she was so beautiful. His pulse quickened when he heard her footsteps, tap-tapping over the floor on her return. He couldn't keep his gaze from the door, waiting for her to appear, suddenly hungrier for the sight of her than the food on his plate.

"Here you go." She set a water bottle in front of him as she passed, hips swaying gently, hair bouncing softly on her shoulders as she took each light step.

He suddenly imagined what she looked like dancing in the studio, imagined her wearing something flowing and clingy as she stretched and twirled on those light steps, hair whipping around her, reflected in the mirrors from every direction.

The thought alone made him catch his breath.

"That's sweet, but you didn't have to wait, Will. I'm sure everything's lukewarm. They dropped it off hours ago. I just haven't had time to eat."

"I hear that. But this is much better than a protein bar so you won't get any complaints from me."

She sat with a smile, and he speared the plastic fork into the sausage dish. She didn't go straight to the eggs Benedict but sampled a bit from each of the other dishes first. Being fair, no doubt. Traditional, he decided, remembering her parents. Reared with an attention to fairness and the qualities of another generation. Was that what made her so different?

"Do you have any siblings, Kenzie?"

The personal question surprised her. He could tell by the way she glanced his way, fork poised at her lips. "No. I'm an only child like Sam." Her gaze widened. "I mean, I assume he is an only child. You haven't mentioned any other children."

"Only Sam."

She relaxed. "I was a later-life baby, but I'm guessing you figured that out when you met my parents."

"I suspected."

"What about you? Does Sam have any aunts or uncles?"

"Two uncles. My brothers. Both younger, not by much."

"They live in town?"

He nodded. "My mother always threatened that if we moved away, she'd move, too. None of us bothered leaving. Didn't want to stress her out trying to decide which one of us she was going to follow."

That made Kenzie smile. "Thoughtful boys. I'm sure she appreciates that."

"I think so. She enjoys being involved. I don't know what I'd do without her help with Sam." He changed direction by finishing the last of the sausage dish and announcing, "This one gets my vote."

She eyed his plate and slid the box with the remainder of the dish his way.

"You're sure?" he asked.

"I tried my bite. Enjoy."

"Make a decision yet?"

She nodded. "I'll ask the caterers to bring me eggs Benedict. If you're a good indication, my male guests will enjoy that sausage strata, and I'll provide the vegetable frittata for an alternative."

"I hope I'm a good indication, then."

"I'm sure you are. And if you're working next door, you're welcome to drop by to eat. If not, you can always come later to grab leftovers. I'm sure there'll be plenty."

That made him smile. "So which is it? Do I always look hungry or you just like to feed people?"

She shrugged a bit sheepishly.

Upending the box, he slid the remaining contents onto his plate. "I'm going to owe you big after all these meals."

She dabbed at her mouth with a napkin. "You've been working nonstop on this building since I met you. How is it you owe me?"

"Renovations were part of the deal."

"I still appreciate everything you're doing. Just works out I happen to have food when you're around. I work a lot, too."

But it was more than that, Will knew. Kenzie was a caring person and wasn't shy about showing how much. He might not know her well, but he could see her caring in the way she looked after the people around her, noticing little things that meant she paid attention. He liked that about her.

And thought her currently off attorney *friend* was an idiot.

Then again, Will didn't have room to talk given his track record. But he couldn't help wondering what her relationship with the pretentious BMW driver was all about.

Instead he asked, "So what's up with this new curriculum you're pitching? I didn't realize divorce mediators were so brainy and academic."

She gave a quick snort of laughter when he wasn't being entirely facetious. He'd overheard some of what she'd said in her class. "Smart is good, Kenzie. Sets an example for the kids who'll soon be your neighbors. They need strong examples."

That earned a more thoughtful expression. "Well, then, I'm glad. Think Sam's going to like his new school?"

"I'm not answering that question until you answer mine."

"Fair's fair, hmm?"

He would hardly call sitting here playing the let's-get-to-know-each-other game when they didn't have time to get to know each other fair, but he nodded anyway. He could afford to play with fire when he knew life would quickly douse the flames. And he liked watching her mouth move when she talked.

"Fair's fair. So how does someone get into divorce mediation? Did you study it in school?"

"I wish. I actually got into mediation because I'm a family advocate. It's a form of social work. I sort of fell into teaching the classes because there was such a need, and it turned out that I love it."

And was good, by all accounts. He unscrewed the top of the water bottle. "How do you fall into teaching classes? There's a story there."

A smile played around the edges of her lips as she took another bite then set her fork down. "There is, as a matter of fact. I happened to be in session in a city building where a class was taking place. The woman who taught the class had car trouble on her way, so an attorney I worked with told me what happened and said there was a room full of people who'd paid to attend the class and needed a teacher. One of them being his client."

"You walked in cold? That's impressive."

"Kind of scary, actually, but my curriculum has come a long way since that class. The fact they'd let someone walk in unprepared to teach tells you what you need to know. We need standardized education—especially now that they're offering classes online. Otherwise these classes are just a money grab for the state, rather than an attempt to improve lives. People go right back out and involve themselves in relationships that won't succeed any better than their marriages did because they didn't figure out what the problems were and deal with them.

"The worst part is that the kids generally suffer. It's hard to be shuffled back and forth between parents, trying to have lives in both places. Start adding new spouses and step-and half-siblings and their family, which is the single most important thing to give them a secure start in life, disintegrates. Unless parents make a real effort to help their children cope after a divorce and that means creating a stable family for them."

"And I'll bet that doesn't happen often because parents are getting divorced, so there's a problem between them already."

"Exactly," she agreed. "Not always, thankfully. But far more often than not."

Everything about Kenzie was passion right now, and her passion was actually an interesting display of gentle firmness and calm-voiced intensity.

Leaning back in the chair, Will twisted the cap on the bottle, on and off, considering her and what she said. "I have to admit that's eye-opening. I never thought about the situation from that perspective."

"You're in good company."

A very diplomatic way of saying that most people didn't think of the impact of divorce on a child's family life.

Had Will? He'd been in this situation, only with more complications. At least he hadn't jumped into another marriage to further destabilize Sam's life.

Kenzie turned her attention to the table, gathering up cutlery and napkins, collecting them on her plate for disposal. Then she sipped from her own water bottle, apparently waiting until he finished before clearing the table. Very traditional, he decided. A woman who appreciated a sit-down meal, probably grew up with her family gathering for a family dinner hour like on old-time television shows from the fifties.

Was that why she was so passionate about family life? Made sense, since she wasn't the child of divorced parents herself.

"I think Sam's going to like his new school a lot," he finally said.

She stacked the empty foam boxes and slanted an amused gaze his way. "My turn, hmm?"

"Fair's fair." He stretched his legs out before him. "What's not to like? More space and there will even be a big playground, which is Sam's favorite part."

"Oh, really? Where's that going to be?"

"Where the maintenance room is now. It corners the building and has some square footage that abuts the easement. We've relocated the mechanical systems so we can free up that space. It's good-sized and walled in. Perfect for a play area."

"Sounds like it. I have to admit I'm impressed."

"Me, too. Building's turning out better than I could have hoped. So far. Still holding my breath."

"Well, that is good, but I was actually talking about the contractor who's making this new building happen. Family Foundations is pretty ambitious, Will, and you have quite a private agenda. But it seems to me that you're using your private agenda to serve a lot of people."

There was so much in that carefully phrased statement. The biggest implication was that his private agenda was his and his alone. He wondered why she'd think that. Her interactions with Melinda maybe? "Did you know about my connection to Angel House? Is that one of the reasons why you didn't vote for me?"

The question was out of his mouth even though he didn't really want reality right now, just wanted to engage with a beautiful woman and hear her soft-spoken voice.

"No, I didn't know."

But she didn't offer any other explanation, didn't mention his divorce, so he left it there, appreciated the chance to backtrack after opening his big mouth. He didn't want reality intruding further when she'd paid him a very nice compliment.

"I'm glad I reassured you, then," he said far more diplomatically, encouraged when she nodded, her smile reaching her sparkling eyes.

"You have, Will. If you run for a second term, I will vote for you."

There was something so earnest in her words that he knew she would not have offered lightly. She was kind, but she didn't sugarcoat the truth. He'd discovered that about her, which meant somewhere along the way he'd earned some respect and rose in her estimation regardless of what she'd heard about him from Melinda.

He couldn't remember the last time a woman had looked at him with admiration. But Kenzie's soft expression bridged the distance in a way that reached inside him to all those places he was trying so hard to ignore.

And finding impossible to ignore.

He seized the opportunity for distraction by gathering the remains of his meal. He took Kenzie's, too, and headed out the door to the break room to deposit everything in the trash, feeling as if he'd gotten too personal, too intimate with a woman he'd only wanted to watch talk.

And that's all he wanted, to talk with a beautiful woman, to feel like a man without a whole lot of responsibility weighing on him.

He hadn't wanted to turn Kenzie's generalizations about divorce into a personal commentary about him. He may have failed at marriage twice, but he hadn't jumped into his second marriage. And he definitely wouldn't jump into a third.

How could Will ever ask another woman to step into his life, a life driven by Sam's needs?

His own mother couldn't handle those needs.

Will wouldn't do that—not to a woman he cared about and not to Sam. Even if he did have the time to find a special someone, which he didn't, so this little break from reality was over. He'd leave the ceiling panels and windowsills until another day.

But as Will ditched the trash and washed his hands, he couldn't help thinking about his meeting with Deanne.

"Closing doors and opening windows," he'd told her.

Maybe Will was the one who needed the reminder. Was Kenzie an opening window, a convenient encounter with a woman because the door had closed on any hope of a real relationship in his life?

CHAPTER ELEVEN

"OH MY GOODNESS, what a perfect day," Kenzie said aloud to no one in particular, leaning her head back on the swing in her parent's backyard. Her hair flowed over the edge as she tipped her face to the sun for a dose of vitamin D.

Everyone in her world was exactly where they should be today. No turmoil. No conflict. No worries about Will showing up or popping through the ceiling.

The *perfect* day.

Insects whirred in the distance, a chirpy trill that always seemed to accompany summer days like this one. She'd grown up in this yard, although the swing hadn't been around then, but there had been a child-friendly wooden play yard her father had built himself. And a tree house. She'd had one of those, too.

The French doors opened and Nathanial appeared, carrying two glasses of a Riesling he'd had on ice.

"Budge up." He handed her a glass. "Mom said to stay put. Geri's running late. She'll let you know when she needs help getting dinner on the table."

"Thanks."

Mom, of course, was *her* mom, not his. Mom

Wright, as Kenzie always thought of Nathanial's mother, couldn't make dinner today because she'd spent the night in Charlotte with Sarah and Sean, and the new baby. So Mom Wright had sent Pop Wright along, pleased not to have to worry about his dinner. Pop Wright and Kenzie's father were in the study, poring over the latest copy of *North and South,* the Civil War Society's magazine.

The Civil War had always been her father's passion, and Pop Wright was the son of an army officer and had served in the armed forces himself. He loved anything and everything to do with the military, historical or otherwise.

"Tell me what you think?" Nathanial said.

"I think today's entirely perfect."

He clinked his glass to hers. "The Riesling."

She'd known he had been asking about the wine and sipped with a smile. The white proved to be a little drier than she'd expected. "Not too sweet. I like it."

Nathanial saluted her again with the glass. "I thought you would."

"I like when you think of me."

"Of course, I think of you. And it's not a red day, no matter how much you like them."

And she did. Malbecs were her favorite. A South American wine she'd discovered purely by accident at a hole-in-the-wall restaurant that made the best figs and cheese appetizer around. She'd discovered the place with Fiona and Jess on one of their girl days, an occasional day trip out of town where they drove aimlessly through the mountains looking for adventure.

That day they'd found it in the form of a restaurant that looked like a total dive in a dilapidated strip plaza between an open-air farmer's stand and a tattoo parlor. But the place had been packed with cars for a luncheon special of *meat, rice, bread and cola* for $3.99. They'd been starving, and if *that* meal wasn't an adventure, Kenzie didn't know what was.

"Living life dangerously," Nathanial had agreed when she'd shared the story.

Nathanial, on the other hand, preferred white wines and was always trying to sell her under the premise she'd discover what she liked if she tried enough good ones.

"You're in an awfully pleasant mood for someone who hasn't left her office much lately," he said. "Doesn't sound like you get home much more than I do."

"True, true," she agreed. Her entire life had been revolving around work even more than usual since receiving a registered letter from City Hall.

She squelched that thought fast.

"That's about to change, Nathanial. I want more perfectly perfect days like this one." Now she clinked her glass with his. "Where everything is perfect and everyone is exactly where they should be. Mom and Dad are home and hosting Sunday dinners again. You and your dad are here, and Geri's on her way. Would be better if Mom Wright was here, but she might be back in time for coffee. We'll cross our fingers. I've got a glass of not-too-sweet Riesling in my hand and a cute guy sharing my sunbeam. Perfectly perfect."

He grinned that grin that had been charming her since kindergarten. "I take it the pitch went well this week."

"Everyone loved it. I did a Q & A afterward that raised a few questions I hadn't considered, so I incorporated the answers for my next presentation. Soon as Geri gets here, I'll get her spin on the things I came up with." Kenzie took another sip. Not bad at all. "Now catch me up on the case. I've been sending good thoughts every morning before you head into court."

"I don't know how you time it, but I literally get your texts as I'm turning off my phone to walk into the courtroom."

"A gift." It was actually premeditated timing on her part, but she wouldn't spoil the mystery.

Stretching his legs, Nathanial let her control the swing. "I can't decide if the partners are testing me to determine if I'm partner material by my performance on this case."

"What else would they be doing?"

"Looking for an excuse to get rid of me."

Kenzie turned toward him, trying to determine whether or not he was serious. He didn't sound as if he was joking. Didn't look it, either, which made her feel guilty for going on about her own contentment.

"You'll be brilliant," she said softly. "You always are."

"You're partial."

She nodded, hoping to reassure him, and his expression relaxed. She slipped her hand over his. "Tell me."

"This is a tough case, Kenz," he admitted. "I'm not going to lie. I've done nothing but prepare when I'm not in the courtroom. I'm driving my assistants insane, according to Chad."

Chad was Nathanial's senior legal assistant, a third-year law student specializing in business litigation like Nathanial.

"What's making this so tough? Is it the case or the partners paying such close attention?"

"They can pay attention all they want." He scoffed. "I'm a performer. You know that."

She did know. Nathanial could walk into any room and take over. He'd always been that way, had walked into their kindergarten classroom, marched straight up to Mrs. Mars and introduced himself. He'd been on a first-name basis with most of the class before the bell rang.

"They're expecting me to pull a rabbit out of my hat. I'm beginning to think they threw this case at me only because no one else wanted to take the fall."

"You really don't think you can win?"

"It's hard enough putting a face on a big corporation, but even getting the jury to empathize with my client... If I don't make some connection with the jury, I'm going to cost the firm a big client and some serious money. I can forget all about becoming a partner anytime soon."

Kenzie knew better than to ask about the particulars of the case, but she also knew how these things worked from listening to him. "If this is such a big case, shouldn't they have put together a defense team and not leave you scrambling around trying to do everything yourself?"

"I have a team, for all the good it's doing me." He scoffed. "That part's my own stupid fault. I smelled the setup but was arrogant enough to let them suck me in because I thought I could use this case as a springboard. And I could if I can turn it around and get a fair judgment."

"Sounds like quite a risk."

"It is, but I'm ready to be a full partner, Kenz. You know that. More than ready."

She was surprised, and not a little. Nathanial was ambitious, but not so much of a risk taker that he'd jeopardize years of hard work. "Any ideas about how to turn it around?"

"That's the only reason I'm here today. Otherwise I probably couldn't have rationalized taking the time. But I needed to clear my head, so I can review with fresh eyes."

She wasn't happy to hear that spending time together hadn't been on his radar today, whether or not he'd thought about her with the Riesling. "Clearing your head sounds smart."

"Fingers crossed. I can't seem to get away from the fact that I have to switch gears and take another approach entirely. If I can convince the jury my client is committed to settling the situation fairly, I might earn a little sympathy."

"Are they?"

He gestured with an impatient hand. "Bingo. Precisely the problem. My client will settle and pay out, but only to end the litigation. They won't own responsibility for the situation. Their brand will take too big a hit if they're found culpable."

"Are they culpable?"

He arched a quizzical eyebrow. "I'm a defense attorney," he said, as if that explained everything.

Of course, all his clients wouldn't necessarily be innocent. But the fact he was in business litigation usually masked that obvious fact. Kenzie knew all this, so why did business litigation suddenly sound so unsavory?

She put the thought right out of her head. Turmoil would not ruin her perfect day. "Anything I can do to help?"

He smiled, but it still looked strained around the edges. "Your texts always help. Listening helps. Getting away helps. I opened my eyes this morning rehashing everything that happened in the courtroom last week."

The French doors opened, and Geri popped her head out. "I'm here. Finally."

"Hi, Geri," Nathanial said.

Kenzie chimed in with, "Glad you made it."

Geri glanced between them with a curious expression. Kenzie could just imagine what Geri was thinking right now, given their conversation about Will.

"I never know if you two are together together," she had said.

"Just wanted you to know I was here. I'll go help your mom in the kitchen." Geri retreated as quickly as she'd appeared.

Nathanial used the opportunity to put the brakes on the conversation. "Don't worry about me, Kenz. I'll figure it out. I knew it was a gamble when I accepted the case. I like challenges. You know that."

She did know. She also knew he was keeping her at arm's length, and Kenzie considered that as they fell into silence. Nathanial likely considering his case or avoiding thinking about it by dodging this conversation. Kenzie wouldn't know because he wasn't sharing today.

And she couldn't help but remember all the questions that Fiona, Jess and Geri had raised during their recent heart-to-heart conversations, Kenzie had but to look at the situation.

The best friend or the hero?

Nathanial had always been both. Even as far back as when he'd been her gregarious friend who was a boy with blond bangs that flopped into his eyes. Her partner in primary school as they'd banded together to stand up to Wade Crucker the crayon-breaker, the much-bigger boy who had tried to push them around.

They'd stood together against a bully and saved their crayons. She had a lifetime of stories like that. Kenzie and Nathanial. Best buds. Occasional friends with benefits. Someday they would get serious about their relationship. When they both got where they wanted to go in their careers and had the chance to think about settling down. But that time hadn't come yet.

There had been times when Nathanial had wanted to focus on them and she hadn't been ready. Hadn't there? She'd dated and had even rented a place on her own in Raleigh for a training program that had lasted nearly a year. But she honestly didn't know for sure. And she'd never asked him the question, didn't want to ask it now.

Kenzie found that very telling.

She would rather sit here and not raise hard questions because she didn't know if she wanted to hear the answers.

There was a problem in that motivation.

Kenzie could certainly come up with some good rationalizations such as now wasn't a good time for Nathanial since he was having trouble with a case.

She needed to be supportive. Her needs could wait.

Their relationship had been ticking along in exactly this way for years, so another month would hardly make a difference.

Too bad her inner child didn't agree.

She could blame all the urgency she felt on Will, and that was wholly unfair to Nathanial. Why should he be impacted because of her crisis?

Because that's what a hero did? Ride in to save the damsel in distress?

Kenzie couldn't remember ever reading one fairy tale about a princess who chose to step back and patiently wait for her prince. No. Princesses kissed frogs. Her very favorite version of the Cinderella story had Drew Barrymore rescuing the prince.

But not Kenzie.

"Why don't you come over tonight, Nathanial? Pack an overnight bag and stay with me. We can brainstorm together. A change of scenery sounds like the very thing you need."

That was all it usually took—an invitation. He'd invite himself over, and they'd shift gears and settle into their comfortable friends-with-benefits relationship.

He'd call her during the day. She'd call him. They'd get together at night for dinner. They'd make love, something they hadn't done since Florida.

She wasn't sure why they'd stopped. But their relationship had always been like that—if they couldn't go forward, they just faded back into their separate lives.

And that's what this was—shared lives, but most definitely separate.

The best friend or the hero?

"Thanks, but no can do, Kenz," he said. "I'm in over my head and can't handle even the prettiest distraction."

His words were lighthearted and sincere, but they hit her with a force she wasn't used to experiencing.

Why did she feel so overwhelmed right now?

Because he'd always been the one to do the inviting in their relationship, and the first time she'd invited him, he wasn't available?

"Are you seeing someone?" she asked.

"No, of course not." He frowned. "I would have told you if I was."

She didn't have a response except that he clearly didn't like the turn this conversation was taking. She saw it in his expression. Heard it in his tone. Sensed it in the way he sat a bit straighter. Maybe not such a surprise given the situation he dealt with at work.

Or was that her rationalization?

He'd cautioned her against becoming interested in Will and yet didn't want to get *together* together.

Reaching for her hand, Nathanial twined their fingers together, gave a contrite shrug. "Sorry. I really have my hands full."

She felt selfish for burdening him. Why had she?

Because she wanted a distraction from Will. Definitely selfish. And desperate. No missing that.

Okay, so now wasn't a good time for Nathanial. That wasn't a crime. They'd been on and off for a long time, a comfortable relationship, Kenzie and

Nathanial, the best of friends. That much felt solid. Shouldn't she be grateful? *Patient?*

They'd get around to them again.

Wouldn't they?

For the first time ever, Kenzie didn't really feel grateful or patient. She was grateful for her friendships with Fiona and Jess, and Geri, too, but that wasn't the same thing as wanting more time with them, wanting to be a priority in their lives.

Was she really being selfish, placing her wants and needs above Nathanial's? Or was she simply discontent because she was comparing her beloved and ambitious friend, who wanted to become a partner, with a new and equally ambitious acquaintance, who advocated for his son and all families challenged with autism?

Because when she compared the two, her world shifted beneath her feet, and suddenly Kenzie's perfectly perfect day didn't feel quite so perfect anymore.

"SOUNDS GOOD, MELINDA," Will said over the Bluetooth in his truck, although the outing with Sam she proposed left Will with a knot in the pit of his stomach.

Wheeling into a parking space in the lot at Angel House, he didn't transfer the call to his cell. Melinda taking their son anywhere was an occasion for a phone call with no distractions. So he sat in his truck with the air blowing at full blast.

"What's the occasion?" he asked.

"My parents' fortieth anniversary. They want the family together. We've hired a photographer to take a group shot."

"Sounds like fun. I'm sure Sam will enjoy seeing them."

"Will he be okay to swim?"

"Sure. I'll bet he'll really enjoy the pool because he's been swimming every day at camp."

"Okay, good." She gave a disbelieving laugh. "Who knew?"

"I know, right?" Will knew exactly what she referred to. When a therapist had recommended swim lessons—an important precaution for any kid—they'd both been skeptical. They could barely get Sam in a bathtub, let alone a pool.

But with the proper instruction, Sam had not only learned to swim, but taken to the water like a fish. The freedom of movement worked for him, maybe, or perhaps it was the way water muted sensory input. Will only knew that given his way Sam would stay in the water until he turned into a prune.

"You will send his swim bag, right, Will? I have summer things, including trunks, but I'm not sure exactly what else he'll need besides sunscreen and a towel."

The question was code for, *"Please send whatever he needs to avoid a tantrum or a meltdown."*

Melinda would be at a big family party, and she got rattled as much as Sam did when they ran into problems. If there were people around, then the pressure was on to make good impressions, and that always escalated the situation.

Which meant Will would have to be selective about what projects he started at Angel House in case the day went south and he had to drop everything to rescue his son.

"One packed swim bag with a spare mask coming up," Will said, because Sam wouldn't go in the pool without a mask. He liked to see underwater, and the rubber pinched his nose shut, which reminded him not to breathe until he surfaced.

"Appreciate it."

Of course, he would have to unpack Sam's stuff the night he returned from camp and do laundry to have everything ready to go in the morning. He made a mental note to remember. Melinda may have swim trunks, but Will would bet money she didn't have the requisite Spiderman beach towel and matching deck shoes.

"Heads up. I'll send his stuff, but make sure you cut out the tags in anything you want him to wear."

"Got it," she said.

While Sam had a bedroom in Melinda's luxury condo in the south end of town, he didn't often spend the night there, and his interests could change fast. Spiderman beach towel one day, and Batman the next. The whole distaste for clothing tags had happened so suddenly Will had been forced to bodily carry Sam from the store wearing only his undershirt, which had a tag. Go figure.

For a change, Melinda accepted the information about Sam well, for which Will was grateful. It didn't always work that way. Most of the time Melinda seemed to resent what he told her, seemed to interpret his instructions to mean he knew more about their son than she did. Which he did, but that didn't mean he thought she was a crummy mother.

He knew how much Melinda loved Sam. He knew how she'd devoted herself to Sam's treatment, even working from home to care for him. But Melinda also saw Sam as a reflection of herself, and the fact they couldn't connect made her question her ability as a mother. She couldn't seem to grasp the fact that not connecting had nothing to do with her and everything to do with autism.

"When does he get home from camp?" she asked.

"Friday night."

"I'll come get him in the morning, then. From the house, right? He won't be with Guadalupe?"

"Yeah." Fresh in Will's memory was the last time she'd dropped in on Guadalupe without making the requisite phone call because that was too much trouble. "What time's the party?"

"Early. Mom wants to make the most of the day."

Early wasn't a time, and Will was about to open his mouth and remind Melinda about the importance of phone calls and reliability, fundamental considerations that he resented having to explain yet again.

Will didn't doubt that she loved Sam, so why couldn't she trouble herself to do something so simple—make a phone call, commit to a time—that was so important?

Normally, the answer to that question was that Melinda was self-absorbed, which explained Will's resentment toward her. Especially when, in addition to unsettling Sam, Melinda inconvenienced others with her thoughtlessness.

But another answer popped into his head, an answer he had never considered before, delivered in a gentle voice.

"Successful parenting partners respect limitations," Kenzie had said during her class.

That reminder stopped Will dead in his tracks. He shut his mouth and quickly reevaluated.

Melinda clearly had a problem with calling before she arrived. Will didn't know why. Selfishness. Denial. Thoughtlessness. He wasn't sure it mattered. What did matter was how he handled the situation. He could introduce tension into this conversation that had been going along well by taking her to task, which would only make her defensive. That much he knew. Or he could offer a solution. "How about I bring Sam to your place? Save you the trip. Just tell me what time you want him."

There was a beat of silence on the other end. "Sure, Will. That'll work. Thanks. How about nine? Sound good?"

"He'll be there with his swim bag packed."

"Great. See you then."

"Take it easy, Melinda." Will disconnected the call.

Then he paused a moment, making sense of how quickly and easily he'd been able to get off the phone.

"Sure, Will. That'll work. Thanks."

And a thanks. He didn't usually get those. Not when Melinda vacillated between resentment that he'd stolen their son and denial about Sam's circumstances and the required parenting skills necessary to fit the situation.

Skills that had to be learned and applied.

And to Will's complete surprise, he didn't feel irritated the way he usually did after dealing with Melinda. He only hoped the day she and Sam spent together would be problem free.

KENZIE GENUINELY BELIEVED she'd had choices in dealing with her reaction to Will. She genuinely believed she could ride out her inner child until the renovations were complete and then get on with her life. Of course, she might occasionally see him dropping Sam off, but Will would officially be out of her side of the building, leaving her with a newly remodeled agency and a bright future that didn't involve seeing him everywhere.

Where he'd left her a beautiful floral arrangement on the reception counter to welcome her.

Where he'd hung her shingle the day she'd officially met Sam for the first time.

Where he'd popped through the ceiling to campaign with her students in the middle of a class.

Where he'd stood in a doorway and watched her until she'd awakened from a snooze at her desk.

Where he'd rescued her from exposed wires, kneeling so close she could feel the warmth of his skin radiating from him.

But now Kenzie had to question whether or not she was being realistic or if she was simply adding a windowsill to the list of places she'd continue to see this man.

At the moment, he crouched in front of the window, and the way the muscles of his shoulders and back were on display as he worked the palm sander over the wood would be embedded in her memory.

He was dressed as the contractor again, in work boots and jeans. He wore a tool belt, too, slung low on his hips, making it impossible not to notice the way his body came together in that area, strong thighs, tight butt, trim waist expanding upward in a V toward those broad, broad shoulders.

The very sight of him proved that Kenzie had been so wrong about having choices. So, so wrong.

Right from the start she'd been attracted to this man, against her will, against her wishes. And she certainly hadn't wanted this unexpected attraction to color her feelings about Nathanial. The latest eye-opener in a string of them.

Her perfectly perfect yesterday had degenerated in a big way. She'd lost an entire night's sleep to answering some hard questions, and she couldn't get past the realization this situation had slipped beyond her control. Her day at work today had been plagued by distraction and an annoying lack of focus on everything she should have been focusing on—like her sessions. Then there had been all the muffled yawning in front of her clients.

Will had walked through the door on time as promised, and in that very moment, all the expectation and edginess, all the interest and impatience had vanished beneath an awareness that made the moment come alive, a feeling so utterly real that she practically hummed from the inside out.

This had definitely gone beyond her control.

The whine of the sander stopped abruptly, and Will sliced a curious gaze her way. "You are ready for this woodworking lesson, right?"

Kenzie stared stupidly for a throbbing heartbeat, as stupid as she'd always been around him.

"As ready as I'll ever be." Truer words had not been spoken. Not by her at least, but she sounded normal. That much at least was a success.

"It might be a good idea to come closer, so you can actually see what I'm showing you."

There was just enough humor in that suggestion to propel her into motion. Covering the distance, she knelt beside him, so close her first breath was laced with a very male scent made up of sawdust and motor, of *him*.

He held up the sander. Their gazes met. "Okay, not hard."

But wouldn't she like him to be?

The breath stalled in her chest at the sheer audacity of *that* thought, at her inner child for dragging Will into bed.

Oh, this was way, *way* beyond her control.

If the man had any clue what was going on inside her head right now, he'd run fast and far. No question.

"I figured I'd show you what to do in here." He seemed oblivious to her turmoil. "It'll be easy to work since you don't have much furniture and just as easy to clean up. And it's the first place people will see."

"Makes sense." What didn't make sense was Kenzie's complete inability to stop reacting to him.

Why had she failed to ignore her inner child so completely?

"First thing you do is put on that mask and those gloves." The mask was an industrial-grade construction type meant to protect her face and lungs from harmful debris as opposed to the medical-type mask meant to contain the spread of airborne germs.

He helped her position the ventilator over her nose. His warm fingers brushed her cheek perfunctorily yet left her skin tingling in the wake of his touch.

Good, at least she could hide her face. She pulled on the gloves, another layer of protection. Now, if only she had a tarp to throw over her head and block out the sight of him.

"Those gloves going to work?" he asked.

She spread her fingers to display the fit. "A little big but fine."

He inclined his head while reaching for a piece of

equipment on a metal tray that looked like a trivet. "This is a heat stripper, Kenzie, and it is really hot. I mean seriously hot. You'll do a lot of damage to yourself if you're not very careful. Got it?"

"Got it."

"All we're trying to do here is strip away the paint then sand what's left so you have a smooth surface."

Will demonstrated by aiming the heat stripper at the windowsill then peeling away the warm paint with a putty knife. "See how it just lifts up? You want to heat the paint until right before it starts to bubble and get sticky."

"What happens if it bubbles?"

"It'll stick to the putty knife. Just wait until it cools and it'll peel off. Do not touch it when it's hot."

"Got it," she said to reassure him. "So why aren't you wearing gloves and a mask?"

A dimple flashed. "I'm familiar with the equipment."

Kenzie could have pointed out that familiarity with the equipment might save his hands from burns but it wouldn't do a thing to protect his lungs from the paint fumes. She didn't. The man knew his business, and she was far too distracted by the sight of him in profile. Shadow cast smudges around his eyes. Or maybe he was simply tired. And his hair needed to be trimmed because it was starting to curl around his ear. No doubt if Will left off a trim for another few weeks, his hair would be as curly and touchable as Sam's.

"Now you try." He motioned her to come nearer.

She scooted impossibly closer, willed herself not to stop breathing when he looked at her, his clear gaze taking in everything at once.

Did he notice the way her breath hitched in her throat?

"Lay this putty knife where you want to work." He positioned her hand on the sill then offered her the heat stripper. "Point that away from you and press the power trigger. Get the feel first because it's touch sensitive. When you stop pressing that button, the heat will stop, too."

Kenzie aimed the stripper away from them, surprised by the force of the motor. Then, with a gentle but firm touch, he repositioned her hands and told her to give it a try.

Her first few attempts resembled nothing of the fluid motions that had yielded him long strips of paint. Not only did she work up the paint in chunks but also managed to gouge the wooden sill with the edges of putty knife.

"Tell me I'm going to be able to sand away all this damage, please."

He smiled. "You'll get the hang of it. Stay on the flat surface until you do. The trim is going to be trickier."

"Oh, wonderful."

Will was a good teacher though, redirecting her patiently, reminding her to keep the edge of the putty knife flat with a gentle touch.

She wondered whether giving patient and clear instruction came naturally to him or resulted from parenting Sam. His ability was unexpected. No wonder friends sent their nephews to train with this man.

She finally pulled the mask down below her chin and said, "I see why you ripped out all the sills and trim on Angel House's side. I didn't have a clue how much work it would be."

He sat back on his haunches, gave her a little space to breathe and eyed her skeptically. "Are you saying you want me to rip out all this woodwork now?"

"No, no. I'm up for the challenge." She laughed. "I'm actually glad to learn how to do this. I've always wanted to renovate an old house."

Will pulled a face. "You're joking?"

Kenzie wasn't sure why he'd find her admission so surprising. "I bought a plantation-style cottage with a gallery on the outskirts of town. It needed a ton of work, but it's coming along. I love it."

"You do the work yourself?"

"I wish," she admitted. "I did the landscaping, but not all the work inside. I tackled only the jobs that didn't have a huge learning curve or I wasn't afraid would cost me more money to fix if I goofed up the job. YouTube really comes in handy."

He smiled at that. "So what have you done?"

"I textured all the ceilings and hung the wallpaper in the bathroom." She didn't mention the teensy problem with repeat on the floral wallpaper.

"Then you'll be a whiz at windowsills. No problem."

She liked that he offered words of encouragement. Nathanial had called her insane to purchase the place with the amount of work that had needed to be done. He'd purchased a brand-new home from a developer in a subdivision so he could choose all the finishes that went in it before the place was constructed.

Kenzie squelched that comparison cruelly. Just because Nathanial preferred to call a handyman rather than be one, didn't make him any less a man than Will.

"I follow this blog about a New Orleans row house that took a beating during Katrina," she explained to dodge the wayward thoughts in her head. "The new owner posts about all the work he does. I've learned a lot. This is my first private lesson."

Will liked that. She could tell by the way his gaze, so clear and cutting, softened. "Feel free to pop over if there's anything you're interested in seeing. When I'm around. The guys won't let you hang around for long since you're not part of the crew." He gave a small laugh. "I didn't peg you for a home improver."

"I grew up around here, Will. Biltmore. Pinebrook. Johnson Farm. Carl Sandburg's house. I love that the city is preserving our history, and I'm really glad to be a part. So thanks." Somehow that came out sounding far more intimate than she'd intended. She could feel it in the silence that fell between them, the way Will suddenly averted his gaze to the windowsill.

He ran a light hand over the surface, came away with a film of fine dust on his fingertips. "Not to rain on your parade, but the biggest reason I ripped out the windowsills and trim next door is because of the lead paint. It's underneath all these layers. Don't want it around the kids."

"Absolutely not. But, um, I'm not going to glow or anything, am I?" She hoped to restore the balance of humor and camaraderie between them, since she was responsible for leaking all her intensity over him and shifting the mood.

"Not as long as the lead paint is covered up by decades of latex or you get rid of it. That's why I brought the mask. Use it." He eyed her as if unsure she was trustworthy. "And don't work with the heat stripper when you're tired. Peeling away all that paint can get eerily satisfying. You can keep going way past the time you should stop. That's when accidents happen."

"Really?"

"Really. I once heat stripped every square inch of wood in this old house over on Buncombe Street. Trust me. It's like playing Spider Solitaire. Or watching reruns of *Law and Order.* Two music notes and a crime, and you don't move for an hour."

Kenzie laughed, steadied herself with a hand on his arm so she didn't fall on her butt. She had a hard time imagining this man sitting still long enough to play Spider Solitaire.

"Go on." Will motioned to the windowsill. "Finish that up so I know I'm leaving the job in good hands."

Seizing the distraction, she flipped the mask over

her face again and got busy stripping away the paint, working the putty knife into the bumpy corners, so aware of Will's gaze on her. But he let her work, allowed her to determine when she'd stripped away all she could. She ran the sander with the same motion he'd used, and when she was done, she turned to face him, found him still crouched beside her, smiling.

"Excellent work." He untangled her hair when it caught in the elastic banding and lifted the mask over her head.

And they were so close, so exquisitely close that she might have swayed forward the tiniest bit to find herself pressed up against the muscular terrain of his body.

The sheer unruliness of that thought made her breath hitch, an audible sound that drew his attention.

And one look into his suddenly smoky gaze, and Kenzie knew she wasn't the only one to notice their nearness.

The realization froze her to the spot, her face raised to his, so close he only had to bend forward the tiniest bit and their mouths would meet.

And he noticed that, too. *Want* was all over his face, as if this moment was the progression of their every interaction since they'd met. As if kneeling here was the most natural place in the world for them to be.

She saw it. She felt it in the very deepest part of her, a swooping sensation low in her belly.

"Kenzie." Her name broke from him as a throaty breath between them. "I can't kiss you."

"No, you can't."

"Things would get way too complicated."

"They would," she agreed.

With the matter settled between them, Will leaned back as if to stand. Kenzie was the one who swayed forward and stretched up on her knees so she could press her mouth against his.

Their mouths met, and they shared a breath.

Then his arms came around her, as strong as she'd known they would be.

CHAPTER TWELVE

WILL KNEW FROM the instant their mouths met that kissing wasn't the cure for wanting Kenzie. Not in this lifetime. Not when her mouth softened against his, so lush and willing that he couldn't have kept from pulling her near if his life had depended on it.

Right now his life just might.

He'd lost a part of himself somewhere along the way, hadn't been whole, but she'd awakened his awareness with her gentle demands and practical caring. Kissing her only proved he hadn't vanished beneath the focused and frazzled reality of life. He'd only ignored a part of himself that was willing to be ignored. It had been for his own survival, probably, which could explain why he awoke now with a vengeance.

For Kenzie, who made him feel like a man again.

She melted against him as if she belonged there, her long dancer's curves pressed into every place that mattered, her kiss tentative but with that calm purpose so unique to her. Composed in the face of his fierce arousal, dragging him in with her matter-of-fact eagerness.

Unable to stop, he speared his fingers through her

silken hair, so cool to the touch, a reminder he'd always known she was a woman designed to touch. He dragged in the fresh scent of her with every greedy breath, the scent that had branded her in his consciousness and disturbed needs so long ignored.

She sighed against his mouth, a longing sound that hinted he wasn't the only one who had been ignoring needs, and that simple revelation urged him to greater daring. Sliding his fingers along the slope of her nape, he anchored her closer, explored the taste of her with his mouth.

Kenzie's kiss was all gentle insistence, suggesting again on some level her need was as great as his, although that hardly seemed possible. But they'd clicked on so many levels and with some part of his brain Will supposed he'd always known they would. He'd seen her respond with careful distance, with concern that had turned detailed to-do lists into cooperation and an offer to strip her own windowsills, with invitations to meals, in her caring regard for Sam.

Will felt it now in the way she swayed against him, as if she'd waited forever to touch him. He could feel it in the quiet excitement of her responses as if she'd imagined how it would feel to press close. And the reality of their bodies swaying against each other made Will glad he was already on his knees, able to brace against her to steady himself.

His body betrayed him. But knowledge of his heated response only seemed to encourage Kenzie.

Dragging her hands down his back, she touched him freely, a bold move that only proved her tranquil demeanor concealed deep emotions. He'd sensed her strength from the very beginning, the deep conviction, the fairness, the matter-of-fact concern. He wasn't surprised to find her passion ran as strong.

And the idea excited him on some gut-deep level. He wanted to melt away her careful control, wanted to provoke the same craziness that was churning inside him, wanted to hear his name burst from her lips unbidden. But her name was the one to break the breathless quiet.

"Kenzie."

Because he was rapidly losing the only part of him thinking beneath the urgency. He trailed his mouth from hers, along the curve of her jaw, along the smooth column of her throat until she trembled, her body so alive, so eager.

And her tiny sigh that sifted in the quiet finally appealed to his reason, to what was left functioning in the face of his arousal, and he broke away from the taste of her silken skin. Raising his head, he pressed his forehead to hers to brace himself steady as he traced the delicate angles of her cheeks, her jaw, her throat. He couldn't stop touching her, proving what he felt was real, that she was real and he could touch her...

She exhaled another sigh, the sound mixing with their ragged breaths and the undeniable intensity of the moment. Slowly, grudgingly, reality intruded, demanding that a choice be made before they wound up naked and making love on this floor.

That they could not do.

Kenzie finally tipped her face to his, and they stared at each other, facing the truth of the chemistry between them, so much more than simple desire. His chest shuddered on shallow breaths. Her mouth appeared moist and red from their kisses. The world had shifted with her one bold move, because now everything was changed. Completely.

Will simply didn't have it in him to resist her just then, yet a dim, rational portion of his mind resurrected her words. *If one parent chooses to act irresponsibly, then the responsibility falls on the other parent to balance the situation as best they can.*

Will was the balance. He had to be.

And with that sober reminder came the realization that as much as he wanted Kenzie, he had to step back from his need for immediate gratification and assess the consequences of acting on his need. For Sam. For Kenzie. And, yes, even for himself.

But Will didn't stand a chance of keeping his hands off her, not without a little distance. Sinking back, he leaned against the sofa, stretched a leg out before him, hooked an arm over his knee. The distance had the desired effect. The storm surge in his body eased the smallest bit, enough to make sense of the beautiful woman in front of him, and how much he wanted her.

She gazed at him with a gentle expression, as if

their kiss might have been everything she'd expected, and wanted.

He recognized her response from some long-buried instinct, the man who had been shut down for so long. Women had once come easily to him, but he'd always been looking for something more than just sex, had sought it in his high school girlfriend, then Melinda. Never a serial dater but a man always trying to grasp something solid, make it his permanently.

That random thought surprised Will, and helped him wrap his brain around a few more realities, a few more responsibilities.

"We've complicated everything," Kenzie said softly, her voice thrumming through him with such power.

He nodded.

A few months ago, he would have rationalized seizing this unexpected opportunity. A few stolen encounters here and there while he worked on the building. Then the renovations would be done and Angel House would take up occupancy, and both he and Kenzie would move on with some fine memories.

But as Will watched her watching him, sitting back and tucking her legs underneath her, looking somehow disappointed with her kiss-bruised lips and tousled hair, he knew that was a few months ago. Now all he could think about was how giving in to their desire had consequences.

"So, now what?" It was a legitimate, if pathetic, question, but Will didn't have anything more in him, not when he wanted her more than he'd ever remembered wanting.

She shrugged lightly, maybe even trying to appear casual. "I suppose we should figure that out."

"Not too much to figure from my end. I'm a lousy candidate for a date."

"How's that?"

He gave a snort of laughter. "I'm committed and overcommitted. I open my eyes to a calendar filled with more things than I'll ever get around to in a month, let alone a day. A date with me involves seconds stolen from what I'm supposed to be doing, which is everything but what I want to do."

He paused, and disliked admitting this. "You deserve a lot better than I have to give, Kenzie."

She frowned. "But there's got to be some time for you in there. Otherwise you'll burn out and not be any good for Sam, or everyone else who counts on you. There are lots of those people counting on you."

"No doubt there." Deanne. Angel House parents. His employees. The mayor. The citizens of Hendersonville. The list went on. He got dizzy thinking about it, which was why he didn't. He simply put his head down and kept placing one foot in front of the other.

But Kenzie didn't seem to get it because she smiled again, as if she thought being counted on was a good thing. "So what's wrong with enjoying your few seconds?"

"When I say seconds, I mean seconds." She seemed

to be ignoring the part about deserving more than seconds. "A relationship can't go anywhere with me. I'm a dead end."

"What exactly is a dead end?"

"It means I'm not free, and I won't be. Sam's got dibs on my time."

"And there's no room for anyone else with you two? I mean, besides Sam's mom, of course. I know you'll always be a family."

Kenzie did know. Will remembered her saying exactly that in her class. But he didn't want Melinda to be a part of this conversation. Just the thought of her helped him put a little more distance between him and his feelings.

"How would that be fair to you, or to any woman? Sam's a great kid. I wouldn't have chosen autism for him if I'd have had a choice, but I wouldn't change a thing about our lives. I mean that. It's different. But for all the complications there are a lot of great things that most people wouldn't be aware of unless they were dealing with the situation."

She appeared to consider that. "Is this why you're so close with the people at Angel House?"

"We're all doing variations of the same thing. We understand the demands. It's nonstop, at least at this stage of the game. I'm hoping that will change in time."

"Okay, I get that, but I'm still not seeing the problem."

Will didn't understand *that*. As far as he was concerned the problem was self-evident. "Kenzie, what's happening right now is exactly what I'm talking about. We kissed. All I want to do is kiss you again, but I come with all sorts of baggage. So instead of kissing, I'm establishing boundaries so I can be fair to you." And so he could handle how he felt about her. But he wouldn't complicate the issue by admitting that.

"Why can't we just kiss and leave it at that?"

God, what did he even say to that? "Because when I was kissing you, I wanted to be doing a lot more than kissing."

"Me, too." Her gaze sparkled. Her expression lit up with such amusement that Will couldn't help but laugh.

His life really was a joke. And not a funny one.

"I don't have a future to give, either, Will. I come with my own set of strings."

"You're talking about your attorney?"

She nodded, tousled red waves distracting him, making him yearn to feel their cool silk beneath his fingers again.

Definitely a joke.

"Do I need to be watching my rearview mirror?" Will asked. "Is he going to rear-end my truck because I kissed his girl?"

That appeared to tickle her, judging by her twinkling gaze. "I think his BMW would lose. You drive a really big truck."

"Glad to hear it."

"Nathanial and I aren't dating, so no worries."

Will had been right all along. The attorney was a complete loser. "So where does that leave us?"

"Why can't we keep doing what we've been doing?"

He'd been getting ready to make his move so he could get her clothes off. "What's that exactly?"

"Getting to know each other, I guess."

She didn't sound too sure. He definitely wasn't. "So we agree on no relationship? We'll be what, then…friends?"

"I can do friends," she said, and something about her admission sounded so wistful. "I'm really good at friendship."

Will guessed there was more in that statement than he could know, but he was so busy looking to his own self-preservation that he decided to simply take her at her word. There wasn't enough distance between them yet. Not nearly enough. His blood still pooled in his crotch, and all he wanted to do was pull her into his arms and kiss that wistful expression off her face, prove that whatever was bugging her about friendship couldn't be all bad. Friendship could have benefits.

He could handle getting to know her. He'd been doing that already, right?

"GIVE ME THAT glass right now, Kenzie." Lou wasn't even through Kenzie's front door before she shifted her grocery bag and reached for the wineglass Kenzie held. "Depression needs something to perk you up, not sedate you. You'll make things way worse with *that*."

Lou made wine sound like a contagious disease.

"How can my favorite wine possibly make things worse?" Kenzie clung to the glass like a life preserver. As if her mood could even get any worse. Not likely.

"The thought of drinking wine is depressing *me*. Don't you know anything about using alcohol as a coping skill?"

"Obviously not." Kenzie gave in before the delicate stem snapped in her hand and she had pricey Malbec all over the foyer. "Can't run the agency without you. Can't tackle depression without you. Do you want a raise?"

Lou chuckled and made a beeline straight for the kitchen, calling over her shoulder, "I should run with this, right? But if I kick you while you're down, then I'll be depressed."

That made Kenzie laugh, for the first time all week because her life had degenerated into two distinct phases—before kissing Will and after. The *after* phase marked the first time she'd ever followed her inner child's urgings.

Only to reestablish that there was a very good reason she taught classes on learning to manage the inner child.

Lou tossed the contents of that freshly poured glass into the sink. Kenzie hadn't even taken the first sip, had been allowing the Malbec to breathe when the doorbell rang.

Her favorite Malbec, thank you very much, Mr. White-wine-is-better. Or Mr. I-can-only-be-a-friend.

She shot across the kitchen before the rest of the nearly full bottle wound up following down the drain. She wouldn't put it past Lou. "I'll bottle this up for another night."

"Good idea," Lou agreed, setting the grocery bag on the butcher block counter. "I've arrived with emergency supplies."

And Kenzie certainly could use them. Her mood had degenerated with every day that Nathanial hadn't bothered to reply to her texts. Every night that Will hadn't shown up after kissing her and saying, "I can't ask if you want me to drop by one night when you don't have a class. That would be too much like a date. So I guess I'll see you around."

In fairness to Will, he had seen her around. He'd caught her in the parking lot on Wednesday night before class to ask how the windowsills were going. He'd called her on Thursday to find out what her schedule was for the following week, so he could have his supplier deliver a new grid and panels for one of the ceilings. There had even been a note on the side door this morning telling her that he would have a crew coming in to take measurements for the stalls in the unfinished bathroom upstairs.

Not romantic. Not even the stuff friendships were made of.

But at least Will had made contact. Mr. White Wine, on the other hand, hadn't bothered replying to her texts to let her know how his case was going. She wouldn't even know he was still alive if Mom hadn't mentioned that she and Mom Wright had gone to lunch and discussed him.

Thankfully, Lou distracted Kenzie when she started unloading the reusable grocery bag.

Vodka.

Rum.

Tequila.

Gin.

Blue Curacao liqueur.

Sweet and sour mix.

7UP.

At least the bottles were pint-size. Except for the 7UP, which was a whopping two liters.

"Are you expecting some friends you forgot to mention?" Kenzie asked.

Lou chuckled. "No. Girls' night. You and me. And the *piece de resistance*. Ta da." She held up a DVD copy of *The Holiday*. "Do you know I actually had to go to a video store to get this? Who knew they even still had those? It's been out for a while. I can't believe you've never seen it."

"I can't believe you brought along your liquor cabinet. Those are the emergency supplies?"

"They are, and you had better be nice, or I'll take you up on that raise. If we have another week like this last one, you will drive me to drink. Or kill me. I haven't decided which. No more trying to drown your sorrows in work, Kenzie. Now get me two glasses. Really big ones."

There was no denying that's exactly what Kenzie had been trying to do—forget the current state of affairs with her love life.

She had believed Will meant every word he said. What she couldn't believe was that he had cast himself in the role of friend rather than seizing the opportunity to be her hero. Not forever. Not even long-term. But for right then.

Or however long *right then* lasted.

A few weeks. A few months. She'd had no clue. She only knew that she'd decided to give in to her inner child and follow what she wanted rather than what made sense for the first time ever. It had never once occurred to her that Will would be the one to consider the consequences. She knew he was as attracted to her as she was to him. Any question about that had ended the moment they kissed.

He wanted more than kissing. He'd admitted that.

And so had she.

Her inner child had positively thrown a tantrum at being denied. But Kenzie's adult understood Will's restraint and respected it. A lot. Especially when it was nothing short of cosmic irony that after questioning Will's integrity, *he* would be the one to practice what she preached.

But even Kenzie's adult had a problem swallowing

the whole *friends again* part, which had left the atmosphere at Positive Partings anything but positive.

Kenzie went to a cabinet, opened it, then shut it again. Depression was an occasion that called for her to break out the big guns. Two hurricane glasses stamped with Pat O'Brien's logo from her and Nathanial's trip to New Orleans while he'd still been in law school.

She needed to make a new memory.

"Perfect," Lou said. "Fill them to the top with ice."

Kenzie headed to the freezer door where the ice machine churned out enough crushed ice to fill both glasses. She set them beside Lou and watched in fascination and horror as Lou began cracking open bottles and pouring liquor into the glasses.

"This might be a good time to mention I'm not much of a drinker."

Lou sliced a glance at the open bottle of Malbec. "Really?"

"I wasn't going to drink the entire bottle, Lou. Speaking of…" Heading back to the china cabinet, she retrieved a bottle from one of a collection she kept specifically for damage control on unfinished bottles. Pouring the remainder of the Malbec into a smaller bottle eliminated room for the oxygen that did so much damage to the taste. She'd been known to keep a good wine evolving for up to a week this way, each glass different but still wonderfully drinkable.

It was a trick she had learned at a wine tasting in Napa Valley with Mr. White Wine.

She really needed some new memories.

Working at the butcher block, she gently poured the Malbec while Lou worked on the sweet and sour mix. Lou looked like a bartender, upending the bottle over the glasses, pouring liberally. She had the looks for it. With her petite build, gamine features and that adorable pixie cut, she looked the part of someone who would be the life of any party.

"You know most people eat popcorn on movie nights," Kenzie commented.

"Oh, cut me a break. It's Friday night. No work tomorrow plus man trouble equals one *Adios Jackass* coming up."

Kenzie almost choked. "What?"

"You heard me." Lou grinned. "Which means you'll have to drink two, so it's *Adios Jackasses*. Plural."

"I'm actually a little scared right now," Kenzie admitted. "You handle my clients' sensitive information."

"Ha," Lou scoffed. "Can you say moonlighted as a bartender through college?"

"You know, somehow I guessed that about you."

Lou drizzled 7UP over the top of each concoction. "We could have done the shooter recipe, but I'm not a big fan of Kahlua, to be honest."

"You're the expert."

"Remember that. And I was not coming over here on a Friday night for popcorn and a chick flick.

Maybe if someone had died…but not because you can't manage your love life."

"Unfair."

"What's unfair?" Lou narrowed her gaze and stared pointedly. "This is me you're talking to here. Unlike your friends, I see you day in and day out. I have a front row seat to the derailment you call your love life. Wait. Let me qualify that statement. You have had a few highlights, but they've never involved Nathanial."

"What on earth does *that* mean?"

"Even when you're with Nathanial you guys are exactly the same. I mean, I don't know what's going on in the bedroom—"

"You're right. You don't."

Lou rolled her eyes. "My point is that you're just Kenzie and Nathanial. Always the same. No ups, no downs, no drama when you're a couple. Now, watching you run around pretending not to notice our city councilman, on the other hand. The sparks are *flying*. That's the sort of thing a love life is made of."

"Oh, this night is going to hell really fast." Kenzie couldn't even make eye contact. She simply corked the wine bottle and took it to the refrigerator, where she hid until she'd wrapped her brain around the fact that she hadn't been fooling anyone. How long had Will known that she became an absolute idiot around him?

She finally emerged when she heard Lou rummaging around in her silverware drawer. "What do you need?"

"Something long to stir these with."

Kenzie produced an iced-tea spoon, which Lou used to gently stir each drink. Then she passed one to Kenzie.

"I do hope you brought an overnight bag," Kenzie said. "Because there's no way you're driving home."

"Way ahead of you. And for the record, I don't wake up until at least ten on Saturdays. I like my coffee black and my eggs scrambled with lots of pepper. Preferably white, but I'll settle for black if that's all you have."

"White it is." Kenzie suddenly felt full inside, grateful for such a friend who cared like this.

Then there was no more time for embarrassment because Lou held up her glass for a toast. "Nathanial and Will…"

"Adios, jackasses!" they said in unison as they clinked rims then squealed with maniacal laughter.

Kenzie took her first tentative sip and found the drink surprisingly, and deceptively, not overly alcoholic tasting. "Not Malbec, but not bad. I might even get used to it by the time I get to the bottom of the glass."

"Oh, you'll not only be used to it, you'll love it. Trust me."

They settled into the living room for some serious movie watching. It didn't matter that they were watching a Christmas movie in the middle of July.

There was no possible way to go wrong with the exquisite and incredibly talented Kate Winslet and the gorgeous Jude Law.

Or Jack Black, who had been insanely hysterical in every movie she'd ever seen him in.

And what woman wouldn't fall in love with Eli Wallach?

Kenzie was well into the second glass when she realized that Arthur Abbot, played so delightfully by Eli Wallach, had nailed the problem cold—*her* problem. And the issue wasn't that Nathanial and Will weren't heroes. The issue was that she wasn't the leading lady of her life.

She was the best friend.

By the time Lou was curled up on the edge of the sofa, passed out with her chin on her chest and Kenzie staring into the bottom of her hurricane glass, she not only felt better—and rather drunk—but she had made a decision.

Unlike Jude Law's character, Will might not have a cow as far as she knew. And he certainly didn't strike her as a weeper, but he did have an adorable little boy and he made her feel alive in a way she'd never felt before. Ever.

She didn't want to let this unexpected feeling pass without exploring the way she felt, without really *living* it.

She was tired of waiting. She was tired of always being the best friend and never the leading lady. She was going to get some *gumption*.

WILL FOUND KENZIE hard at work at the windowsill in one of the session rooms. This was one of four windows lining the east wall offering a view of Main Street. Apparently she'd made good progress in the week since they'd kissed—he'd already been in the reception area looking for her, and the sills and trim on all the windows there were stripped and sanded, ready for her to decide whether she wanted to paint or stain them.

She was wearing the face mask and gloves exactly as he'd instructed, and he drank in the sight of her, jeans riding low and giving him a shot of her creamy skin. He savored the moment where he could appreciate her unobserved and drink his fill of the sight of her.

His careful restraint took an unfortunate hit. Her every fluid motion with the heat stripper—she certainly seemed to have gotten the hang of it—forced her to lean forward enough to make those low-riding jeans ride even lower, revealing her trim waist and the gentle slope of her hip.

The ponytail swung in time with her movements, reminded him of what her hair had felt like beneath his hands, tortured him with his purely physical response to this woman.

But he was an adult, Will reminded himself. He could handle this. He'd had a week to rein in his reactions and live all the valid reasons why he couldn't become involved right now. And he had. For the most part. Having Sam at home again helped a lot. Life was back to normal. For the most part. That was exactly the reason he was here tonight.

To be a friend.

Still, he waited until she clicked off the heat stripper before he said, "Kenzie, it's Will."

She startled at the sound of his voice. Lifting away the mask, she said, "Oh, hey. How are you?"

Of course, the elastic bands got caught in her ponytail as she tried to lift the apparatus over her head. Two short strides and he was there to help. To touch.

"Sorry to disturb you," he said. "Do you have some time to talk?"

She was so close. Close enough that she had to tip her head to meet his gaze. Close enough that he might slip his arms around her and pull her even closer.

And Kenzie was aware, too. She was gauging him, assessing why he would make an appearance now after a week of painfully casual contact. He wondered what she thought. Whatever might be going on inside that pretty head of hers, she swallowed hard. Her chest rose and fell on a hard breath as she took a careful step away and set aside the face mask, removed her gloves.

Friends? *Right.* More like awkward wannabe lovers in full-on denial. A week hadn't cured her of their chemistry, either.

"Listen, Sam's mom is at the house spending time with him since he's home from camp, so I don't have to rush anywhere to pick him up. You want to grab a beer?"

She smiled. "Are you asking me on a date, Will?"

He could hear the laughter in her voice. She clearly didn't believe he'd changed the boundaries of their relationship, and in that moment, he resented his inability to be a man. Nothing but a man who wanted to become involved with a beautiful woman.

"Friends can go out for a drink, can't they?" He tried not to sound defensive.

"I've got nothing on the agenda tonight but the windowsills."

"Great. Do you care where we go? There's the pub up the street. We can walk." He wasn't ready to tackle the intimate quarters inside the cab of his truck.

"Great," she said, following his lead.

"I'll take care of the equipment if you want to go grab anything or lock up."

"Thanks."

Slipping out of the room, she vanished without a word. By the time Will had unplugged everything and gathered the bucket she'd been using to store discarded paint, she still hadn't returned. He headed outside through the side door and disposed of the bucket's contents in the construction Dumpster he'd had parked in the lot for Angel House's debris.

Will hoped he wasn't setting himself up to fail the test of being with her. He needed to give her a heads-up about the media storm about to break, needed to reassure her that her agency wouldn't get caught in the fallout. That's what a responsible council member would do since he'd involved her in the Family Foundations project in the first place.

That's what a friend would do.

And they damn well needed to get to some reasonable place where they could function for the duration of this project without winding up with their hands all over each other.

Still, when Kenzie appeared in the reception area with her hair freed of its ponytail and a purse slung over her shoulder, Will thrust his hands into his pockets to resist the urge to touch her. He wouldn't even trust himself with a simple hand on her waist to guide her through the door. The gesture might be instinctive but it was so dangerous given how tempted he felt right now.

He held the door open with his foot instead, a desperate jerk trying to do the right thing for once. He didn't have to wonder why so many people let their desires lead them through life—it was a hell of a lot easier.

Kenzie locked up, and then they were on their way up Main Street, walking side by side, him measuring his pace so he didn't force her to run.

"So what's up, Will?" she asked as he'd opened his mouth to comment about the city's efforts with downtown renewal. "Should I be worried?"

"No. That's why I'm here. To give you fair warning so you don't worry."

Her step faltered and she glanced at him, her beautiful features golden in the spill of light from the streetlamp. "What's going on?"

"You want the good news or the bad news first?"

"Good news, always."

"I go for the good news first, too." The observation popped out of his mouth, a shared bond he shouldn't be pointing out.

"My mother always says to remember the blessings first so we can accept the disappointments graciously."

"I like that," Will said. "I've got a friend who always wants to feel good before he gets knocked down. Swears it doesn't hurt as much."

Kenzie's gaze widened. "Sounds like quite a character."

"He's that, all right. He's also the uncle of the kid who drywalled over your outlet."

She didn't get a chance to reply because they were suddenly crossing Main Street to reach the pub on the other side. Will did touch her then, just a hand on her elbow as they stepped off the curb against the light. Then he grabbed the pub's door and she swept past.

They were led to a booth not far from the bar, but with enough privacy they could talk.

"Are you hungry? I know it's kind of late but it occurred to me I missed dinner." Nothing like feeling stupid to remind him this get-together wasn't a date.

"Peanuts and a protein bar don't last long, do they?" The corners of her mouth tipped up, almost a smile. "They have a dessert here I love. The Irish Crème pie. I could splurge."

"Go for it. You work hard." She probably ordered only so he wouldn't feel rude eating alone. But he liked that about her, liked the way she thought of others and came up with equitable solutions.

That ability was some gift.

She ordered the house cabernet, explaining, "This is actually a good vintage and it's not too high on the alcohol count, which is good because I need to be able to think in the morning."

"I'm going with a Guinness, since I don't have to put my son in the truck."

"Nice to hear. Alcohol around children can be one of the tougher points of negotiation between a divorcing couple."

"I had no clue. Kind of sobering to think there are that many alcoholics."

She made a face and laughed. "Often one parent will have a problem the other parent is concerned about. Sometimes one parent wants to micromanage the other, and alcohol is a convenient target. Sometimes parents simply have differing opinions about what constitutes acceptable consumption. Some people feel as long as they're below the legal limit, it's okay to get behind the wheel. Others feel even one drink is too many when there's a child in the car. I guess I know where you fall on that topic."

"And you, too. Kids can be distracting under the best of circumstances."

That earned a soft smile, approval if he read her right. "So you were about to share the good news..." she prompted after the waiter had delivered their drinks.

"Right. The good news is your agency is officially the long-term tenant of one of Hendersonville's historic buildings with first option on renewing the lease," Will said. "The renovations will continue until they're completed and whatever happens with the rest of the building won't impact you."

"And what's happening with the rest of the building? Please tell me there isn't a problem with Angel House."

He took a long draught and let the cold brew take the heat out of his admission. "A friend who covers a beat with the local paper told me today that a controversy could be brewing. There were some letters to the editor about Family Foundations that sparked an interest in the recipients of the city's funds. Naturally, they're calling attention to Angel House's religious affiliation and questioning why a group should be eligible for public money. The first of the series of articles will run in Sunday's edition."

"Will there be fallout?"

He shrugged. "Probably, but the mayor's office has a plan in place—has from the beginning. The bad press isn't unexpected. That's why we worked so hard to cover all the demographics with Family Foundations. People get touchy about religion."

"But Angel House serves all children, right?"

"Any race, religion and socio-economic group. If a kid needs the services Angel House provides, that's the only qualification. The parents also must provide transportation—we don't have buses or vans to transport kids. Yet, anyway."

"I really don't think where a program began should impact the way the city provides services."

"Personally, I don't think it should, either. People affiliated with religious organizations are still a segment of the population with the same rights as everyone else. Unfortunately, that's not mainstream opinion right now. The minute religion comes up, the media uses it as a platform for social issues. Then people get riled up."

She folded her hands on the table, considering. "And the mayor and the council back up the choice of Angel House?"

He nodded. "I wouldn't have pushed for any of this without their support. It's going to be tough enough to overcome the negative."

"I don't like the sound of that. You don't think they'll withdraw their support if the public backlash gets too loud, do you?"

"Not if they can help it. The mayor understands the need and knows the services are not being provided at the levels of current demand. It's her job to provide for all segments of her constituency. It's all our jobs whether we're career politicians or average Joes like me. We've agreed to represent the people of Hendersonville. Not just the ones whose issues are garnering the most media attention. It's pretty black and white. That said, I can't realistically expect her or any of the council members to damage their reputations by going to bat for my cause."

"I *really* don't like the sound of that. It's called bullying, and it's an unacceptable way to handle any situation. There are ways to negotiate difficult compromises."

"You'd be the expert on that. Let's hope Angel House gets a chance to overcome the opposition." The thought of that opposition and having to defend their position put a big dent in his appetite.

"What happens if they can't, Will?"

He reached for his glass, took a fortifying swig before admitting the simple and brutal truth. "It'll be the end of the road for Angel House. We've tapped out our resources. We rely on the church's support, several grants we have in place and fund-raising, but it's not enough in this economy. There's a waiting list for enrollment a mile long, but we're not able to continue services for our kids now without more financial help. I've found a grant we're eligible for, a big one that will put us on solid financial ground so we can cover our overhead. If we can get this grant, we'll be relying on fund-raising and donations to grow the program rather than simply maintain it."

"What's the catch?"

That she read between the lines made him smile. "We have to have a permanent location that serves the community."

"Family Foundations."

"You got it. No other way to make it happen. We can't continue on the income we're bringing in now. You've got to realize that as a ministry, we're already circumventing a lot of the basics. The church gave us the house we're located in, so we don't pay rent. The woman who runs the program doesn't take a dime for a salary, and with the exception of the certified faculty and staff, the rest of the paraprofessionals like classroom aides and dietary and custodial staff are volunteers who are willing to undergo extensive training. Most of them from the church."

Kenzie shook her head, clearly disbelieving. "The government couldn't possibly provide that level of care, and yet people would rather sacrifice all those services because a church is involved?"

"All I can tell you is parents of kids with autism are all about believing in miracles. Church involvement is not an issue." He hadn't expected this conversation to become a tell-all, but Will wanted Kenzie to understand, needed her to know the reasons he couldn't drag her into his world even though he wanted to.

And he wanted more than he had ever had before.

CHAPTER THIRTEEN

KENZIE WAS A huge believer in being in the right place at the right time, but she had no clue she was stepping into one of those situations on her way outside to unload the paint scrapings into Will's construction Dumpster.

She'd pushed open the door to the parking lot when a shout stopped her in her tracks. In one startled instant, Kenzie took in the unfamiliar car parked in the lot, and the dark-haired child barreling toward her at full speed.

"Sam!" a voice rang out, and Kenzie saw a blonde woman lunge around the front of the car.

The former Mrs. Russell.

That was Kenzie's only thought as she leaped into Sam's path, which had him aiming right for Main Street.

He crashed into her with surprising force, and the bucket clattered to the asphalt, knocked from her hand. She stepped backward to balance herself, steadying both of them with a hand on Sam's shoulder as she knelt in front of him, ready to stop him if he attempted to take off again. But by then his mom was there, grabbing him by the arms and pulling him close.

"Oh, my God, thank you." She exhaled the words on a breath, then did a double take as she glanced at Kenzie.

They didn't get a chance for reminders about where they'd previously met because Sam began to struggle against the restraint, huffing with obvious frustration and sounding as if he was trying to say something.

"It's okay, honey," Melinda formerly Russell said. "It's all right. Let's go find Daddy."

Sam wasn't having any part of her reassurances. He struggled in earnest until his movements threatened Melinda's grip on him. His actions were accompanied by noises that were getting louder and louder.

"Come on, honey. It's okay. Don't be upset."

Kenzie stood there unsure how to help, so she scooped the dried paint peelings into the bucket. A couple jogged down Main Street past the parking lot, their gazes locked on Melinda and Sam. They couldn't have been much older than Kenzie, and they ran with their dog on a lead.

"Can't figure out why some people bother to have kids," the man commented loudly as they passed.

Kenzie overheard the comment. So did Melinda, judging by the stricken expression on her lovely face. She glanced at Kenzie, who felt a pang. This woman was so, so beautiful.

A perfect match for Will, in appearance, at least.

"He doesn't want me to leave," Melinda explained as if Kenzie, too, might pass a similar judgment.

Then hanging on to Sam with a death grip, she maneuvered him around to face her. "Honey, Mommy has a work function tonight. I have to go. I'll come back in the morning. I promise."

Kenzie recognized two things. The first was that there was a noticeable difference between the way mom and dad handled their son. Mom tried to reason verbally with Sam. Kenzie remembered Will being noticeably concise, every interaction of minimum words.

The second thing she realized was that Melinda could use some backup.

"Would you like me to get Will?" Kenzie asked. "He should be working inside."

"Oh, please. Would you mind?"

"Not at all." Kenzie set the bucket on the curb and took off, letting herself in the unlocked side door to Angel House.

She found Will in the labyrinth of rooms that occupied what used to be Madame Estelle's prized recital hall.

Will was crouched in a corner working with a saw. When she got close, she recognized the miter box. A professional version of the ten-dollar plastic one she'd used for her baseboards.

"Kenzie." Will glanced up and saw her. "What's going—"

"Sam's mom could use a hand outside."

That was all she had to say. The electric saw ground to sudden silence, and he was on his feet without another word. She didn't run to keep up with him, knew she'd helped the little bit she could. Her place wasn't with their family.

And that knowledge ached inside her. *Ached.*

Slipping back outside, she intended to quietly grab her bucket, but the scene she walked out on was an intimate one.

Will and Melinda kneeling in front of their son, Sam's mouth working so hard to speak, maybe to share what he felt. Kenzie didn't know. She only knew the little boy was frustrated and angry because he pushed against Will's restraint when Melinda said, "We went for ice cream and had a good time."

Will only nodded. "Wave goodbye, Sam."

Sam clearly wasn't having any part of waving or anything else right then. He flailed wildly until Will finally hoisted him into his arms and told Melinda, "Go ahead. Don't worry. I'll text to let you know when he settles down."

Melinda looked so torn in that moment, raw emotion obvious on her features. Then she nodded.

Will caught Kenzie's gaze and inclined his head in a silent thanks before disappearing with his son inside Angel House.

Melinda had tears in her eyes as she watched them go. Then she blinked past them and turned to Kenzie.

"It took me a second to place you, but I recognized the name of your agency. Thanks for your help."

"I hope everything worked out," Kenzie said softy. "You have a very lovely family."

Tears welled again, then Melinda circled her car and climbed in.

Kenzie made her way to the Dumpster, and everything about her felt heavy. She ached inside for a little boy who'd been so upset because his mom was leaving.

She ached for the mom who hadn't been able to console her little boy.

She ached for the man who was running interference between the two, sacrificing himself to be there for his family.

She'd had it all wrong from the very beginning. Melinda hadn't mentioned her son's special needs during their meetings, and Will hadn't even mentioned his son during the election.

Because they'd wanted to protect him from people who didn't understand? People like the runner who'd passed judgment after one glance.

Or because they ached for their son and were trying to provide for his needs in the best way they could?

Kenzie suspected the answer was a bit of both.

She tried to imagine what it might be like to be in Melinda's shoes. How did a mother cope with not being able to make things better for her child? Kenzie couldn't even imagine, had zero frame of reference. All she knew was that Melinda had been hurt because she couldn't console her son.

Will had stepped in and taken charge, as she suspected he always did, comforting both Sam and his mother in the process.

God, Kenzie hadn't understood him at all.

She had thought she'd had all the answers about love, but she hadn't even been asking the right questions. She'd believed Will had failed at love because he had two divorces behind him. But those divorces didn't define him. No, what defined him was his commitment to his family, his dedication to his son.

That was the mark of someone succeeding at love.

Kenzie hadn't understood at all. With Nathanial, she'd been allowing friendship and familiarity to define their relationship. Then she'd waited, avoiding any real commitment, never testing herself against her inner child, loving but never actually being in love.

Until Will had come into the picture.

And ever since, she'd been on a roller coaster of emotion, more alive, more in love than she'd ever been in her life.

"DOESN'T THE MEDIA oversee what's written anymore?" Will folded the newspaper and handed it to Deanne. He didn't want to read any more. Not another word or the top of his head might blow off. "Whatever happened to integrity in journalism?"

"All I ever hear about is slanted media. And in the advent of the internet all bets are off. Anyone can write anything they want." She glared at the paper and gave a huff of exasperation. "Okay, that's not entirely fair. There are a few publications that stubbornly wield their power for good and not evil."

"Just doesn't feel like it today."

Crossing the hall in a few steps, she leaned into an empty classroom and dropped the paper in the trash. "No, it doesn't."

They stood in the hallway at the old Angel House location while Sam was working with the speech therapist. School didn't begin for another three weeks. And they needed two of those weeks to move and get Angel House up and running in the new location, which left him only a week. Seven days.

Where school would begin became the question.

Not only did the entire place still need to be painted, but all the flooring, wall covering and lighting were sitting in one of his warehouses, waiting for his crew to finish installing bathroom fixtures.

But instead of concentrating on finishing the renovations in record time, Will was knee-deep in the backlash from the exposé on Family Foundations. The mayor, the council, Angel House parents...they'd all expected some opposition but hadn't anticipated the spill-over effect of the previous presidential election year. People were still raw from the constant bombardment of controversial social issues.

An advocacy group now picketed at the original Angel House, making sure they called every media outlet so the protest could be documented live. The mayor had immediately responded by going on record stating that Family Foundations served, and would continue to serve, all representatives of Hendersonville's population without discrimination or bias. She touted the careful safeguards Will had put in place, from Kenzie's agency to the work of the Main Street Advisory Board.

Hendersonville had been well covered.

The mayor had also made Family Foundations financials and guidelines available on the city website for any who wanted to see where Family Foundations spent money. She also posted links to direct people to all the public records that proved Angel House was a legitimate nonprofit organization serving the public based on need.

Angel House had done the same on their own website, providing documented and historic proof they served kids from all backgrounds. Their defense was total transparency.

The dust still hadn't settled.

And while Will didn't think the mayor would give in to the bullying by refusing Angel House the Family Foundations lease, he was now worried about the effect of the public controversy on Angel House's chances with the Ramsey Foundation.

Serving the community was a criterion for the grant, but picketers and inflammatory letters to the editor didn't demonstrate a community embracing the service. If Angel House didn't win the grant, then all this work with Family Foundations, with the move, with the renovations would have served no purpose whatsoever because Angel House wouldn't be able to keep the doors open, anyway.

"The Ramsey Foundation emailed me again," Deanne said.

"They want a date?"

She nodded. "The application process is complete, and all we're waiting on is the walk-through. They said we may have a problem scheduling if we wait any longer."

"So you need a date." Not a question this time.

She didn't reply, simply waited with a somber expression. She knew he'd have already given her one if he'd had it.

Leaning against the wall, Will dragged a hand across his forehead to relieve the pressure there. God, he was tired. He couldn't remember the last time he hadn't been tired. "Are we going to have anyone left to move this place with all the preparation for the Apple Festival?"

Answer a question with a question. He'd bought himself a few more minutes.

"Our wonderful pastor told me not to worry about that part. He said he'd ask for help from every committee at the parish if we need it."

What did Will even say to that kind of support? *Thank you* didn't begin to cover his appreciation to people who so generously offered hope whenever and wherever it was needed.

"I'm surprised they're even willing to touch us with all this media fallout. Instead of telling the world about the amazing work they do at this parish, we're going out of our way to disconnect from them. They deserve so much better for everything they've provided Angel House."

Her expression softened thoughtfully. "No doubt about that, but they understand what needs to happen for Angel House to grow. And keep in mind the parish isn't involved for recognition, although recognition would certainly be appreciated. The parish is involved because it can fulfill a need. It's really that simple. That's what everyone around here does. They help people who need them."

"They may wind up with picketers in the church parking lot for their effort."

"Then I'd say a prayer for the picketers because they'll get a lot more than they bargained for when Father gets a hold of them."

Will chuckled. Deanne was always so quick to give him perspective with reminders of how he needed more faith in people and more trust in miracles.

"Come on," she said. "Sam's still going to be a bit. Let's get coffee in my office. We can talk more there."

Will followed to the break room, mentally reviewing the list of things still to be finished before he could give her free rein to begin moving into the building.

Once ensconced in Deanne's office, Will took one look around at the books and computer software stacked on her desk and the empty shelves lining the wall. "Coffee, *right*. You want help packing boxes."

"Drink that before you fall down and land in one of those boxes yourself. When was the last time you slept?"

He considered that. "Got a few hours between the cops breaking up the picketers and the mayor's press conference."

Deanne eyed him from over the rim of her cup. "You can't complete the renovation if you kill yourself."

"My mom's been coming over to spend the nights with Sam so I can leave after he falls asleep. I need those hours."

She didn't reply, only half sat on the edge of her desk, inadvertently tipping over a stack of books that knocked over another stack then another. There were several muffled thumps as books landed on the floor.

Deanne watched everything topple over with disinterest. "That's my life at the moment."

"Join the club."

"So what are we going to do, Will? Book the walkthrough? I can try to get the very last day. Unfortunately, we'll also be opening our booths at the festival then. That whole week will be labor intensive, and we need all our key people at the center for the walkthrough. The Ramsey Foundation will want to see the place in action. They'll want to talk to teachers and therapists and students and parents. We'll need all hands on deck for the performance."

"We can't possibly have the space ready for the week before the festival."

She nodded. "I'll ask Father to find us some help. We've got days of chopping vegetables for the American booth and making churro batter. If we can get some people into the booth for opening day, we should be okay."

"Book the walk-through," Will said decidedly. They hadn't come this far only to trip at the finishing line. If he had to work around the clock from now until then, he'd get everything done. "If I let you into the offices this weekend and next, will that help? I can't have lots of people running around during the week. It's still a work site."

"I'm not going to lie, Will. We're already cutting it close. I've had Laura, Beth and Fred packing up classrooms for weeks. There's just so much junk."

"Want me to have a Dumpster delivered?"

She paused, considering the offer. "Thanks, but don't bother with that now. Maybe later. Father already said we can take as long as we need to clear this place out. Let's get moved in and get school started. Then we can deal with whatever mess is left over here."

"One less thing to worry about is a good thing right now. It'll probably be in our best interests to move in slowly, anyway. Might keep the media off our trail for a bit before all the fanfare of moving trucks on the big day."

"Big *days,* you mean. But that's a good idea."

He hated the thought of picketers showing up to grandstand at the new location. They would never be content at the rear entrance to Angel House. No, they would only be satisfied to march up and down Main Street garnering the most visibility. Kenzie wouldn't be able to get to her front door.

God, he wanted to see her, just one smile.

"I'll focus on getting specific rooms finished and bringing the new shelving and storage units out of the warehouse. That way everything will be there when you're ready to start unpacking."

"So, we're going to take a leap of faith?" Deanne asked.

Will nodded, tucking away his thoughts of a beautiful redhead who was his to enjoy only in the privacy of his mind. "Looks like that's exactly what we're going to do."

"KENZIE, WHAT BRINGS YOU by tonight?" Nathanial glanced away from his desk, where he and his assistant had been crouched over some sort of documentation.

"Hey, Chad," Kenzie said then met Nathanial, who approached her, reaching for her hands and kissing her cheek.

"Nice to see you, Kenzie," Chad said. "Please excuse me. I'm going to seize this chance to grab something to eat from the vending machine since my maniac boss won't break for dinner."

Kenzie smiled as Chad headed through the open door that he pulled shut behind him. "Does that answer my question about how the case is going?"

Nathanial nodded, then dragged her over to the sofa. "What's up? You don't drop by unannounced for no reason."

"I'm only unannounced because I didn't see the point in taking the time to text when you never reply."

He hung his head. "I'm on overload. It's really that simple. Sorry I've been so rude."

"If you can't trust me to understand, then who can you trust, right?"

He leveled his gaze at her. "Okay, now my flags are flying. Hit me with it."

She smiled. "No, I won't. Not when you've got so much on your plate that you can't even handle texting me. That's never happened, and it tells me everything I need to know. But I do want to tell you something and ask you a question. Can you handle that?"

He leaned forward and took her hands, giving her his undivided attention. "Shoot."

Kenzie took a deep breath. The moment of truth. "I respect that you're drowning right now, and you don't want to share. But I want you to know I'm here for you no matter what."

"I know that, Kenz."

His touch was strong and familiar, his voice soft, reminding her of their conversations late at night, snuggling in bed. She had so few of those memories, but the ones she did have had kept her hoping for a long time.

"Promise me you'll remember that, Nathanial. I'm here and always will be. Today, tomorrow or whenever. Nothing will change that. You're my dearest friend in the world, and I can't imagine life without you."

He exhaled heavily, seeming to gear up for what he sensed was coming because he knew her so well. Or maybe he simply was so burdened that he couldn't handle what she was saying. Kenzie didn't know. For the first time ever, she couldn't read him, felt distanced enough that his needs weren't her priority. Her need was, and everything inside her that felt so momentous, and urgent, and necessary didn't feel the same way to Nathanial.

That was the reality of the situation, and it was no longer good enough for her.

She squeezed his hands gently, opened her mouth to ask if he wanted her to wait for him. She intended to explain that she couldn't promise she would but she'd consider it.

But as they sat there in that moment, no words between them, only the companionable silence that was uniquely theirs, Kenzie realized that Nathanial's answer wouldn't make any difference.

She didn't want to wait.

She wanted to feel alive the way Will made her feel, flustered by the mere sight of him, giddy from his kisses, awed by his dedication to those he loved, frustrated by his unwillingness to consider any possible scenario for their relationship.

She wanted to be challenged, to help him understand that what was happening between them was too special not to explore no matter where it led.

And in the wake of that realization, Kenzie knew that asking Nathanial whether or not he wanted her to wait would only be putting him on the spot for no reason.

He'd already told her how he felt by his words and his actions. She'd been the one who hadn't wanted to accept them.

She'd been the one willing to wait.

Would they ever get around to realizing their plans?

Maybe, if she forced the issue. But even if they did force it, she might be told, "Not right now," as she had in her parents' backyard not so long ago.

She was done with waiting.

"And I wanted to ask you to be honest with me if you ever feel as though our friendship is in jeopardy. Give me a chance to address the problem before any damage is done. Will you promise me that, Nathanial?" The question popped out of her mouth, the words miraculously there when she needed them.

He held her gaze, those beautiful blue eyes revealing a play of emotions that suggested he was hearing everything she hadn't said. He understood that this time was different.

"It's Will Russell, isn't it?" he asked.

She nodded. She had no reply, didn't need one. Nathanial had sensed something was up even before she'd recognized the seriousness of her feelings for Will. He'd warned her against getting involved, but hadn't chosen to resume that part of their relationship, to help her tackle what she'd been struggling with or to even fight for her.

And she respected his choice.

In that moment, he looked so handsome, the embodiment of everything she'd ever dreamed of for her life. "I'll always be here for you, no matter what happens."

And she couldn't say anything would happen because Will was so set against involving her in his life. But she couldn't wait for Nathanial anymore. She was going to try to change Will's mind, going to try with everything she had in her.

Nathanial rested his forehead against hers, such a familiar gesture, the two of them all alone against the world.

Best friends for life.

There was nothing for him to say right now. He could have tried to stake his claim, but he didn't. Like her, he was willing to wait for them, risk them, allow other things to be more important than them.

And that told Kenzie everything she needed to know.

Letting go of a longtime dream should have created a gaping wound in her heart, but somehow it felt peaceful, and empowering, and promising and...

Right.

WILL SAW KENZIE'S CAR on her side of the lot when he pulled in. It was late, after nine, but he remembered she'd mentioned Lou would start delivering presentations to potential clients this week. On impulse he glanced in the bed of his truck, where he'd been driving around with her grid replacements since he'd picked them up from his warehouse yesterday.

He had five thousand things to do at Angel House, and Kenzie had already given him a free pass to put off the remaining work at Positive Partings until he was ready. She understood he was out of time. And she cared enough to want to help.

But in that moment Will needed to see her, so much that the need was an ache inside. The grid was the perfect excuse. Kenzie's life would be so much simpler if she had another room available instead of coordinating with Lou to use the large session room. Replacing the rusted fastenings would take him twenty minutes tops. He'd feel better by making her smile. He'd feel better just seeing her.

That was all the rationalization he needed.

A mere twenty minutes then he'd head to the Angel House side, to shoulder the pressure of that ticking clock and everyone who depended on him to clear out his crew by the weekend.

Will let himself in through the side door, but didn't find Kenzie in her office. A quick tour of the place didn't turn her up, which meant she was either in one of the bathrooms or only her car was here. So much for seeing her. Will headed up the attic stairs with the grid and dragged it into the crawl space.

He'd just disconnected the first set of rusty bolts when he heard the music. And knew.

Kenzie was here.

He needed to turn around and slither right out of this crawl space, climb down the stairs and straight out the door. And he would have done just that but for the music. She was in the studio dancing, moving her beautiful body with an effortless grace that belied the exquisite discipline of her training.

He could envision her fully without even closing his eyes.

Now that he'd kissed her and felt her body close, Will had nothing to protect him from this crazy need that only the feverish pace of his life helped him keep under control.

Barely.

And the knowledge that as much he wanted her, he had nothing to offer. He wouldn't change his life, but he wouldn't invite Kenzie into it, *couldn't.*

That helped him keep his need under control, too.

But tonight, when he was frazzled and fried and so unsure he could pull off his end of a miracle, Will had no resistance to the soft strains of music lingering in the dark crawl space, to the knowledge of the woman who would be moving her beautiful body in rhythm with the music.

Just a glimpse.

That's all he'd wanted tonight, one glimpse of her so he would feel better.

But even as his head warned him to get out of the crawl space, Will inched forward on a steady course.

Just a glimpse.

And there she was, showcased through the missing ceiling panels. The exquisite lines of her body softly illuminated in the overhead light, reflected in mirrors on the walls. Her body lithe and in motion, shifting from one perspective to another, fast, graceful, strong.

He might be half-dead from exhaustion but his body reacted to the sight of her, the blood pooling in his crotch—that one part of him more alive than the rest of him together. Will stretched out on his stomach, so he had to shift to get comfortable, and... *clang!* He nailed the metal support with his boot. The ensuing groans of the stressed T-bars didn't stop for a lifetime.

Busted.

Kenzie had to know he was there. No one could have missed that racket. Especially Kenzie who already knew he had a penchant for lurking in the rafters.

But she continued dancing, never glancing up at those empty ceiling panels. She didn't call him out. She raised her arms in a series of graceful moves and freed her hair from whatever contraption held it in a ponytail.

Suddenly red-gold waves tumbled around her face, shifting and swaying in time with her movements, curls catching the light as they created their own dance around her face.

Will watched her, unsure what to make of the situation, riveted to the sight of her. The only thing he knew was that he could never resist this assault on his senses.

And it was an assault in every way.

Before his eyes her movements lost their precision, her athleticism, yielding to a much sultrier performance. Her every motion lengthened as she swayed, a new kind of dance, one that emphasized the lean lines of her body. Bare arms rose and fell above her, around her, drawing his gaze to the way her hips rolled to the tempo of the music, the way her breasts lifted upward as she surged forward only to fall back again in a sinuous display.

He remembered the stage in the big hall that had graciously supplied the square footage for classrooms and remembered that Kenzie was more than a dancer. She was a performer.

She knew he was up here, and she danced for him.

He knew it with a gut-wrenching certainty. Every sense ground to a stunning stop until he could no longer hear the creak of the catwalk or the steady strains of the music.

There was only Kenzie.

And the way she moved. Her body so pliant, her motion earthy as if her dance was a seductive ritual. Her tempo quickened. He couldn't say if the music did because he only followed the rhythm of her body, the music of arousal.

Red-gold waves whipped over her face as she swept forward to touch the floor with outstretched fingers in an impossibly fluid move, then soared back again to reveal the swell of her breasts, rising and falling with the unrestrained intensity of her dance. Again then again.

Then she leaped forward in a graceful jump before compacting her body tightly on the floor to begin a different sort of dance. She rolled over sinuously and stretched her legs, never losing her rhythm but presenting her body from new angles as she arched upward, braced on an arm, breasts lifting skyward, hair flowing behind her to graze the floor.

She presented such a sensual display, from the way her mouth parted around her breaths to the flexing muscles along her legs. He was so caught up in the sight of her that he wasn't prepared when she spun around and lifted off the floor, stretched her arms upward.

Toward him.

Their gazes collided across the distance.

Her gold-flecked eyes half-hooded with invitation. His surely dazed by the effects of her dance.

Desire was all over her face, and he had never wanted more in his life, would never want more. *Ever.*

There was no thought of resisting. He had no thought left in him. No reason. No fight.

He'd been fighting for so long already.

Rolling off the catwalk, Will hung suspended for a moment before dropping down through the empty grid.

He landed in a crouch that vibrated through his joints, and for one breathless moment they faced each other, assessing. Her arms still outstretched. She didn't shy from her desire though it left her vulnerable. His pulse faltered as he realized with one flash of blinding clarity the course he committed to.

Once he touched her, he wouldn't have the strength to deny her, or himself.

And he wanted so much more than a glimpse.

So much more.

Then he was on his knees, gathering her into his arms, kissing the breathless sighs from her mouth as she melted against him with a need as great as his own.

They began their own dance of exploration. Their mouths came together, and he drank in the taste of her, the warmth of her mouth, the intensity of their shared breaths.

They'd fought their need for so long.

Skimming his hands along the curve of her neck, he touched her with complete freedom, trailing his palms along her shoulders, and down her bare arms. Twining his fingers into her hair, he coaxed her head back until all the smooth skin of her throat lay exposed to his touch, and he kissed her there, too. He dragged his mouth over her smooth skin, tasted her the way he'd fantasized about for far too long.

Resting light hands on his shoulders, she swayed backward to grant him greater privilege. His name broke from her lips as he nibbled at the hollow between her neck and shoulder then trailed his mouth down the smooth expanse of her chest.

She shivered.

Her hands fluttered around his shoulders, his neck, finally cradling his head and guiding his descent with an encouraging pressure that proved her need. He tasted her quickening pulse, the desire that made her tremble as he inched his tongue beneath her collar, hinting where he'd like to explore.

But Will couldn't resist the lure of her kiss for too long and lifted his face to hers again, caught her mouth.

Oh, could this woman kiss.

Her soft mouth slanted across his, so warm and eager. She teased him with inviting strokes of her tongue, brushed their mouths enticingly, and shared her breaths. She met every hungry stroke of his tongue with a demand of her own.

And Kenzie wanted.

Her need revealed itself in the way she sighed his name, in the way her kisses grew hungrier and her hands began to roam, in the way she arched against him, a full-bodied motion that brought his body to aching response.

Molding his hands over her bare shoulders, he explored with her, the feel of her skin, much more tantalizing than in memory.

The straps of that clingy dance thing she wore got in his way. So he slid them over her shoulders. She lifted her arms through and brought them around his neck, arching backward until her breasts crushed his chest, and he could feel her heartbeat join his, beating in tandem.

There was no reasoning between them, no rational arguments or good intentions. There was only this moment and the feel of her against him, those bare arms draped around his neck, the swaying motion of their bodies together. Their own dance.

Then he explored the length of her, learned the bow of her spine, the indent of her waist, the smooth curve of her bottom. And he couldn't help but anchor her closer, cradle his arousal against her warm body. She responded by rocking back and forth, taking advantage of their closeness.

He groaned out her name, a broken sound.

Kenzie.

Then he started peeling away layers of the clingy thing she wore, revealing her body inch by luscious inch, her skin pale in the soft light, so sleek and enticing.

His hands felt clumsy in the awe of the moment. This was insane. There was no place to make love.

There was only the two of them.

And a moment that could be theirs.

He wanted to see her reflected in all these mirrors. He wanted her underneath him. Or against him. Or on top of him.

He wanted to wipe away the last vestiges of her calm until she came unglued in his arms.

He only wanted Kenzie.

And when they were finally both naked, *finally,* Will pulled her on top of him.

Finally.

CHAPTER FOURTEEN

KENZIE COLLAPSED OVER WILL, too weak to open her eyes. All she could do was cling to him, boneless, because if she let go, she'd roll right off his lap and tumble into an undignified heap on the floor.

What had she been thinking trying to seduce the man...*seducing* the man inside her studio? She hadn't been thinking. She'd been acting. With *gumption.* Besides, there weren't many other places to make love. The sofas in the reception area or her office, maybe?

But either of those would have meant relocating, and there had been no stopping once Will had dropped through the ceiling, put his hands on her...

They were still locked together, her sitting on top of him, the quiet only punctuated by the ragged sounds of their breathing. His chest rose and fell sharply, and her heart throbbed almost painfully. Resting her cheek against his shoulder, she drank in the feel of him, all male, overwhelmed with the proof of how incredible they were together.

Right.

Kenzie finally opened her eyes and had to blink several times to make sense of the decadent sight they made in reflection. His glossy hair against her pale skin. Her bare arms draped around his broad, broad shoulders. Her knees tucked around his hips, holding him close.

The sight made her tremble again.

He noticed because he braced himself on one arm, and slipped the other around her waist, supporting her. He was such a caring man. Such a beautiful man, outside and in. From all these angles. She pressed a kiss to his silky hair, couldn't resist.

Kenzie had always liked kissing. But she especially liked kissing Will. She liked the way his kiss reached all the way down into the deep inside of her and awakened places she normally didn't notice, made her hum with anticipation.

She liked kissing him.

And she liked making love with him even more.

A sigh slid from her lips, the sound of contentment.

Tipping his head, he met her gaze, those clear eyes half-hooded and searching. He looked raw around the edges, exhausted and spent with his mouth unsmiling.

So utterly handsome, though his expression was *not* one of a man who had just made her body tingle, a man who had come unglued in her arms the way he'd made her come unglued in his.

His expression was all pensive concern.

"Now we've *really* complicated things between us." His throaty whisper broke the quiet.

Ah, he didn't stop caring for even an instant. Not even sitting here naked with their intimate places pressed close. Kenzie wondered if he knew how to stop caring.

She hadn't realized how hard he'd been struggling to resist *this,* resist her.

Through the filter of their lovemaking, she recognized so much of his struggle in his gentlemanly concern for her, in the careful way he'd been shielding her from the unique pressures of his life, the challenges that had molded and shaped him into such a caring, committed man.

She pressed her mouth to his softly, unable to resist.

"Only if you don't trust me to make my own choices. I know what's best for me, and I know what I want."

To be with Will.

WILL LEANED AGAINST the wall and inclined his head toward Kenzie's side door. He hadn't been here since last night when they'd made love in her studio, when they'd done the only thing they could do—give in to need and table the consequences until they could make time to figure things out.

Until *he* could make time.

"Knock, will you?" he told Bob's nephew Jason, who had been coming every night to give Will a hand.

Jason shifted a worried glance between Will and the door then knocked sharply. Kenzie's car was the only one in the lot, which meant she didn't have a class. The sun hadn't gone down yet, so he stood a chance of getting her to answer the door.

He controlled his breathing while they waited. This was crazy and still wasn't sure how he'd gotten himself in this situation.

Jason knocked again, harder this time. "Are you sure you don't want me to drive you."

Will shook his head, grateful for the distraction. "I need you to get those light fixtures up. Are you sure you're good with that?"

"Piece of cake, man. Don't worry. They'll be up by the time you get back."

That confidence alone was enough to make Will nervous. Unfortunately, he didn't have any choice but to leave Jason to finish the job he should have been finishing.

The door cracked open and Kenzie appeared, looking somehow angelic silhouetted in the light from the hallway behind her. "Hello, may I help—"

"Kenzie, I need a ride," Will said abruptly.

Her expression transformed at the sound of his voice, and she pulled open the door. The instant she saw him, she asked, "What's wrong?"

Judging by her expression, he must look like hell. He was sweating a lot. That much he knew. "Would you mind giving me a lift to the emergency room?"

Her gaze riveted to the hand he cradled against him. "Ohmigosh! What happened? Are you okay?"

"Hurt my wrist."

"He slipped off the ladder and broke his fall with

his hand. It looks broken." Jason filled in all the details that made Will sound like the total idiot he was.

"My right wrist," Will said lamely. The wrist he needed to do absolutely everything from install the fixtures in the classrooms to brushing his damned teeth. "Can't drive."

"He won't let me take him." Jason shrugged. "Sorry to bother you."

Kenzie shook her head at the kid, clearly flustered. "No problem at all. Let me grab my purse. Do you want an ice pack? I have a first aid kit."

"No," Will said at the same time Jason said, "Tried that."

Kenzie glanced between them with a scowl meant only for him.

"Thank you but there is no way anything is touching my wrist. Period."

She didn't bother arguing but vanished inside, and Will asked, "You have my keys, right?"

Jason patted his pocket.

"Then if I can't get back before you're done, just lock up and go. Keep your phone on in the morning, and I'll catch up with you to get the keys back."

"Just call, man. I'll bring them by. If you want, I'll ditch afternoon classes and help out around here."

"Thanks." Will meant it. Closing his eyes, he willed himself not to fall down. God, he was so tired he could barely keep his eyes open. And he was starting to feel sick. Not even the temperature drop of a mountain night was doing a thing to cool him down.

And he was standing around here like an idiot with only two days left. That's all the time he had to wrap up everything so Deanne could start moving in and to get the place functional for the walk-through. If he worked around the clock and pulled every guy he could from every job site, he still wouldn't be finished, even if he hadn't done the stupidest damned thing imaginable.

He couldn't even turn over the ignition of his truck with this hand, and if they put a cast on...

"You okay, Will?" Jason asked.

"Yeah." That single word was about all he could manage.

Then the door opened and Kenzie said, "We'll take my car. That's it over there."

The lock rattled then Will had Jason on one side of him and Kenzie on the other, helping him to the car. He sank into the front seat and promptly shut his eyes again.

Will heard Jason say, "Just wanted to say sorry about the outlet, ma'am."

"I appreciated your help," Kenzie said warmly. "The drywall looks great."

Will really liked that about her. *Kind.* That was the word he'd use to describe her. She cared about everyone who crossed her path. Whether she cared for a few seconds to say a nice word to a kid who'd screwed up, or for a lifetime like she had with her not-at-the-moment loser *friend,* she genuinely cared about the mood she left a person with.

She would be the only woman he'd want around Sam. One who would see all the good stuff. Sam might not have found his words yet, but he had a wicked sense of humor and contagious laughter. He might need time and tools to figure out everything going on around him, because it all came at him at once without filters—which would be overwhelming for anyone—but he was the most loving kid. There was nothing, absolutely nothing, like having Sam throw his arms around Will's neck and hug him with that absolute abandon.

Kenzie would appreciate those things, too.

Will must have dozed—no real wonder since he couldn't remember the last time he'd slept all night—because he didn't remember hearing her door shut or the car take off, but he awoke to the sound of the engine humming steadily.

"Kenzie." He didn't open his eyes.

"We're almost there." Her voice was soft, a familiar beacon in the drowsy darkness. "You doing okay?"

No, he wasn't okay. His wrist throbbed so hard he might be sick, and then wouldn't she be sorry she offered him a ride? "I respect you to make your own choices."

"We don't have to discuss this now." He heard the exasperation in her voice. And the humor. That was there, too.

He tried to laugh, but his own voice came at him from a distance. "If not now, when?"

"Will—"

"I'd rather talk about us than obsess over everything I could be doing at Angel House if I hadn't slipped and fell." One stupid misstep.

And he had given *her* a safety lecture about using the heat stripper late at night. She must think he was a joke.

"I'm going to trip at the finish line."

"What exactly does that mean?" she asked.

"It means that, because of my carelessness, all this work will be for nothing."

She didn't reply, so he turned, forced his eyes open.

While he'd been asleep, the sun had set and now he could see her in profile, her features glowing in the light of the instrument panel. She had that mildly amused look on her face, the one where she humored him. Not exactly the response he'd been going for. He'd made crazy love to her one night only to need her to rescue him the next.

That's exactly what this felt like.

"I can't believe this is happening." He wasn't sure if he was referring to his wrist or the fact that he wanted to lean over and kiss her. He'd always known getting in the confines of a vehicle with her would be death on his restraint.

Then again, after last night, his restraint was moot.

"Okay, then, let's talk about us," she said.

"I liked making love with you."

That got a better response. "I liked it, too."

"It's not that I don't want to be with you. It's just that it wouldn't be fair. You get that, right?"

"Fair to whom?" she asked. "Sam? I know I don't have a lot of experience around children, but I like them. I really do. Especially Sam."

How did she even come up with that? Of course he knew she was good with kids. He'd seen her with his son already. "I'm not talking about Sam. He likes you. He'd fall in love with you if he got to know you better."

Just like his father had.

There, he'd thought it. Brought it out into his consciousness. He'd done exactly what he'd sworn he'd never do again. Of course, through the fog of pain, he heard some nagging voice pointing out that the third time might actually be a charm. His common sense countered with, "Three strikes you're out!"

"Who's out?" Kenzie asked.

Man, he was screwed up. He was confusing what was going on in his head with what was coming out of his mouth. Or was she just messing with him? He couldn't think past this damned throbbing in his arm.

"I need an acetaminophen. Got any?"

"Afraid not. Left my bottle at the office in the first aid kit. How about we ask the doctor for something when he checks out your wrist? Sound good?"

"Sounds good." His arm sure didn't look good. Even looking at the way everything from elbow to fingers swelled made it throb more.

"Will, who are you worried about being fair to?"

"*You.* I told you this." Or had he only thought that, too?

"So, you don't think you can be fair to me because

you're so busy because of your life with Sam. Do I have that right?"

"And my business, and Angel House, and the city council." He dragged a hand across his brow. Great. He was still sweating and now he was clammy. Why was he suddenly so cold? Was the air-conditioning on? He reached toward a vent. Nothing.

"But what if your devotion to your life and all the people in it is one of the things I love about you?"

That stopped him. He frowned.

"What if I love the way you love your son, with your whole heart and soul? You're moving mountains to give him opportunities. And what if I love how generous you are? You could have moved those mountains just for Sam, but you've made sure others benefit, too. And not only the people you know at Angel House, but you're making sure autism gets noticed in the government, so people you don't even know, people who are dealing with the things you and Sam are, can benefit, too."

She made that sound like a lot bigger of a deal than it actually was. "Kenzie, I had to run for city council to push Family Foundations otherwise we couldn't get in this building."

A hint of a smile played around her mouth. "And what if I love the way you're so committed to helping people, that you don't even realize how special what you're doing is? What if I love that about you, too?"

"What's your point?" If she'd made one, he'd lost it in all those words.

"My point is you're worrying about all these things being unfair to me, when they're all the things I love about you."

While he was still trying to come up with an argument, he watched her small smile grow until she sort of beamed in that glowing light.

"I very much appreciate your special circumstances," she said. "And I respect the fact that I'm not living your life, so I can't know all the demands. Don't you think you should give me a chance to find out?"

That stopped him. He hadn't actually considered that before. He'd simply made up his mind that he would never put these demands on any woman. Melinda couldn't even handle Sam.

But Kenzie wasn't Melinda.

And that really wasn't fair, even to Melinda. He understood better than anyone why she had such a tough time dealing with their son. He hoped that would eventually change as Sam continued to grow his skills and as Melinda made peace with the fact that she wasn't responsible. She couldn't have done anything differently to prevent or alter Sam's autism.

"Don't you think that if we have something special, we should at least give it a try?" she asked.

"You think what we have is special?"

She glanced away from the road, her gaze as soft as her smile. "Don't you?"

That's when it hit him—she was a mediator, a skilled negotiator. She was using her skills on him, mediating on her own behalf for all she was worth.

Something about that made him smile, too.

Then she wheeled into the parking lot, and he could see the emergency room sign illuminating the darkness.

"I'll pull through the circle drive and drop you—"

"Just park in the lot," he said.

She frowned but didn't argue. Once she'd pulled into a space, she tried again. "If you'll wait here, I'll go grab—"

"I'll walk."

And he did. With her arm around his waist to direct him. He walked every damned step even though he felt like his arm might fall off. Actually, he wished it would.

Of course, he had to swallow what was left of his pride and ask her to grab his wallet out of his back pocket.

She slipped her fingers into his pocket, taking advantage by feeling up his backside in the process, then sat quietly beside him as he dozed between triage and x-ray and the interminable wait to have his fractured wrist set.

And sometime during the night, Will remembered what it felt like to be cared for, instead of being the one to do all the caring.

"WHERE IN HELL—" The growl reverberated across the house, startling Kenzie all the way in the kitchen. "Where in hell am I? Where's my phone?"

She replaced the coffeepot and carried a mug of steaming coffee into her bedroom.

Will was sitting up in bed, disoriented and frantic, a man wholly unused to not having life firmly under his control. He looked like a wild man in the midst of her white lace bedding with his glossy black hair askew and stubbled cheeks drawn.

"Where the hell—" He stopped in midsentence and did a double take when he saw her. "Is this your place?"

She nodded.

"Where's my phone? I have to—"

"It's okay. I spoke with your mom last night while you were having your wrist set. She has Sam, and she was going to call Melinda. One of them will get Sam to Guadalupe's on time this morning. She said not to worry and to call her when you wake up."

Kenzie grabbed his phone off her dresser and brought it to him with the coffee. Poor man. They'd drugged him last night, and he appeared to be having trouble shaking the effects. She wanted to ask how he felt, but didn't want to bombard him with questions. She had no idea how he awoke in the mornings, whether he hit the ground running or needed time to face the day.

She wanted to know.

But now was the time to help him regroup. She pointed to the boudoir chair, where the clothes he'd worn yesterday sat in a freshly laundered pile. That had been the best she could do since they'd arrived home so late. "Clothes."

He lifted his hand then winced, taking in the sight of the cast. He scowled and thrust his left hand through his hair instead, making the dark strands stand on end.

"Oh, man. Nothing can ever be simple. Did they mention how I'm supposed to shower with this?"

She nodded. "And the doctor said when you follow up with your orthopedic surgeon, you might be able to have that cast replaced with a waterproof one to make life a little easier."

Her good news didn't have the effect she'd hoped. The frantic edges were creeping into his expression.

"Did they say how long I'd have to wear this? I don't remember."

No surprise there. Will had been operating under the assumption he was exhausted last night when he'd actually been in shock. "Sounded like it could be six weeks. I put your discharge papers with the doctor's orders by your clothes."

Blinking, he opened his mouth as if to speak then closed it again, apparently robbed of any response. He closed his eyes as if he might block out reality.

"The doctor said you were very lucky, Will." She gave him some good news. "He said, and I quote, it was a miracle the fracture didn't sever tendons. If that had happened you'd have spent last night in surgery and could have had permanent damage."

Will inhaled deeply, an effort from where she stood.

"If you're interested in showering, I can grab what we'll need to wrap your cast."

He opened his eyes, and that clear gaze cut across the distance, a gaze with the ability to drop the bottom out of her stomach. To her surprise, he managed that charming smile of his, dimples flashing. "Yes."

She whirled and headed out of the room, her heart suddenly pounding hard. And by the time she returned to fit a plastic trash bag over his cast and secure it with duct tape, her pulse still skittered at their closeness, at the sheer maleness of this man all rough-edged from sleep.

He'd dropped the bottom out of her world, too.

"Thanks for taking such good care of me." His voice was a throaty whisper.

"It's been my pleasure." She wondered if he truly understood how much she meant that. When he slipped a warm finger beneath her chin and tipped her face toward his, she thought he might.

"Am I remembering last night right?" he asked in that gravelly voice. "Did you totally take advantage of me?"

"I did," she admitted, not just a little proud. "I seized the opportunity. It's called gumption."

"Really?"

She nodded. "You were so busy being noble that you left me out of the equation. I wanted to weigh in."

He exhaled a small laugh. "A control freak, hmm?"

"I can't honestly say I'd argue too hard with that assessment."

His gaze settled on her mouth, and she knew right

then he was thinking about kissing her. He pulled her onto the bed beside him instead, didn't let go of her hand, but twined their fingers together as if testing the fit.

"I'm not noble, Kenzie. Just wanted to do things right. I've been married already."

"I know."

He arched an eyebrow and admitted, "Twice."

She squeezed his hand. She'd known that, too.

"Melinda mentioned that while she was divorcing me?"

"You knew we'd met?"

"It took a while to put two and two together, but yeah. She'd mentioned when she'd first gone to see you."

Kenzie wasn't sure what to say. She'd tried not to judge, had been very well aware that she didn't have the whole story about this man…and that she had formed so many impressions.

None of them good.

But many were based on her own idealistic views about love and marriage. While she still believed in what she taught, Will had helped open her eyes to the bigger picture, to what was really important about love.

"I was too young to get married the first time," he admitted. "Way too young. But I tried to do things differently the second time. Did everything different, in fact, and it still blew up in my face."

Maybe he had. There were some pretty special

circumstances that had surely factored into his second marriage. That much Kenzie knew. "You figure out what the problem might be?"

"I think so. Maybe. Probably should get a lock on it before I attempt another walk down the aisle. How long are you willing to wait?"

"For a marriage proposal?"

He chuckled, so close to her ear the throaty sound rippled through her, sparking that incredible awareness that only he could ignite in her. "I don't want to wait to have sex. In fact, if I didn't smell so ripe…"

His words trailed off beneath the sound of her laughter. Exploring their relationship and waiting for his marriage proposal seemed like exactly the right thing to do. "And I can't think of anything I'd rather do than have sex with you." Kenzie tipped her face to his and they sealed the deal with a kiss.

WILL TRIED TO keep the situation in perspective while sitting beside Kenzie in her car as they left her house. The sight of her in contrast to his drowsy memories of the night before helped a lot.

She looked lovely and fresh and ready to face the day, with the calm that was so uniquely hers firmly in place. But Will knew beneath that exterior was a kind and caring woman whose gentleness was actually her source of strength, a deep strength that didn't waver in the face of opposition or adversity or challenge.

The kind of strength that weathered life's storms

and made her emotions run equally deep. Emotions like loyalty.

And passion.

The memory of the way Kenzie had danced for him, had made love to him and come apart in his arms stunned him. How had he ever gotten so lucky?

He didn't know how they could make a relationship work given the parameters of his life, but they would figure that out together. He was determined to keep understanding the skills that would help him be a more effective parent and a partner worthy of the blessings he'd been given. At the moment that included not freaking out because he'd need a doctor to sign off on a release before he could even drive his truck again, which created more problems than he could even comprehend at the moment with transporting Sam and traveling to job sites.

That meant accepting the fact that he'd blown precious hours needed to complete the work at Angel House. He remembered what Deanne had told him, "You can't finish the building if you kill yourself."

He hadn't killed himself, but he hadn't listened to her, either. Had he not pushed himself to the edge, he might not have been so careless last night. He had only himself to blame. He knew the rules, knew very well accidents happened on the job when workers were tired or distracted.

Those rules applied to him, too.

Reaching across the console with his uninjured hand, he took Kenzie's hand. "Thank you."

"You're welcome. But you already thanked me."

"I thanked you for last night. Now I'm thanking you for not taking no for an answer."

"Then you're very welcome. I'm really pleased with the result of that choice, too."

He chuckled, bringing her hand to his mouth, brushed a kiss against her smooth skin. He felt a peace he hadn't known before. She was so lovely, so completely right for him and Sam, and he found himself touched by the way her breath fluttered and her mouth parted, as excited by him as he was by her.

How had he ever gotten so lucky?

God only knew. *Seriously.*

The color rode high in her cheeks and she slanted a glance his way with sparkling eyes as she turned onto Main Street not far from their building.

Will braced himself for the sight of protestors as he had every day for the past few weeks, for the emotional drain of standing his ground in the face of opposition.

But the scene was worse than Will imagined when she wheeled off the side street. The lot was packed with cars and trucks, busier than he'd seen it yet.

"Oh, come on." He groaned. "You'd think they'd at least have the courtesy to park in a public lot and not take up our spaces."

"Who?" Kenzie leaned forward to gauge the distance between two cars that hadn't left much room to pull through.

Will opened his mouth to reply, but then it hit him.

He hadn't seen any protestors on Main Street, and the big van on the far end of the lot wasn't a television van but a panel van with a magnetized logo that read: *Atteberry Construction*.

He glanced more closely at the cars and trucks in the lot, mostly trucks with toolboxes and equipment packed in the back.

Kearney Developers.

Tom & Al's Redi-Rooter.

Nunez & Son Flooring.

Van Brocklin III Painting.

"What is— How is this even possible?" he said, disbelieving.

Kenzie put the car into Park and turned to face him, beaming. "Well, you have Jason to thank. Apparently he called his uncle last night and told him what happened. Then his uncle called while you were having your wrist set. I answered your phone, and we had a nice conversation. He said he would take care of everything. He cares about you a great deal."

Will could only imagine a conversation between Bob and Kenzie. The very idea might have made him laugh if he still wasn't still trying to wrap his brain around the fact that all these people weren't on their jobs but his. Guys he knew well. Guys he'd only worked with occasionally. But he could guess that Bob had sounded the alarm and folks had responded.

The magnitude of such generosity was so big that Will could only stare through the windshield at the crowded parking lot, so overcome that he had no words, couldn't even look at Kenzie because the enormity of his relief and profound sense of gratitude felt a lot bigger than he was right now. But he could practically hear Deanne reminding him, "God provides."

Big-time.

And somehow Kenzie knew, and in that intuitive way of hers, she did exactly what he needed. Twining their fingers together, she gave a reassuring squeeze, a gentle touch that seemed to say simply, "All is well."

He finally turned to her, met that dazzling gaze and felt the warmth of her smile from the inside out.

And he knew all would be.

Even better than he could have ever imagined possible when he pulled her into his arms and they kissed.

And kissed.

When Will finally lifted his head to peer into her beautiful face, her expression so filled with pleasure, all he could think to say was, "So, while I was getting poked and prodded, you were pretty busy."

"Oh, Will." She faced him with an expression he'd never seen before, a mischievous one that could barely contain her excitement. "You have no idea."

And she was right. Will couldn't possibly have imagined that, after facing so much negative press, for every protestor there would be three people willing to step in and help Angel House achieve its goals.

Not only did Bob, with Jason's help, rally friends and business acquaintances from all over town who had shown up to complete all the projects Will couldn't on his own, they wrapped up much more work than he'd even hoped to get done.

Every piece of trim installed. Every wall painted. Every vent and light and plumbing fixture mounted and wired and caulked. They were professionals who knew how to work together on job sites, and there was lots of laughter and good-natured complaints and lots and lots of jokes about Will's accident.

To support the generosity and efforts of the construction crew, Kenzie rallied her friends to help out by running a buffet at Positive Partings to keep everyone fed while they worked.

By Friday night, the work was completed and all the contractors' trucks cleared out of the parking lot.

At the crack of dawn on Saturday, the moving trucks arrived. Kenzie's dad moved the buffet outdoors, setting up his grill in the parking lot, marinating his special barbecue chicken and feeding the workers and movers from Angel House.

The contractors who had worked maniacally for two days showed up again, only this time to sit in lawn chairs and talk shop. Main Street from West Orchard to South Wall took on the appearance of a block party, a full week before the Apple Festival was set to begin.

Even Kenzie's not-at-the-moment loser *friend* had turned up to lend his efforts to the cause. And to Will's surprise, Mr. BMW wasn't so bad after all. At least once his status permanently changed to *never-*

again boyfriend, now only friend. His loss was Will's gain, so Will could afford to be generous.

Monday morning saw Kenzie's parents packing up the grill and her friends heading back to work, her included.

But by then Angel House had things under control. The place remained a flurry of activity with teachers working around the clock to install the school in its new permanent location. Parents came and went, helping out when they could in between setting up for the Apple Festival, which would take place only a few blocks up Main Street.

And when the day of the walk-through finally arrived, there were protestors with their signs, but they were swallowed up by the crowd of supporters eager to present Angel House as the community effort it was.

Even Melinda surprised Will by showing up, taking her place beside him as the parent of an Angel House student. But this particular parent had an extensive background in public relations, so whenever Deanne and the Ramsey team fell silent, Melinda stepped into the breach to seize the opportunity to do what she did so exceptionally well—manage Angel House's reputation by communicating all the ways this one resource center served not only the Hendersonville community, but also provided a yardstick for the global community that so desperately needed innovators and leaders.

But the biggest surprise of all came when Deanne's

assistant arrived midafternoon as the group gathered around an observation window of a classroom, where one of the faculty and an aide worked with several kids, including Sam.

"Forgive me for interrupting," she said to Deanne. "But I wasn't sure if you knew about the media outside. They're here to cover the building rededication."

Deanne managed her surprise for the benefit of the Ramsey team, but still had to point out, "The building rededication isn't until five, when the mayor kicks off the festival."

Her assistant shrugged nervously. "Looks like they're a bit ahead of schedule then. It's a pretty big crowd."

"Thanks for letting me know." Then Deanne turned to her guests. "Would you like to be a part of the excitement? I'll bet it's not every day you conduct a walk-through during the rededication of a potential grant recipient's new permanent location."

The Ramsey folks were very interested in being a part of the festivities, but Will could tell Deanne wasn't sure what to make of the situation. He *knew* Melinda wasn't pleased. Too many unknowns when they were trying to reassure the foundation and a lot of those unknowns had to do with protestors who could undo some of the good work they'd done this morning.

"Did the mayor say anything to you about this?" Melinda asked under her breath as they headed toward the main doors.

"Not a word."

"I wonder what's going on." She plastered a smile on her face and braced herself to do damage control.

They made their way outside, but as he and Melinda trailed at the rear of the group with a few other parents, he couldn't see much more than a sizeable crowd and some local news trucks.

This didn't look good.

Deanne was immediately called into action, but not before whispering, "Will, you're on."

He had no idea what she meant, but Melinda was already herding him through the group, sticking like glue to his heels. He heard Deanne explain to the Ramsey team, "I mentioned earlier, Will's a city council member. He works closely with our mayor who works with our governor."

Will didn't get a chance to react because both the mayor and governor were standing right there on the front step, presiding over a crowd that filled the circle drive and blocked access to the street.

An aide he recognized from the mayor's office handed her a portable microphone.

"Good day, my friends," the mayor said. "Welcome to the kickoff of our fair city's Apple Festival. Today we're rededicating the newest addition to our Main Street Historic District and we have a very special guest, the chief executive of our excellent state of North Carolina, our governor, Pat Smithson. Please join me in a warm welcome."

When the applause finally died down, the mayor

said, "Thank you for accepting our invitation, Governor Smithson, and welcome to Hendersonville."

She passed off the microphone and the governor addressed the crowd in the pleasant, media-friendly persona that had made her the first woman to ever be elected to the governor's office.

Will exchanged a glance with Deanne, who could barely contain her excitement. The Ramsey Foundation group appeared to be suitably impressed. By the governor's enthusiasm about Angel House or by such influential support, Will couldn't say, but he was more interested in the woman who appeared in the wings when the governor spoke a few words about preserving the state's history and blending the past with the present and the future.

Kenzie.

She was dressed as she usually was for business in one of those formfitting skirts he favored, the kind that showed off her legs. She carried a champagne bottle, and led the small procession with the governor and mayor at its head around the building to the cornerstone on Main Street.

As the governor rededicated the building amidst a frenetic flash of cameras and rolling video, Will finally caught up with Kenzie. There was no opportunity to talk, and no need. He slid his hand into hers, content to be near her, sensing her excitement. And he knew that somehow she, with her network of connections all around the state, was responsible for this media opportunity and illustrious visit.

He could wait until later for the details.

"Governor, I hear you're responsible for fixing my potholes," a gruff voice called out from the crowd.

"What's your name, sir?" the governor asked, her voice amplified, an eruption of flashes popping off rounds like automatic gunfire. "The man with the potholes?"

"Chuck Ridgeway." A grizzled old guy stepped out of the crowd and, sure enough, it was the man from Kenzie's class.

Will and Kenzie exchanged a glance. What were the odds?

"Did you vote for me, Chuck?"

"In fact, I did, Governor. But that was before I knew you were responsible for my potholes."

There was laughter from the crowd, and the governor didn't miss a beat. "Well, I'd like you to vote for me again in the next election, so file a report with the Department of Transportation. I'll have my office follow up. Does that sound like a plan, Chuck?"

"Sounds like a plan, Governor."

There was applause and more flashbulbs, then Kenzie leaped into action, leading their procession through the parking lot, laughing her lovely laugh that filtered through him in such a physical way.

"I think Madame Estelle would be so pleased," she whispered.

Will sent up a silent whisper of thanks to the dance instructor who had shared her talents with this woman by his side. There was still one dance studio in the building, and Will intended to make sure it was put to incredibly good use.

Because in this moment, his impossibly busy life didn't feel like an exercise in stealing good moments from days spent putting one foot in front of the other. Instead, it felt like a gift.

Such a gift.

EPILOGUE

HAD IT ONLY been months since Kenzie had been on schedule making progress with her five-year plan, ticking along with her plans for the future and thinking she had all the answers?

It *felt* like another lifetime.

In reality only eight months had passed since she'd revised her opinion about love at first sight. Now she had an entirely new lease on life. Her wonderful new office felt like home, and her five-year plan had been updated.

"All done?" she asked when Sam showed up at her desk with his homework sheets in hand.

He set the papers in front of her showing the pictures he'd colored and the lines he'd drawn to match items to words.

Toaster.

Toothbrush.

Dog.

Swing.

Man.

In this case, Kenzie suspected *man* was actually Dad because Sam had colored the hair black and the eyes gray. But no cast. For a while there, Sam had been including that in his drawings, too, but Will's arm had healed and the physical therapy sessions had ended, so he'd retired the wrist support he'd been wearing—permanently, to hear him tell it.

"Good job," she said and meant it, her heart melting around the edges when he smiled at her with laughter in those big blue eyes.

Then he grabbed his checklist.

He crossed *homework* off the list in orange marker, then slipped the dry-erase marker into the slot that kept writing utensil and checklist together. He pointed to the next item, which was his reward for completing his homework.

"Wii," she said.

Sam smiled and nodded, slipping his hand into hers and tugging her along. Kenzie hopped up from the desk, grabbing the clipboard before he led her from the office and upstairs to her studio.

He knew the drill.

Didn't matter that she still had stacks of folders on her desk. She'd get to them later. Today was Saturday, and Will would be working at Angel House until he installed the new appliances in the kitchen— a donation from one of Angel House's newest community partners.

There had been quite a few new partners.

Not only had Angel House won the Ramsey Foundation grant, but all the media exposure—good and bad—had put Angel House on the map. Melinda had been working closely with Deanne to make the most of the opportunities, and they'd found so much support among the community.

Kenzie smiled when Sam abandoned her in the doorway and made a beeline straight for the TV she'd set up as his personal space. After flipping on the power, he rocked back and forth on his sturdy sneakers, impatient while waiting for her to untangle the controller cords.

"I'm getting there." She laughed. "Trying to, anyway."

Who'd wrapped up these cords the last time, anyway?

Finally Sam chose the device he wanted, then took off as far as the cord would reach, eager for the game to begin.

"Dad will be back soon," she reminded him.

Will had only run down the street to the hardware store for some spackle because the container he kept in his truck had dried out. It shouldn't take too long, but until then, she and Sam had some time to enjoy together.

They'd been getting to know each other during the months since Angel House had officially taken residence in their new home and she and Will had become an official couple.

And they were officially a couple.

He made time for dates, which was part of his new

balanced-perspective-on-life plan. They went to movies and wine tastings and farmer's markets and hiked along mountain trails.

She accompanied him to political events, which meant she got to shop with Fiona and Jess for evening wear. He accompanied her to networking functions and to family gatherings.

They did fun kid things with Sam.

They also spent lots of time at Angel House, where she learned about autism and met so many wonderful people. Will's new lease on life had prompted Melinda to become more involved in Sam's life, and the very happy result was her relationship with her son appeared to be going more smoothly.

This had been great for Kenzie and Will because they got to spend long nights together. They explored their incredible chemistry, sometimes at her house and sometimes at his. *Always* they wound up marveling at what they'd discovered together.

They were enjoying their present and looking toward the future, which they fully intended to spend together.

They'd already begun making plans.

But while they made those plans, they enjoyed every second *now* as they faced the ups and downs of every day, shared time with family and friends and *lived*.

Will had been right about another thing, too—Sam

did love her. Probably because she was pretty good
at playing Wii Sports.

And Kenzie loved him right back.

He was a funny and smart little guy, who laughed
easily and loved to hug and was an absolute fiend at
bowling. Sure enough, that was the game he chose
to play now. No doubt so he could crush the competition. He was also competitive and knew her weak-
ness—she was so much better at baseball.

Will said they would venture out to a real bowling alley soon. Apparently the last attempt had been
a bit of a disaster because of the noise level. But
thanks to Wii Sports, Sam not only seemed to have
gotten used to the clamor, but immensely enjoyed
trouncing her fair and square, so much so that they
cheered and applauded along with the game after a
good throw.

Today Kenzie spent more time groaning at her
own lousy performance than clapping, which made
Sam laugh all the more. They were so into the game
that she never heard Will return until Sam bowled
a strike. Then they were cheering and clapping like
two maniacs. Sam was the one to notice Will first
and with all the excitement of the moment and that
joyous abandon so unique to him, he ran to Will, yell-
ing, "Daddy!" and wrapped his arms around Will in
a bear hug.

That one word echoed through the studio, stunning
in intensity, articulate in pronunciation and context

Kenzie caught Will's stunned gaze in the mirror, dissolved inside at his stricken expression, the disbelief all over his face.

Sam had found his words.

"Daddy, Daddy, Daddy, Daddy!"

Will sank to his knees, and Kenzie had tears in her eyes as she watched those two dark heads bow close together.

"Good job, Sam," Will said in that gruff voice she'd come to love so much.

Sam flexed his newfound vocal muscles, apparently wanting to make up for lost time.

"Daddy, Daddy, Daddy!"

And Will laughed through his tears, holding his son like he might never let go.

Kenzie stood there, her hand pressed to her mouth, her eyes misty. Then Will caught her gaze. In those clear depths she understood everything. All the uncertainty gone. All their hopes fulfilled. All his prayers answered.

In one beautiful word that would open the way for others.

They exchanged a glance. She knew exactly what he wanted because they were intimately connected. She went to him, was pulled into a family hug that made Sam laugh and cling to her like a little monkey.

Had it really only been eight months since she had finally started to live? Because that's exactly what this was—*living*.

The one thing Kenzie had known all along was that families came in all shapes and sizes.

There was room in this one for her.

* * * * *

Be sure to look for the next
Harlequin Superromance novel
by Jeanie London!
Available September 2013.